COLLECTED POEMS
AND STORIES

ADELE SCHWARTZ

Full Court Press
Englewood Cliffs, New Jersey

First Edition

Copyright © 2011 by Adele Schwartz

Published in the United States of America
by Full Court Press, 601 Palisade Avenue
Englewood Cliffs, NJ 07632

Also by Adele Schwartz
Yesterday's Breakfast
Black Ice

ISBN 978-0-9833711-2-0
Library of Congress Control No. 2011925500

Editing and Book Design by Barry Sheinkopf for Bookshapers
(www.bookshapers.com)

Cover Photograph, "African Mask," Copyright Barry Sheinkopf

Colophon by Liz Sedlack

Dedication

Before I enrolled at The Writing Center, my poems and stories lay wrinkled on the floor and ready to be tossed away. I'm lucky to have found Barry Sheinkopf and grateful for his confidence and support in my work, and for showing me how to know the music of poetry (alive in every class).

I'm grateful to Yehudis Abramowitz for the endless hours she spent listening.

For Stefanie, my daughter, Gregory, my son, who are at the soul of my thoughts.

For my mother, father, and sister, for their unwarranted praise throughout my life.

And for Oliver, who always knows the difference.

> *"At the end of every rainbow*
> *lies a wreckage or a poem*
> *and you've made your move*
>
> . . . .
>
> *No no the Fates do not find*
> *poetry amusing"*
>
> —*Barry Sheinkopf*

About the Author

Adele Schwartz was born in Hackensack, New Jersey. She lived in East Paterson, where she East Rutherford High School. She studied at Syracuse University and received her B.S. in Secondary Education and taught in Fairlawn High School. She lives in Edgewater, New Jersey.

She started writing poems at the age of eleven and has never stopped. This volume assembles all her previously published work, as well as newer material that appears here in print for the first time.

She believes the following lines sum up much of her sense of language and the purpose of her life:

> *I guess my folks were disappointed*
> *over my female birth.*
> *They never said it—straight out—*
> *just spoke of a switch in the newspaper*
> *announcing me as a boy (named Adam)*
> *and how the press goofed,*
> *and how, when they focused*
> *on my eyes, my nose, my mouth,*
> *they swore that I resembled*
> *no one in the family really:*
> *"Too Irish, Italian, or something," they'd say,*
> *no signs of their dark gypsy blood*
> *boiling in my veins.*

TABLE OF CONTENTS

Yesterday's Breakfast

☙

The White Pigeon

Black Ice

The Fourth Wall

Yesterday's Breakfast

A FLORIDA POOLSIDE

Sitting at the senior citizens' pool
I saw a petite figure
walking, dark, straight toward me
without a wince—no hesitations—
and I thought it was you

there were no signs of anger
for visiting someone else's mother
to never know my son and daughter
those twinkling eyes
the impish laughter
your girlish playfulness

you sit in my chair now
calm with pain
as I often do
you turn around—I see my face looking back
I knew—I'm sure I knew
that brief moment
when I *thought* I saw you!

AFTERSHOCK

I'm always losing something since then,
sometimes not knowing exactly what—
sagging in chaotic looseness,
pockets vacant, untidy,
free of costly vices
and dabblings in self-pity
ravenously rising
out of newfound valleys of weeds
and fathomless displacements,
sweet quiet velvet mournings
lost now in iambic pentameter.

The tattered red flag of battles
grows a bit taller every day,
rooted in deceptions and lies,
sweating out words without appeal—
until next time.
You can't stop me!
I wear these anguished days
yet, still intact with an occasional glow,
even wave a white flag every now and then.

ALIVE AND WELL

He's alive and well somewhere.
It makes me nervous to know
    that he still leaves sprouts
        that rape the soil,
    overfeeding the well fed
        left then to starve in blank fate
frothing in an unrelaxed honesty
        in parlor games
    like an uninvited guest
        on chance journeys
    to familial haunts,
        never resting
    like the safe night falling down on him.

ALIVE AND WELL II

Don't worry, pretty thing
the dogs won't bite
the bees won't sting
you won't fall while
you fly your kite

your skin worn thin by time
not touch

taught to stay alive and well—
but not by much!

AN ISRAELI BAR MITZVAH

The exhausted Holy Wall
ruddy and laden
with paper prayers inserted into cracks,
wilting in a still wind.

A vernal sun shines
        on your newly appointed manhood,
alone and obvious in this celebration,
        gorgeous with inner sorrow,
        budding with permitted wisdom,

white handkerchiefs held high
        by circles of dancing men
        around you, facing east.

ADELE SCHWARTZ

CENTRAL PARK ZOO (A VISIT)

Tightly grasping strings
of yellow and gold balloons
I stood at the marvelous lions' cage.
    Eventful eyes wandered to
    spectacular tall buildings,
    glittering distant figures,
    regal strutting dogs.

Yellow and gold balloons rise impatiently
leaving formless, insignificant strings.
Sudden hysteria
evoked clamoring voices,
(like early morning hens—"she lost her
balloon, poor thing!")

endlessly declaring my tears unconvincing—
"You're never satisfied—be happy
you're at the zoo."
Seeing the other balloons rise up!
I knew
I'm through with visits to the zoo.

CON JOB

"Mom, can I borrow three thousand
today?
I really need an expensive medicine, it's hard to get."
"Anything—anything, my son."
(No death—no death.)
"It will be okay. Don't get upset."

"Hi, dear, are you all right?
I tried to get you day and night.

Hello, hello! So what's the news?"
"I'm really just fine, Mom, just needed a cruise."

DICK AND JANE

Dick said to Jane so true,
"Marry me—I love you!"
Jane said to Dick, his eyes deep blue,
"Oh yes, I love you, too!"
So down the aisle went Dick and Jane
and all was A-okay.
Dick, Jane, and Spot, their bonds so new,
one poignant day had "nothing to do"—
then Dick went preying,
Jane went praying;
he found Maud,
she found God.
Seething in court for days,
Dick and Jane went separate ways.
This scene's not old or new—
sad, empty, hours we've muddled through.

DID YOU KNOW HER

Did you know
her hair was like apple blossoms,
her eyes dark
and strong as chestnuts?

Her mother watched her lively walk
and feared what dusk would bring,
as she bent toward the table
and fell forward in fatigue.

When the golden sun
turned pale and weak,
the girl came home
to smell the despair,
the ruins spreading like rust stain;
the facade was over.
The girl's hair flattened
and frayed under steamy clouds,
her eyes dewy and anonymous
as rain on pebbles.

So my friends
that have disappeared,
did you have empathy or sympathy,
apologies, theologies?
Did you have two eyes
to cry with?

ENRAGED

Scrooged villain!
    Your "empty" pockets fill up
    with my last fruits of labor—
    gummy-Valu coupons and cauldrons of pennies
    will not save you.
Your presence leaves
    canaries to whine
    rabbits to crawl
    and fish to die on their backs.

My maniacal laughter
    at your plastics and scanty polyesters
    flow endless tears.
Bright, abundant, bountiful sun,
    dry my tears
and blind me from you.

FORECLOSURE

The woman stands before her home.
The doors are chained together.
She's peering through familiar windows
just to catch a glimpse of what's there now.
The place is dimmer, sterile—
walls become parched of old tears.

She's the marked one in this town,
where geraniums gush blood
and sparrows circle like vultures
to devour all that remains.

FOR GAME CREEK FARM, ALASKA

My sentiments are with you
back at Game Creek.

I'm now in jungles of high-rises,
brassy-carpeted elevators,
materialistic giggles,
leaving lipsticks and trendy sunglasses
on dashboards.

After calling you Jesus freaks,
I escaped your heathered, dry houses
and weathered tabernacles
soaked in potato sacks and Gideon Bibles

as two grand American eagles
swooped toward me,
gulping and clamoring
excerpts from Noah's ark
and a final "God loves you!"

FOR GREGORY

I wouldn't have sent the food back
if we would be together
    just a little longer.
I wouldn't have complained
    about the weird taxi driver
if we could talk about this life's peculiarities.
I wouldn't have told you to hold on and on
so that your boyish sighs would fill my room
    (just a little longer);
any confusion—any delay—to have held us together

FOR LITTLE MIKEY
(August 8, 1981)

Let's stop for awhile
      to think about little Mikey.
Let's pretend it's only a scary movie
      and that he's playing hide and seek.

Look at the sun—it's bright and happy
      and the clouds aren't loose
and hanging in sadness.
      He never had time to talk—

hitting, kicking rocks and obstacles
      that turned into our tears.
He'd always come back
      with a daisied, sullen look.

Are you hiding again, Mikey,
      just behind the pillows and barricades
of a dallying, gold sky,
      holding back tears in your darkest August?

GOOD-BYE TO A FRIEND

I spotted you on Third Avenue—
that airy, recognizable stride,
savvy in your warm merlot
at Melons,

stammering in haughty theories
at bloodshot eyes around you.

Oh yes, that quirky charm
rustling through helium days
in silly conceit,
pulsating your way into bogus galas
to stave off emptiness—

I will not phone you at noon
to hear that muffled
late-morning staleness
half-breathing in satined sleep,
forgetful of your recent DWI hearing.

Your Disney sunset scorches still.
Not enough left in me for you.
Good-bye, old friend. Adieu.

GOOD-BYE TO MY MOTHER

My mother too polite that day,
  a ready smile
   quickly changing to a loose roller coaster.

"She's worried about her dress,"
  says the stiff-shouldered nurse.
  "She still has a price tag on it."

Sterile hospital odors camouflage
  the stench of sickness.
Gazing out into the soft rain,
I deeply breathe the jasmine scent of summer.
Slate clouds move in to darken the room even more.

Sitting at the foot of a half-raised bed,
I watch my mother try a new nail kit.
"I ruined this one!" she says,
  like a harried woman at a salon.

"I love you, Mom," I say,
  rubbing her soft knees,
  heeding my father's warnings
  not to press too hard.
"It's okay—let her, just let her," she insists.

Leaving the pale-green room,
I watch my mother
glancing intermittently at Channel 13's *Safari Hour*.

"Giraffes are the most beautiful creatures!"
  she declares, and turns
  toward the narrow metal closet
  with stormy, uneven eyes,

concerned about the ivory-flowered dress
waiting delicately, formlessly,
to be worn home.

GRADUATION DAY

Sitting in the hot bleachers on a clear June day—
      the Class of '61
leaping, thrusting forward, waving to parents
      siblings, aunts and uncles—
her chest swells underneath the dignified gray gown,
      an obvious red ribbon 'round her neck
(for three years on the honor roll)
      flashes out to a crowd of strangers
(the serious cap and gown become light
      over her heavy heart).

She presses her wrist against her strained eyes
      on a pathetic watch, like some forsaken eagle
looking for her own.
      The diploma's handed out in silence.
Clouds stop moving as life pours from her.
      She hears cries from an old school
with a red door on the side of the building,
      where a five-year-old
waits in a vacant classroom, waits
      for a familiar face,
till the sky's ink black—

erect and separate from the crowd,
      she sees black specks
clot again in the distant horizon.

HER CHEEKS WERE ROSY

Her cheeks were rosy
from his praises,
her face aglow
from pleasures with him,
gliding through airy days.

Then stinging winds moved in
and Satan's long, hard strides
crossed over her
with balls of fire

leaving her, at last,
so raw and parched
before the excuses
of a clear and powerful heaven
and the confusions of a frail hell.

HUSBAND

Sandy was anxious about getting home
      that day (an uncomfortable feeling
            in the pit of her stomach).

Dinner was simmering on the stove
      in anticipation
          of a quiet meal.

The housekeeper was laid out
      on the couch,
          white, drawn, her finger

pointing upward, toward the bedrooms.
      Sandy ran upstairs.
          Her husband's closet

was empty, including the unopened tennis balls.
      On the dresser was $200.00
          and a class picture

of their son Zach,
      his wispy hair blonde,
          touching his shoulders

with a wise-lost look.
      A leaky pen
          (left carelessly behind)

had spread ink over the photo
      and the money, leaving them
          untouchable, black.

HYDROPLANING

The road is Satan's roof—
sleek as a wet seal.
Suddenly daring white lines lose form
spinning like a tossed coin
guessing either heads or tails.
My slicker entraps my torso
and I'm mummified.
Cars come to a gasping halt
and angrily flash me onward
to keep going, keep going
despite the splintered debris
I leave behind.

INCLEMENT DISMISSAL

Glittering metals at rest exaggerate the mist,
spotlights on small bodies—
hunched with book bags,
tousled, fatigued, wrapping up another day.
Out of the abstraction I see my sons's eyes
like two poached eggs
drawn toward the familiar green wagon.
He dives into the back seat,
his face stained with chocolate,
playground smells on his jacket.
His soft-padded hand kneads into my shoulder—
knotting with my wet hair.
Turning around, I see him gazing
at the sealed window.
He looks back at me knowing
more weather is coming.

INTERMISSION AT THE PHANTOM

Bright lights gleaming
on a falling chandelier,
endless eerie music of the night,
a masked lover lingering
purple satin around us. . .

During intermission, a young boy asks,
"Is he a ghost or a real man, Mom?
I know that he's a ghost!"
"I think so, too," I say excitedly,
noticing a strangely grimacing
mother-in-law face,
and tapping, fretting feet
before she comments,
"Really. How can you love a ghost,
love a ghost, love a ghost. . ."

JUSTICE

Vested barristers in pin stripes
    like tigers,
swaying with pockets of tricks,
    salty verses,
white smiles like old movie stars,
wheel in and out of brown rooms.
I, white as bleached laundry,
sit with the orange people,
chained and washed over,
as granite-eyed judges in serious black,
with silly and worn-out decisions.
Last pleas are shredded ribbons evaporating
    floating transparent tickertape
    protesting,
unresolved and messy,
wandering to somewhere, anywhere—
blue children somewhere else,
scattered in open fields,
bent like twigs forced to bloom
without the sun's warmth,
our grief our only possession now,
bleeding all over this blue-green world.

LETTING GO

He's kneeling into the earth
his eyes aglow like fires
to seize what's deep down
with tenacious paws
sliding toward me breathless and muddy;
leaves fallen creatures at my feet;
skips back with blackened cheeks
and dives into his mud pillows once more,
primal, proud, to leave yet another love token.

Now with long determined strides
his innocence evolves as savvy, stoic;
kneeling into mud stones,
I look for these gifts alone

MOVING BACK

When I found out about the move,
I vomited in the locked bathroom for hours.

The austere van pulled away
from Hewes Street and Lee Avenue,
the only home I remembered
(past Ellis's Deli,
my Sunday haven in club bread
and glowing hot pastrami).

Rozzie, my closest friend,
waved me off feverishly with swollen tears,
vowed she'd call me every day
(I guess she meant it at the time).

I cried mildly and leaned
on my mother's soft shoulder,
shared her deep breathing,
and went with the rhythm
as she murmured nervously.

East Paterson was a reunion for my father,
a separation for my mother,
unanswered questions for me—
the lawns and flowers seemed prissy
(growing outside the Brooklyn Botanical Gardens),
and there were no banners or Welcome Back signs
from friends, as my sister had promised,
to shut me up.

Some dressed well
and others not so well,
just strange, I thought.

People were less exhausted
and smiled more than I was used to.
The kids at the Gilbert Avenue School
looked corn-fed, and after calling them
"a bunch of hicks," they beat down on me
after school and never spoke to me again
till high school.
I took refuge in my back yard,
contemplating the huge New Jersey acorns
that fell slowly,
deliberately in clusters.

ADELE SCHWARTZ

MY MOTHER ON HAND AND FOOT

My mother on hand and foot
pushed the portable server
so my dad could watch TV and eat
(well, there was nothing new to say).

He'd chew his meat yet never swallow it—
he was a vegetarian of sorts.

He loved her for that
and her acceptance
of never to dance
or the dreams after a New York show.

She was too busy picking up
the clothes that fell off our backs, anyway.
Stayed up to 3:00 watching
the Late Late
with her sweet late snacks.

I'm not one to judge, grown and alone,
yet the pity I have
for the reasons she stayed
I hope will remain.

ON MY DAUGHTER'S GRADUATION
(for Steffi, June 1985)

Tangled in dark woods,
my burning feet
are lodged in quicksand
paths to the stadium—
please, please

The clear and simple air of June,
the caps and gowns
covering diversities of ripened children,

you there
square cap crooked,
one eye blinded
by a golden tassel,
the gown's folded hem
sweeping the ground,

you erect, stiff,
obediently in place,
walking on the mountains
of the pomp and circumstance's
pensive beats,
you who wait still, still
on the hard seat,
spotting the empty space
near your brother.

Gold and blue angels toss
their halos in the air
to father and foe,
to spread and root like vines
on red-brick buildings,

as is expected,
like a mother's presence at a graduation.

What
can I, then, expect of you?

PEACOCKS

The peacocks loiter in the neighborhood,
prancing as if on high wires,
sliding softly with stretched necks
       toward the heavens.

The woman looks out of her half-opened window
       with dizzying eyes;
they trot in packs, with omnipresent smiles
at torn safety nets and those blinded by
       the hard fall off their tightrope.

Their weightless chatter grows louder and teasing;
       the woman's mind whirls;
enraged, she shuts the window tight,
cloudy with sighs chooses a humble costume
 that will please their glassy eyes that day.

PERFUME BOTTLES
AND MUSIC BOXES

In Aunt Lainey's bedroom,
I'd lock the door on visits
to stay away from my doll-like cousins,
Jane and Liz, as flat
as their matching heart-shaped lockets
holding photos of each other,
who'd kindly give me Best & Company
hand-me-downs.

I'd try the door again in Lainey's bedroom
to secure my privacy,
and strap her green silk high heels on
to dance dramatically
with the pink-netted ballerina
on the mirrored dance floor of the music box,
remembering Aunt Lainey's dear assurances

when she referred to me as "little sunbeam"
and "far prettier than all your cousins,"
especially when wearing their old Best & Company's
very best. I'd dab some scent on
from each of many bottles,
fall into the folds and crevices
of Lainey's purple satin sheets

above which hung the picture, much discussed,
of five quite naked dancing ladies
holding scarves in soft pastels
and bright bouquets of lilies,
like Isadora Duncan dancers.
I'd caress this splendor where Aunt Lainey
slept with her third dazzling husband—

to be woken harshly by Aunt Betty
(Jane and Liz's mother)
in her sensible tweeds,
inquiring
if I'd ever be a little girl
as good as hers.

POEM

I was going to write a poem
        growing up in Harry's corner store—
        button candies, mini Mary Janes,
        bright yellow yo-yo's,
        the reliable ruddy-aproned knish man
        pushing his greasy patties
        forbidden to me
        for fear of an appendectomy—
        the green store near P.S. 16
        where we shared Lenny's philosophies
        on half sours.

I was going to write a poem
        of that long, high-ceilinged hallway
        that led to the only door that locked,
        weeping at the sight of strange
        bright redness flowing unaware, afraid,
        heavily drawing Nagel's new
        "natural" lipstick,
        eyeing the soap that would remove
        its sultry glow.

I was going to write of
        tight schedules in shiny German cars,
        moonstruck watches holding malignant time,
        square rural footages
        of bland kisses and bruised rooms.

Someone's princess
        someone's slave
        someone's miracle
        someone's monster—
            was going to write a poem.

REMEMBERING THE GROUP
AT HOLLOW HILL

Unpeopled, vacant now,
it was once there:
tamely toughing it out in the tightest tee,
fiercely discontent in sun-streaked rain,
> so there was always a joint around
> in some back cabaña,
> while Edie's come-hither looks
> at Carol's husband never ceased,
> as Jeff tossed tennis balls
> too far back as he watched
> Franny run after them
> in her short-short tennis skirt.

The kids kept busy in weekend day camp,
> never noticed,
> reminding us only occasionally
> of their needs,
> like when Jill's favorite doll
> was thrown in the pool
> and left her
> on an obsessive search all summer.

We were so tired
> of making love not war—
> our privileged group that vanished so
> to different corners.

I want to dive to the bottom of the pool,
> and save my daughter's drowned doll
> at the deepest end of the green darkness,
> and kiss away
> the crusted tears of Hollow Hill.

SECOND BORN

They called it after-birth pain.
The horror of it—
when I thought it was all over,
it just started, sharp and cruel.

"It happens sometimes," said the nurse,
"only after the first child."
"There's no time for this!" I shouted,
knowing somehow the desperation of time.

"Just stop this! I must see my son!"
Thus the moment, brief,
before a memory too quickly bursts—
his content, sweet smile,

blue, round, and moist.
"Such a good baby," they agreed.
I begged to hold him
just as his obedient body held onto me.

But time's our enemy,
and armies of our pain
keep us moving, just missing each other,
on parallel roads.

SEPARATION

I was the kind of kid
who held onto my mother's ankles
that life-threatening first day of school.
She stood faithfully at the school window
covered with nostalgic leaves of a dying summer,
slowly edging away—I escaped a stunned classroom
>　to find her,
>　to find her,
>　always to find my mother.

SHE HANDED BACK

She handed back my book of poems,
decided they were unreadable now,

her elegant hands above her face, perplexed.
She walked to her distant room,

cuddled in fetal form, and wept.
She wrote a large note—the letters

smudged by tears.
My fingers stiffened,

and I dropped the ink-filled weapon.
She picked the pen up and placed it

in her breast pocket
(in keeping, perhaps, for another time),

and, with a half-smile,
forgave me for awhile.

SHE WANTED TO

She wanted to go to England that summer
       wanted to see her first grandchild
       and would gloat with each awesome kick—
tiredly carried my groceries
       those last two waddling months.
She wanted to be a blonde by August
       and promised not to back out this time.

Her diagnosis sounded
like a hoarse and brooding cello.
       Dad lost his lively walk;
his smile at best became a forced grin:
       "Dammit all! She waited too damn long!"
It'll be okay, though, he went on
       with a troubled, enduring stare—
the constant MRIs throughout the summer,
       her gaunt cheeks turning sallow,
a sullen little-girl fright
       with each tight-clotted cough,
the smothered sobs on wide-eyed nights,
       skimming through pages of *Why Bad Things
Happen to Good People*, not absorbing a word
       of its bloody instructions.

ADELE SCHWARTZ

SUMMER CAMP

Wasn't your life
       turbulent enough
that summer we sent you
       to camp?

You were so lonely there
       with cool and distant counselors—
moody bunkmates
       and shivering nights with screened walls.

You came home thinner,
       paler, with lice in your hair.
Oh, sweet Steffie—
       your lovely silken hair.

SUNDAY RELATIVES

My childhood visits come back—
bland peach Sundays,
Hungarian meatballs simmering,
as thin tight-lipped smiles stretch out
　　　with my words:
　　　　"I think it'll work this time!"

Looks hissing like the flat tire of a Mack truck,
I play the obligatory relative
to my mother's pink-kneed sister
and her son enamored of initialed shirts
with matching cuff links,
sitting still, sweet with polite reasonableness,
their napes resting stiff
against matching leather chairs,
exhaling sighs to release last trickles
of family cold wars,
running off warning commentaries
on "the tough streets out there"
and "if only you had. . . ."

My whirling ambitions move out
faster than ever
to the coolness of strangers
who help soothe high-noon burns
and shoo away ancestral wolves.

THAT JULY

We sat in the living room like dried compote.
You cleaned up all your what used to be's
down to your silkies.
Your oily harsh framed hands
shoved garbage down our throats
unexpected open mouths
like sparrows.
Cedar shake boards around us,
warped and splintered,
littering the streets where peacocks strolled,
we became unknown in our shameful shawls,
counting pennies for tonight's feast
of gamey organs,
too tired to tape the wide cracks
of our once gilded doors.

THE ACTRESS

Waking at noon
     in peeling rooms,
the mild stench of forgotten garbage,
cockroaches speedily turning in,
she sits erect
     before her mirror,
draws soft kohl lines
carefully around her eyes and lips.

Smudged sunlight seeps
through a streaked window,
contrasting her refining art:
     a final look,
     the usual frown,
     a spray of Fabergé—her oxygen.

She grasps a tin
of leftover Diet Coke,
a ten-minute-late look
     on her dusty midnight face,
forcing energy and glee
     on flashing cameras,
     lashing voices—
     "Next!"
     "We'll call you—"
waiting on her last table,
inhaling her deep last drag. . .
     the note
     the unheard answering machine.

THE BABY SITTER

When my daughter babysat
I'd worry,
hopeful that her younger brother
avoided thumb tacks
or other inedibles.

My friends would say, "Relax,"
eating their dinner leisurely,
for absence of worry
somehow guaranteed
a sweet calm
in charmed dwellings.

My daughter, usually hysterical—
thinking she might have heard someone
in the yard, bathroom,
maybe the kitchen,
she wasn't sure—
always concerned
over her younger brother,
who, wide-eyed and with blotched cheeks
assured her that no one was there,
stronger at seven than she at twelve.

Yet the wisdom of five more years
was not in vain;
she worried about a man (she'd call Daddy)
she heard every day
but never really knew—
who would steal her brother
and her world.

THE CURLED CUL DE SAC

The curled cul de sac
wraps itself in neatly lined
bi-levels and splits—
cedar on brick, brick on cedar,
matching shutters
as individual as the perfect geranium beds.

Hazy silhouettes move about
within mauve and peach walls
that absorb daily mutterings
of late BMW lease payments
and two tuitions due at BU
and that "great cruise"
Sandy and Bob took last summer
and why can't we?

THE FIXED SUNDAY

I phoned my daughter at half past eight;
she hung up quickly—guess she was late.
I phoned my sister at 8:32.
"I'm at the door, we're off to the zoo."
I saw my neighbor at 9:03,
I saw him—he didn't see me.
I waved to him—worked out and gray.
He smiled and said, "Have a nice day."
I bolted the door at 9:08,
muffled the phone,
x'd out the date.

THE MOTHER

Glue-eyed and heavy footed
I entered the misty vapored room,
sounds of a frantic storm
tossing and turning with fever,
my daughter's cheeks like two jelly apples.

I lurked helplessly outside her door
like a lost alley cat
to heroically spoon dosages of pallid fluids,
her room glowing of iridescent disinfectants—
then the calm steady breathing,
smooth as a jet plane;
pulling back the wisps of her moist brown hair,
I move toward the dark gray sill
    as street lights become
    honking cars
    and hustling feet of a healing morning.

THE RED BOOK AND MY SISTER

Bent over the book, pupils dilated,
my sister glanced around to assure her privacy.
I gave her the signal—A-okay, all's clear.
"This is the 'sex book.'" She grinned.
Comrades we were in that rare moment,
two shadows sitting like eagles
ravenously flipping through glossy pages,
groping for their hidden magic
of what had brought us here.
Words bounced off the pages
like water beads on oil,
our faces blank, our minds like Teflon.

THE SHORT ESCAPE

His schoolboy tantrum
ended in generous, caressing
August foliage,

Yellow-green moss his calico blanket;
mosquitoes lullabied him to purring sleep,
protected by a diligent, maternal moon.

A wrinkled crayon drawing of a square house
with square windows
and a door off-centered, square,
fell to the green velvet ground,
judged only by armies of insects.

THE TWO LIVE-INS

"John,
   did you get those tickets for the
      Sondheim show?"
"We'd better not. It's gonna snow!"
"I'd love to see Hopper at the Guggy, too."
"There's a parade—the city is a zoo!"
"Gee, Joplin's gigging at the Met."
"Are you kidding? It's raining, we'll get wet!"
"Mary,
   did you look for that job in the *Sun?*"
"You know, John. . .
   the day ended before it had begun!"

THE VISIT

I pushed open the door.
Reclining against a yellowing white pillow
was my father,
his eyes vacant.
The phone was trapped
in his half-open, motionless hand.
The coiled wires spiraled lazily
against his frail, pale thighs,
as if giving up.

He looked at me blankly.
"What's wrong, Dad?" I said.
Impatiently, he stared,
as if I were to blame,
as if my own unsettled life had gotten to him.

My shrieks stormed through the vacant air.
I touched his cold lips,
knelt beside his body stiff,
the lost currents of his life
rolling through me—
as if I were a burning thorn
disturbing his deep sleep.

THE YOUNG GIRL

One Friday afternoon the young girl
          returned home at the usual time.
          Distinct in chaotic order,

her house was sullen, confused;
          odors of stable, proper meals lingered
          on the gray shawl of the young girl's mother,

who, nervously upset, tended
          to early spring's tight leaves
          and spitefully closed buds.

They looked around for signs of movement
          and a brazen hint of warmth,
          but the neighbors shut their tight doors.

Fearful of "getting involved"
          in the oddly transformed "turn of events,"
          the neighbors stayed safe and sequestered—

complained about
          the stubborn ways
          of this cold spring.

Summer came with its thick grass
          and soft marigolds;
          this pleased the neighbors,

who loved survivors and blossoms,
          the two women left the home
          with a strong sun above them,

the young girl's childlike shadow stayed behind.

THERE ARE MANY KINDS OF STORIES

This is a legend re:
a big shot,
obvious as his nose,
with a smile as square as a grill.

As the moon rose,
he moved far away
until no one could see him,
his transparency aglow with glitter,
adorning castanet queens,
rolling up his LL.B.
into a weed,
smoking it on flimsy routes—
what a nifty fellow!

Must give credit where it's due.
He was choosy about whom to screw,
usually brown, dimpled types
with definitive boobs.
He passed quickly through his urbane life,
sealing his honesty in a deep scroll.

THURSDAY'S TULIPS
(for Greg, May 25, 1972)

Thursday's tulips
bushes, firmed to their petaled best,
stand up clean and crisp
as spring seersucker.

I was born for this day—
no need to do
a thing now,
give a damn
outside of you
sweet folded
in the blanket of my gut.

My throbbing womb still aches;
it has no mind, no will,
just gives, gives flawlessly.

TODAY WE LEFT

Today we left our house
on the rounded dead-end,
the carefully planned chocolate brown door,
still glossy against worn cedar shingles,
closing in the ghostly, plumaged rooms,
pictures on walls a bit
more crooked now.

Today we left
with quick-breathing minds,
firm-footed on the unkempt, rusty sod patches,
needling our tired soles,
needing a moment to ponder
the stump of the unwanted apple tree
dead rooted in this town's infamous radon.

We left no residue
like that of Grace's plant,
with spattered hearts still in multicolored
Halloweens and sparkling Fourth of Julys,
courageous as the red brick behind.

To woeful jobs,
sorry ties,
ceaseless, unwanted remarks,
knowing this place was not really
for us.

TO MY DAD

I used to jump up and down
to hear your quiet footsteps after a long day,
used to feel bad when you looked sad
and said, "I'm tired,"
used to leap into your arms to feel that strong loving
grip on my chin,
to know my vices were yours, too,
to see through your proud eyes and hope one day
you'd see through mine,
regret these things you never used to know.

TURNED BACK

Turned back
 like Lot's wife,
  to see the sunny places
    where a few bucks
    and some clever remarks
      get you somewhere
   holding on to charlatan jobs
     (from who knows who)
   and obvious marriages
     till whenever
   trying to be positive
     approaching the millennium.

Turned back
 like Lot's wife,
  see the old dark moon's
   stained eyes,
      more vital than ever,
    looking down on spotless gardens,

whirling salt and old dust,
  getting closer to the stars,
    the road unknown.

UNTITLED

Once upon a time,
there was a house
where love reclined under chairs.

Once upon a time,
there was a house
where children grew sturdy, happy as morning,
with rooms of hugs and kisses that flattered life.

Once upon a time,
pets wagged and tumbled through days
snuggled in popcorn nights.

Once upon a time,
there was a house
where love reclined under chairs,
where love reclined under chairs,
once upon a time.

WAITING ROOM

We sat closely in the waiting room
of the intensive-care unit,
my daughter clutching her moist tissues
blackened by mascara,
absorbing her prayers
for her father's recovery.

I wait with forced patience
and determined indifferences
for one who removed us
from his table of feasts,
leaving us only a mysterious strength.

Sitting stiffly, barely there,
I'm saddened by my daughter's
innocent, unearned concern.

She grasped my hand when informed
of his positive prognosis,
thanked me for being there for her,
and all that seemed strange and nonsensical
suddenly made sense.

WILLIAMSBURG

Being there was neurosis
of the stuffed: veal, kishka, cabbage, chicken

it was about listening to Cantor Moishe
over sweet-sour meat

it was visiting neighbors with aching, watered eyes,
revealing branded numbers on arms,

long-sleeved unraveling in clusters of children.
Williamsburg, with pure white Rosh Hashanahs

and whiter Yom Kippurs
as cathartic as banked lightning,

it was about the small purse of a seven-year-old
loosely dangling on a coat button

on a celebrated Saturday noon
in fear of Shabbos-goy mimickings.

WINTER BREAK (1983)

My son standing close to my agitations
over a silver server too tarnished to shine,

this was the place of family ties,
his Batman mask hanging loosely around his neck,
sun-stroked bangs covering
his startled and too-wise eyes.

Purposefully lifting his mask over his brow—
"Swiping down the monsters,"
he says with a theatric Mom-I-could-do-anything stance,
follows me through the house
as I turn lights on in dusk's quiet rooms,
listening for his father's end-of-day footsteps,
he starts to stretch out his arms,
then fiercely holds back,
ripples of loss all over his turned-up face.

Impure changes begin here,
through cloudy and debt-ridden hallways,
passing abandoned stuffed animals,
holding on
and letting go of justifiable hatreds,
biting the still wind's rougher passages
through cracked doors.

YESTERDAY'S BREAKFAST

It was absorbed
        somewhere,
all that was worth the process——
        the elegant crimson love seat,
        oriental birds strong in flight
        on a water-stained silk screen,
        there in transparent form.

The rooms are empty
        and the paint on the sills and woodwork
        is warped and chipped.
A soft beam rests on the hot pink carpet
        in my daughter's room;
        the plum pansies on the wallpaper
        sag in old moisture.

I left my cheerful yellow gloves
        on the kitchen table,
        near yesterday's breakfast,
        the last time I was there.
Bet they've turned a hard and dirty gold
        from waiting.

The White Pigeon

ABOUT POETRY

The writer's block,
the phone off the hook,
the nervous breakdown—

you give up
the blank stare
outside the window,

the sky's black and gold,
the crickets' night music,
owl's orchestration,

a ballet of bats,
a young couple
lost in all this.

A DAY IN HEAVEN

Bitter toxins seep through seaweed grains;
  we're wrapped in the black, fetal moisture
            of the Dead Sea's pearly mud packs.

Naked reflexology points press down
            on the toes of our souls;
            tight disciplines escape and blend
            with lavender vapors.

We float like petals on a soft pond,
            tired years drowning
            in herbal, peppermint-green froth.

Our faces gleam
            like a new moon
            through mysterious smoke.

Sapped of anxieties,
            we leave our day in heaven
            brilliant, light,
            grinning as if we were twelve!

A HUDSON RIVER VIEW

Hudson River beauty:
still movements between seasons,
stiff meringue peaks in winter frost,
the soft caress of summer blossoms
in urban pinks and golds,
cleansing and meditative
on smoky, silent days
in moist gauze clouds—

you move with the lights, the breezes,
defying the rigidity
of a skyline that always
looks down at you.

A MOMENT

"What do you mean?"
"You know what I mean!" he said,
wiping the sweat off his neck and his brow.

She stood looking down
with her hands on her rounded hips.
"Yeah, but I don't understand what you're saying."

"Let's cut out this game. You know just what I mean,"
he said, shoving his stained handkerchief
in his shabby, beige jeans.

"Oh, Richard, you just beat around the bush—
get to the point. I'm so tired of this!"
She frantically brushed her long chestnut hair.

"Why, by now it's become more than obvious.
Jesus, the way that he looks at you.
Sickening."

"I can't control his dumb,
lost-puppy stares. He's meaningless to me,"
she said in her best breathless sigh.

Ramming his baseball cap back on his head
with the peak to the back,
he stormed out quite drained,

his eyes deeply circled, and, turning, he shouted,
"You always had something about you
that I never wanted to know!"

A MOMENT AT THE CAFE

Hysterical tongue floating in salivary waters
like slippery algae in warm seas—
I, amused at this one-way dialogue
of a fragile daughter with child?

Or rhetoric of thundering red days?
Silent other, patient as a still pond,
your heart grows in a swollen ear.

A MOMENT AT THE DINER

A woman with braided salt-and-pepper hair
sat at the counter,
nursing her eighth cup of coffee.

"They turn away when things get mixed up,"
she said to the well-dressed older man
with a wise air.

"The balloons start falling
on your head, don't they?"
he sympathized.

She opened her compact in a frown
(her symmetrical cheekbones sunken
as if the world had pressed in on them)
and grinned. "Yeah, the crowd thins out,
and there's always bird shit on your car,
and that's not good luck."

The man looked through
the lottery section in the paper
and chuckled. "You win the Lotto, dear,
and the process starts again.
They come back, kiss your ass,
to fill your hours with bogus crap,
and suddenly the wind blows
in a different direction."

The woman snapped her compact shut,
blew her nose in a used hanky,
replaced it in her worn-out purse;
she squeezed his rounded, shrinking shoulders,
softly moaned, "I have a cold.
I think I'll sleep alone."

AND THE STREETS
SPARKLE OF GEMS

O solemn, long-faced social worker,
don't push me—sore, scaly, mangy—
to the aching green walls of the flophouse.

I have only a few changes and miss
the ferocious dancing fires
of burning news headlines

near a private cardboard room
with spacious acres under the West Side Highway,
and the spring scent of summer ferns

from half-open shutters on my corner
at spiffy Waverly Place.
Tight-lipped volunteer,

find something else to do.
No iron-post bed with yellowed hard sheets
and rattling windows that assure immunity

to safety—to sleep with one eye open
as stubble-bearded men
with white calcareous hands

slip into the fruitful end of my pack,
through dirty laundry and beaten-up mementos.
Life's too deliberate out here for sniffles

and tearless sobs,
and the sidewalk's a symphony of roaring trains,
and the streets sparkle of gems still!

A PARK SCENE

Two hand in hand
bent in summation of their years,
white headed, eyes gleaming
with the innocence of youth,
deeply lidded wise eyes—
the music of two hand in hand.

My five-mile run now done,
I'm pensive on the lost moments
        of my youth,
bitter about middle years
        when life's gong
echoes away,
        my bland heart,
        deaf ear,
        my empty hand.

A TYPE OF WISDOM COMES

When I call my cousin
to spend some hours at his new pool
and he says he's having friends over,
some other time,
(I feel as if I've just had root canal);
or when I give my book of poems
to my ex-mother-in-law,
and she rips through it defiantly
and says, "If you could afford
to write poems, that's great,"
or when my live-in life
becomes despair,
and my immovable pain
pushes me to the front,
to the world of singles,
alone in this new career,
my black-and-blue wounds will fade
without surviving in spurts of warmth.

Yet I stay alive in cold uncertain moments,
waiting for the next lesson.

BECAUSE I STOPPED

Because I stopped at the flashing lights
     of a school bus
     and saw flickering eyes peer through
     the spotted windows,

I was reminded of new freedoms,
old commitments—
        how lucky not to have to meet him
        at weary 3 p.m., to see his bright day face
        dull as he searched for my car,
        (and, since he wasn't breast-fed,
        I suppose it led to displacements).

Relieved of frustrations,
        encouraging those veggies,
        he defiantly munched on his junks,
        those sleepless nights of giggling kids
        making faces as they praised
        my too-doughy toll-house cookies,
        glued morsels stuck to their teeth,

I'm left with stories, the ones I started with,
     perhaps.

BLACK EYE

When I was eight
my cousin Barbie hit me in the eye
(I never knew why).

She made up for it
by doing my homework for a week.
I wore that black eye

valiantly, forgiving,
vulnerable
("Nice Jewish girls don't hit back").

Bonnie O'Leary,
my best friend, though,
vehemently disagreed.

Years later,
I had my revenge when Barbie
was an estranged divorcée

(pathetically independent)
and I was still
engaged in proper marriage,
to speak always

of my beloved husband
and bright kids and all the torches
fate bestowed on me.

She helped me do
my homework once again.

I think I now

know why she hit me
in the eye.

BLOCK 29

Vanishing stars barely illuminate empty pages
unrevealed words
once sharp, daring, open,
a yellow star is sewn into your heart,
nobody knows you, Anna,
your mysterious bleeding blends with burning flesh,
empty fingers grope to write,
finding a tooth dipped in blood,
avoiding words, fearing words,
surrounded by human transformations,
naked bodies white as chalk,
glazed eyes, ears astute
as those of frightened deer,
kneeling, urinating on splintered bones,
as thumps of goose steps
and twisted emblems of twisted minds
pull souls out of their shells.

COLLAGE BY TWO

Black circles and bitter pieces of white root
        swirl in and out
        of waning shadows—
a folded childhood, pale and ego thin,
like the delicate tissue paper
        over pebbles,
adding neatly executed boundaries,
monotone lines in one direction, stuck
        like strange luck.

Effortless red petals touched by dewy hands,
        smiling like cherries on white linen,
        to fight the sallowness
        as the second touches this piece
        with partial photos
        of pearly faces and grinning dogs
        against a background
        of green birds and opening tulips—

a complete work now
        in dark shadows and tawny shades,
        flattened and framed,
        indistinct, misunderstood.

DAISIES AND WEEDS

Simple foliage,
the farmer's nightmare,
unwanted, free,

with each pluck,
the thicker you grow—
straighter than the lilacs,
greener than the rose,
jagged in tedious rain,
palsied in snow,
growing reckless and wild in rough fields,
blades of lead with crowns pure white,

bastards of nature,
defying the day,
standing up to night.

DAPHNE, THE RABBIT

Runs to the door
so much like a dog,
licks smells on my clothes
and wounds of a frantic day.

She sheds on dark clothes, too—
a ploy to not forget her
and her hunger,
placid eyes
that wait for me to fill her plate.

She sniffs the grains, turning toward me,
ears flop over, head atilt,
in a silent gaze of love,
of loyalty.

DECEMBER'S DAY OFF

Woke up to a jagged, icy sun.
My forehead warmer today,
I indulged in that needed five minutes more,
reading a poem by Emily Dickinson
(great for a recluse, I thought).

Chills flowed from my shoulders down
through my legs.
Vaguely drawn to the clear window,
I felt the snapping air seep in.
Oddly frustrated
by quiet traffic and chattering evergreens,
I embarked on a shadowless panache,
slow to catch up
on whatever's left at 3 p.m.,
December 24.

DILEMMA

I found you
that hazy night;

then you followed me
around every dark corner

and sunlit bus.
You were really crazy

about me. . .anyway,
I dodged you, darted you,

pushed you away,
then relented—

to hold you at last.
So you could walk off, too.

My legs crumbled downward
toward you.

DIVORCE

She jogs to sublime elevation.
A scary vacancy hangs in the air.
The lies, the twisted conversations,
"walking on eggs" M.O., dispersed in the wind.

"Got a lemon, make lemonade," they say.
But all those preparations
(the blueprints, the fresh break
in the foundation,

carefully measured built-ins,
final floral touches)—
the death of this
for the boy whose lips

resemble his mother's,
and the girl with her father's eyes.
They're burning leaves outside.
She wipes the ash dust off

and heavily relines her lips,
puts on the unworn black strapless,
insignificantly hums a tune
that blends with the cackles of any fall.

DREAM

I sulked all day,
      feeling apart
            from life's festivities.

That night
      I dreamt
            about a man in my building

who always seemed
      exciting, upbeat, joyous.
            In my dream

the building was sketchy,
      hazy, and surrealistic;
            there were no walls or doors.

I walked toward him,
      as huge clouds
            passed through us.

I could tell
      he loved me
            from the way he spoke.

He talked about
      his girlfriend,
            her tough life, and how

he'd helped her
      "get back on her feet."
            He drove near the lot,

and blood was gushing
        out of his mouth;
                he left his car and jumped

in front of a bus.
        Knowing he was quite ill,
                I tried to stop him,

but a thin, frail hand
        held me
                back, and when I looked,

it was his girlfriend,
        her eyes demonic,
                piercing. . .so many

obstacles, passions,
        sorrows
                at least in this dream.

DREAM KILLERS

In drama class it was explained
only two per cent will
rise to fame.

In pre-law it was said
fifteen percent will pass the bar—
that is, those that get ahead!

In science lab we were told
that thoughts of cancer cures,
for now, are far too bold.

Historical dilemmas,
wise as they may seem,
kill.

EASTER SHOW

The late morning tingled with excitement;
her parents took her
to the Easter Show at Radio City—
and it was a good thing—
for her incurable clumsiness.

It was a glamorous day,
her father in his white-lapeled suit
and wider tie,
her mother in that gray Marlena Dietrich
sarong dress, with a matching hat
worn at a slant—
a veil mysteriously
covering one eye.

The theater glowed
as the Rockettes kicked out
with glistening, molded legs
in perfect unison.

The girl watched without flinching,
her breath faster and louder
with each high scissor step,
the sparkle of costumes showering on her face,

and yes, with pie plate soles
and hermit-crab feet,
she kicked above her head—
not missing a day of it—
with sparkling skirts and feathers
around small shoulders,
danced and danced,

arms linking to imaginary figures
in a chorus line—

and it was a good thing—
the make-believe audience
applauding
her poise, her beauty, her sacred duty.

EREV ROSH HASHANAH

Pale blue clouds soften the red of Indian Summer,
anguished memories of tired,
tumultuous days without you.

The clear golden day here glistens on your stones:
Ida Lebowitz, Beloved Mother, Grandmother, Sister;
Irving Lebowitz, Beloved Father, Grandfather, Brother.

Aunts and uncles right behind,
as they were on weekend highways;
other relatives
just below, surrounded by unfamiliar names,
rounded dedications,
engraved silences of the bosom
that comfort my touch
when I lay a stone on your names
before the trembling holy days,
kiss letters in stone
to follow my sister,
absorbing beloved ghosts.

ESTRANGED

I know you think
you're not what I expected,
so you hide from me
the way you did back then,
when things became hurtful, uncertain.

Give me your hand
and hold on, squeeze hard.
There's time on our side.

Driving along the Hudson,
I see the sunset sparkling around
your building, just close enough
to catch a glimpse
of you in the light.

You're unattainable these days
and keep a safe distance between us.
I pick up the car phone
and put it down again in one swift motion—
I'm afraid to call and hear
the usual distant response
but try to forget you,
to forget,
and all those things
no one will see
quite like me.

FADING FACES

Dark spots on sun
reflect man's tragic scientific blooms—
almighty chemicals
that simulate life.

Fate sneers at fading faces
that rush volcanically with marqueed hopes
always to be a part of Times Square's raucous
serenades
and the immediate unfailing New York skyline
at any cost.

FANTASY

I dreamed I caught you smoking
and eating red meats,
harming yourself,
wasting others.

I sit at a desk
and you are astute in a chair
opposite me,
actually listening.

A gush from somewhere outside
catches your attention,
and you look away, become absorbed
in the sound of water

rushing downhill
soothing your burning pain.
I expect you to put out your cigarette
and munch on greens and beans,

but you light up and eat a bloody hamburger,
our session together coming too late.

GRIDLOCK

Gridlock's not a religion
      or a matter of sexual proclivity yet,

Yet it's there, here,
      impervious to the quick-tempered nerves
      of the indestructible New Yorkers
      who wish Clinton and the other heroes
      would all stay the hell home.

Even New Jersey's and Connecticut's
      calmer 4 X 4's can't bear it—
      sagging, tired tires
      loiter through glued streets
      (Which way's one way?
      How come? Two ways?
      Wind up none.)

New York's too splendid
      for pulsating indecisions,
         inanimate traffic noises,
         tortuous fumes
         taut middle fingers going
         up and up and up
         unintentionally violating
         roller-bladers,
         fathomless schedules crushed,
         dangerously late!

HANGOVER

Strange percolating sun
contrasting this ugly morning,
eyes heavy as anchors
holding down a floating head.

The ball ended over a sleeping city,
guests drowning in champagne moments,
glowing in pink-yellow lights,
drinking to release spontaneity,
drinking to dull pain,
drinking to allow that fleeting charm to shine,
drinking to love,
drinking to drink.

Rising to a tucked-in city,
damp and weak,
I pick up the usual stained denim jacket,
  exit for
    aspirins—
    a slow walk,
      having died a little today.

HEAVEN'S GATE MASSACRE, MARCH 27, 1997

Purple shrouds decorate their last triumph,
triangular sleep to a passive somewhere,
falling too gently like blossomed petals
   (in ritualistic order)
melting the hearts of those who shake their fists
   at earth's injustices,
roaring ,thundering, trudging heart-sore for threads
   of hope,
always avoiding that trip
to those rigid gates of heaven.

HER EX TELLS MADELINE

Her ex tells Madeline,
"Marry that guy you live with."
On the other end of the line,
he studies the crinkled photo of the kids,
the sparkling yard and lovely Madeline,
their faces warped, cracked,

realizes the neglect—
the need for laminations over time.
He touches the photo,
pictures it as smooth and even,
and how all the shiny plastics in the world

would have kept their smiles
crisp, clear,
and how he would protect them all now,
and, if he could, how, probably, he would.

HOME

"I'm going home,"
I said to a newfound friend
          at the pub—

the word a painful one
          to me,
but where does one go
          after the good brew
          and worn-out laughs?

I'm going home!
I'm going to a place where
          "when you have to go there,"
          said a wise man,
          "they have to take you in."

So many homes had I
          in time,
          yet so few places to live in,
          when the days are done.

IDIOM MAN

So, big shot,
  you're a space cadet, a piece of cake,
  cried wolf in tall stories.
  Caught you red-handed
  trying to kill two birds.
  You pulled wool over our eyes.
  You're busted—eat crow!
  Let the cat out of the bag—
  you'll pay through your nose,
  lose your shirt.

Let's see eye to eye:
  I hit the ceiling, smelled a rat,
  went ape,
  put 2 + 2 together
  through lots of red tape.
  Too much elbow grease.
  Got under the weather.

Snowed from your snow jobs
  (it's raining cats and dogs),
  I feel like turning over a new leaf.
  You're not my main man,
  and that's the word.

IF I KNEW MY GRANDMOTHER

She'd have a great nickname
with lots of rolling vowels—
she'd be petite and strong
with blue-gray eyes (like my Dad).

She'd stir over the stove for hours
to test-taste her Eastern European dishes
of homemade varnishkas (from scratch)
and moist meats with their thick, red, cozy sauces.

Everything would fall in place;
somehow she'd create perfections
from little or even nothing
and hint at the basic joys—

"Thank God for just a nice clean house
and a full stomach—"
and repeat it till it grew cathartic
as a mantra.

She'd greet me on special Friday nights
with a glow from burning, flickering lights
straight across our faces—
not remain the void I see.

ILLNESS

A small lump,
        white blood cells working overtime—
                my arm blows up, taut, red.

The pale green hospital room,
        and antiseptic sheets
                come off bland yet scary.

My clutched fist enhances
        one good vein yet not quite
                obedient enough to take the intravenous.

The Hungarian doctor glances toward me
        with a reassuring look
                over my shoulder, and says,

"It vill be fine, dahling,"
        but he doesn't
                meet my eyes.

I bite my lips
        as the other three physicians
                circle in a huddle, whispering softly,

then more softly (are they saying
        "amputate"?). The one from Hungary
                tells me to relax, relax, *relax*

(he still avoids my eyes)
        as a nurse drains vials of blood
                with an exaggerated grin.

"I know I have AIDS!" I shout,
    but I'm
        hardly promiscuous

(but who knows?).
    I refuse more blood tests;
        the assistant can't release

my fingers (digging in her arm).
    I hide beneath the sheet for days;
        the fever breaks, the swell subsides.

"We found the right antibiotic,"
    he explains. "It vas
        peculiar virus, dahling."

The rain outside looks like
    so many clear balloons in celebration.
        I check my elbow

for the lump
    and feel the cushion
        of my daughter's hand.

"You look real tired,"
    she says. "Lie down." I do.
        I do not close my eyes.

INTERVIEW

He scans the resumé,
and she reiterates the story
of her sales of varied wares,
her hobbies, tennis, poetry, etcetera.

He listens, says not much
(with a fixed, tight smile).
He thanks her, mentions
some upcoming interviews.

She kicks open the apartment door,
goes right for the refrigerator,
finishes off last night's ice cream.

She carefully removes the suit,
setting it aside from all else,
goes through the paper—
can't help noticing the ad from Tiffany's,
(looking at things she always wanted),
the travel section
(her innate capacity for diversion).

She irons the navy linen suit,
hangs it up;
it cools wrinkly and drab
except for the shine
that comes from her persistent wear.

I ONCE SAW A MOVIE

I once saw a movie
in which the vulnerable criminal
would not drop his weapon at gunpoint.

I think about that when I write poems
tenaciously gripping my pen.

IT MADE SENSE

Joyce, my best friend,
it made sense—
        straight A's,
        rapid advance in school,
        solid as a brick,
        yet crisp and soft
        as fine chintz ribbons,
("She always smelled of Ivory soap,"
my little niece would say.)

Joyce, with silky amber brown braids
perfectly parted in the middle
        ("Another Margaret O'Brien,"
        all my neighbors would say.)

I tried so hard to be like her
and one day was determined
        to feel that special way,
        shopped around and stumbled on
        the taffeta dress
        gleaming in hot pink and purple iridescence,
        layered frivolously with canary yellow ruffles.

I breathlessly showed it to Joyce,
who embarrassingly turned away,
        trying to smother her giggles.
        She turned toward me again,
        this time composed in a sweet smile
        (too wise for an eleven-year-old).
        "Delly, that's the most beautiful
dress I've ever seen."

JENNY IS HAVING A PARTY

Jenny is having a saffron party
      with intertwining arms
      and skipping souls
      head-to-toe chilled glances.

Jenny's fringed invitations
      welcome
      peripheral charades
      to conquer
      tempestuous cloudy hearts
      drawn to impatient sweaty passions.

I hope you don't return
      from your tan trip, Jen.

I really don't want to go
      to your party!

JOSH

I went down to Rod's Animal Care;
my rabbit Josh was dying there.
It wasn't day, nor was it night;
the terror sucked me up, all right.
I cried. He died.
His fluffy fur went stiff and dried;
his glossy eyes, his deadened stare,
left me abandoned—all alone—there.

KNEE SOCKS

It was spring,
      hardly a time
            for wool knee socks,

but Mom knew about
      early spring and its
            unexpected "chill in the air still."

No short anklets, no school,
      I thought
            and stood at the foot of the stoop

with stiffly folded arms,
      my book bag on the ground
            its strap trapping my feet in place.

LIFE'S NOT FAIR

Once he got his power ax going,
      she fought for the least heap of rubbish,
           thundering her words—
for advocates had not the time.

While the hard-nosed sick
      were laughing,
           the poor were crying,
the bad weren't trying,
as the good were dying.

The night's not dark enough now
      and the day's ozone hardens the good light.
           Flies are less shy
defiantly around her,
as on a tired donkey, killing time,

while they, the hard-nosed sick,
      were laughing,
           the poor were crying,
the bad weren't trying,
as the good were dying.

LITTLE CONSPIRACIES

The donkeys we admire
have learned
there isn't always fire
behind the clouds of smoke

or twisted breezes
that distort the trees.
Golden days turn black
in the frigid heat

of public lights,
and winter heeds her hard cry.
Premeditated spring winds
blow on elephants

as white as milk
with sweaty spots of red.
Both continue
their dart games

of right-wing pain
and left-wing love,
losing their way.

MESSAGE

Must sell my gems—don't need them no more
to flaunt at dinner tables full of baby blues.

No bushing around the beat—
truth hits in the eyes, hard-fisted at times.

That vague haunting sibling thing's gone, sister.
I'm boned to the billy, unfrilled to the silly,

the old blowing horn's flirtatious song
now worn, brooding, numb, and strong.

MORNING MAN

He stands on the corner of Salem and State,
contrasting the clarity of sunrise
liquored through his bones,
his cheeks flushed and obvious
against a matted beard embroidered in saliva.

He isn't moved by the wild ducks of calm spring
and the emergence of opening tulips
or bothered by black ice on vapid streets
of broken compacts.

In an unsure stance, he's stoic with forced control,
on the corner of Salem and State,
speaking now and then to those who pass,
who hardly know what he means,
and waves to the usual commuters—
too perfectly postured
and overly proud of his role.

Oh morning saint of young days,
where in the world do you go
when the day grows old?

MR. J.P.

Eyes opaque,
visions unabsorbed like atrophy of the soul,
he closes up in metals and in golds—
a leafless search
to tell his tale untold.

He looks my way and doesn't ask my name.
Leaves rustle still—
        a crimson tear on his cheek like a ruby
        will stay,
too ingrained to ever wipe away.

MS. HAMMELL DIED TODAY

The sky is a sickly yellowish green-brown
                like a giant melanoma
        a tribute of kicks:
                Ms. Hammell died today—

going up the grades,
                so fearful of the fifth,
        her ready impositions on life's impossibilities
                when we thought there were none—
horrific Hammell with her enormous amethyst
                on an indexed fang
        that struck across those warm young cheeks
                then fondled her crinkling décolleté
        under a prissy lace blouse
as we gazed on with bland, amused eyes.

I'm staying home in the golden, protective arms
                of residual possibilities and hopes,
        not playing sick.
                It's just that Ms. Hammell
        got exhausted from autumn's hard rulers
                and pitiless slaps,

now accepting the deep earth's cruel purple dirt
        going straight down.

NIGHT TALK

Stars wink and tease the steady unwilling moon,
both nag the flaying night,

and clouds escape in whining leaps;
this scene cuts through my fearful window,

mimicking the stillness here
with uncanny insight.

NOBODY LIKES A LONELY WOMAN

After all, there's always the tattooed man
who's homeless,
or the guy down the hall,
thick-headed, with missing teeth,
red-faced from gin.

Come on, lady,
there's lots of lost cities to explore.
So you're not Scarlett O'Hara anymore.
Nobody likes rotting flesh
doing weekend errands, contriving chores.

OBVIOUSLY SAFE

She felt alone in the house,
and no one would be coming home—
she knew she couldn't
survive the emptiness.

She looked out.
The yard's southern exposure
deepened to a golden haze over the roses,
yet no bloated shadows muffled sounds.

of rock and roll inside,
and the usual noises of a settling house
became suspicious.
She checked the hallway and closets twice,

feeling tipsy, decided to shower,
remembering the shower scene in *Psycho*
(not a sign of Mr. Bates, his knife,
or bloodstains), got out, shaken

but safe, obviously quite safe.

ODE TO FIFTY YEARS AND OVER

Don't mind my freckled, sun-kissed hands,
       immersed in collagen creams,
pushing upward, upward,
       counteracting gravitational mishaps

or if I stay in soft light
       thus to lessen piercing glances
at the lines I've earned from life's calamities.

With pen in hand
       I find this time
       amusing—sadly jovial

so much more to say
and so much less to lose
       Impervious to those sultry blues.

ODE TO VALENTINE'S DAY

Like spirits of Christmas past,
you impose on this tired aching
bent winter's eve,
silvery eyes that mirror the graffiti and flaws
cut into me.

Have I disappointed you, my shadowed friends?
You dissolve weightlessly to silent waters
like promises unkept.

I'm stone now
and sing my usual lullaby
not in the usual way;
glued lovers like groomed poodles
jingle about,
submerged in seas of red wine and chocolates—
I'm passionless in a new song.

ON MY EX'S BIRTHDAY

I look for signs of madness:
hot pink angels tossing their halos about
as God directs terrible plays
full of conflicting characters.

I look for falling stars
and rainbows in shades of gray,
a Hiroshima over young, dying flowers.

Yet I smell roses
and see only cheerful girls and boys
playing hopscotch in green fields

(and know less obvious signs
could mean much more).
Unfulfilled and forlorn at day's end,
I wait for June 22 to come again.

OPEN THE SKIES

Open the skies,
pound the stars

for a suffering rhyme
of weeping trees

and ruddy lonely men near clamoring tides
above Trojan horses,

kneeling for that momentary stab of insight,
words to curse or praise vices of the arts
without ill-at-ease squirmings,

words that seep into waiting ears
on dim cozy eves,
splitting bittersweet hearts.

PIGS DEVELOP A CURIOUS
WAY OF EATING

Pigs develop a curious way of eating
         their food—
served to them in a dish,
         inevitably they turn it over
         and lap up the contents from the ground.

Instinct, we call it,
         find it foreign, illogical,
         amusing,
nervously fidget with our china plates,
         pleased and assured of the distinction.

POETRY

Poetry I was told should be
      the donut not the hole,
      the cherries not the bowl.
Poetry should be
      the baby not the cries,
      the epic not the sighs.
Poetry should never be
      the limb but the tree;
      this limb a poem left in me.

RACHEL'S THING

Rachel asked for surgical masks on visitors
        when Carrie was born,
sterilization of infant's formula, utensils,
    toys, vaporized a steamy apartment,
her hand-washing ritual all too obsessive
        even for Lady Macbeth,
the place, a cross between boarding a spaceship
        and an operating room.

My family found this disturbing.
I never analyzed or understood
        my older sister's ways,
just carried lots of Lysol around
        (when I had kids)
and nervously said, "God bless you,"
    after their a-choos as if praying.

REINCARNATION

Time's running out.
I'm feeling odd about
life's quarrels,

but I (mother, daughter,
sister, ex-wife, vaguely thought of)
will be back

to this old world
maybe as a ragged mouse
wise enough to find the cheese here.

SESSION

Eighteen-year old Mary says she's pregnant
and can't imagine what it will be like
without a husband. Outside,
a baby sparrow awkwardly flies,
hoping to find its nest.
"You don't get it," says Paul. "It's like
coming down when you lose your girl,
knowing an hour later you'll get high."

"But what about when you lose it all
in one day, that day that didn't like you?" I say.
I think of my sister, who's absent tonight,
on her own for the first time
since she lost her husband
(regressing to little girl helplessness)

and how she cried to the rabbi
about "being hard to live with all these years"
and that guilt trip when someone dies and becomes
angelic, and how the remorseful living
deserve the misery of going on alone.

After the session, I go to a coffee shop
where I see a family
(the kids playing with their food)
and feel the undercurrents
(the mother minimizing with small talk
about little league, school, tennis,
while the father daydreams about other women
and another place,
though less than two years back
his dreams were there with *them*—

alarm clocks, rushed morning kisses,
your troop out the door, against the world). . .

And when all this ends,
we survive the survival
yet still want to take off
even in the midst of the kids' growing quirks
and shadows of scandals
that become acceptance.

The new man in the session
sits next to me.
We talk in funny, strange,
and unexpected ways,
smart enough to not hold back—
two dark silhouettes in the corner booth.
He drives me to the old marital house
with its grayish-brown sod;
the keys I lost a while back suddenly show up,
scintillating in the dead grass;
I leave them there.

The wobbling sparrow lands in a nest,
probably not the one it started in.

SILENT AS LICE

It's the usual scene—
the couch deeply ingrained
with old sweat,
his refusal to open up,
to change.

Not a chance.
She starts to slap his face,
his knees.
His eyes grow stiffer,
grow immovable.

He's silent as lice,
doesn't even ask her to stop,
so she doesn't—
she goes for his wrist,
her hands smudged with blood,
his eyes fixed on her.

She's startled by the sound
of neighbors outside,
barbecuing, laughing, eating.
Could it be—is she the same species?
She looks at her hands,
examines them closely,
stops.

SOPHIE MY NEIGHBOR

Sophie trying so hard
fiercely washing Friday's windows
eight floors up
(inside and out!),
cleverly sliding back in
(what a relief).

Unflinching
strong-footed
gloating over the silky clear panes—
"Help cleans only on the surface,"
she declares, gasping of ammonia,
straightening a bent and fragile back.

Sophie tries so hard—
20 lbs. overweight,
perspiring as she lines
newspapers on half-dried linoleum,
steadily pulling down her pleated skirt
over her rounder spots,
Casablanca flickering on the TV.

On a different Sophie face
(red lipstick too far above her lips,
overly defined arched eyebrows),
catching a glow
from her clear windows
and neon floors.

SQUIRRELS

(In Memoriam S.S., July 13, 1998)

Cedar Lawn just below the malls and highways,
the sun here's unusually dense,
brooding over our heads.
Odors are pungent, painfully sweet.

On empty stomachs and void hearts we say good-bye.
How long have we?

Your body's half moist still,
and the gap in the ground is expecting you—
you might have been overdue (knowing you)—
and the sulking days you stood up to
give way to the covering evening.

Dazzling squirrels quicken their pace
to and fro, scattered, dumb,
checking out the prospects.

SUBWAY BLUES

So leave all those
      too-loving good intentions
      verbal slaps and dangerous pretensions.
Ride the subway, lady.

Get it left and right and center:
      a tainted mouth of nails
      chokes on kind food and patient drink.
      She throws the pain right down an angel's sink.
Ride, ride that subway, baby.

A quiet in her rises in the underground's
      black, clashing shrieks.
      She sits upon the tarred and shaky curb
      clench-fisted and with bloated veins.
Ride, ride those sparkling subway trains.

Crazy with questions
      of an imponderable plot,
      a vacant lot, the next stop;
      there, with a thin, unmarried look,
      frail words unheard,
      she's stiff with knives in her,
      her patience absurd,
      waiting for anything lost to be got,
      for something that now is not.
So ride that subway, live to the next spot.
Ride it to its final stop.

THE ACTRESS

Waking at noon
        in peeling rooms,
the mild stench of forgotten garbage,
cockroaches speedily turning in,
she sits erect
        before her mirror,
draws soft kohl lines
carefully around her eyes and lips.

Smudged sunlight seeps
through a streaked window,
contrasting her refining art:
        a final look,
        the usual frown,
        a spray of Fabergé—her oxygen.

She grasps a tin
of leftover Diet Coke,
a ten-minute-late look
        on her dusty midnight face,
forcing energy and glee
        on flashing cameras,
        lashing voices—
        "Next!"
        "We'll call you"—
waiting on her last table,
inhaling her deep last drag. . .
        the note
        the unheard answering machine

FINE-TOOTH COMB

When I came back
        from summer camp (three weeks prematurely),
I'd just developed breasts
        or got too fat from all that starch
(no one knew the difference);

strangely enough, I missed my father
        more than my mother,
dreamt he'd died.
        Did *he* miss *me* that much?

I pretended I couldn't swim
        or throw balls
so I'd get
        kicked out,

stopped showering
        (couldn't fathom
standing naked
        among my bunkmates).

What got me home
        was lice,
lovely little friends
        crawling on my scalp.

Oh the warmth of that fine-tooth comb
        lovingly gliding through my hair.

THE GIFT

A gift of pearls
to fit so perfectly the neck of life:

At proms crisp in net blue gowns
they stand out stark white, stiff,

ripening to ivory just in time
to set the lace and satin off
with smooth round beads that glow like happy faces
over a three-tiered wedding cake.

Their yellow cast on the woman in black
at serious second weddings
and young funerals,

the twists and turns, wear thin the strand—
graying beads
drop like tears on a pine floor.

THE LADY AT THE COUNTER

The lady at the counter
    with the floppy green felt hat
    and the mothball smell she lives by
    sat beside me and asked
    if I were "staying or leaving."

Securing her place, her deeply lined face
    and shriveled features revealed
    smoky days of drinking bouts,

as did the oversized
    and worn black patent-leather purse
    from which awkwardly protruded
    a residual pint.

She scratched her head and with narrowing eyes
    read the comics, occasionally looking side-
ways,
    and I caught a glimpse of leftover cheer
    from somewhere way back.

She stayed longer than usual;
    the stars came out too early to warn her;
    she fumbled through cobwebs
    of frayed and layered cloth
    that wrapped her small frame,
    reluctantly leaving on an uncertain stagger,
    shuddering with the insight of a gypsy
    past the usual pubs
    and, with the struggle of Circe,
    decided to go home.

THE RECURRENT DREAM

Creased and spun out
I tumbled into that last day of class
the room was round and dark
    like the final cycle of a washing machine.
Impatient pedantic hands
    distributing the test,
he appeared masked and silent
    like an intent doctor.

I, apprehensive, unprepared, dangling
  in front of the others, packed together into ice,
  looking at me judiciously, like a mother-in-law,

I woke up glazed and sweaty
to breaking waters
    that pushed out my first child—
    my replica,
    my achievement.

THE WHITE PIGEON

A pigeon on my terrace
        immaculate in white
doesn't squat or beg in hunger
        but poses like a swan
            poised to a chilly glance

with a certain point of view
        from city stone parks
where life's sadly untrue.
        I offer her seeds
           she cautiously sniffs

her deep eyes wise and tough
        from scorching lessons.
She stays awhile,
        one foot curled up
           against her breast,

the other sturdy, still
        (unknowingly picturesque);
she dips her head to thank me,
        and she feasts;
           she even clasps some seeds

(a souvenir perhaps),
        then floats off, regal, bold,
drifting in murderous cold
        above her menacing and clumsy clan
           in iridescent purple grays—
           slightly above motley days.

THIS THANKSGIVING

We weren't the Thanksgiving cliché this year,
    the table set in silence
except for a buzzing fly and nagging radiator,
    not yet ready for discussions or joyful about
        the Pilgrims' intrusions here,
    drinking deeply like horses from a trough,
    comforted by glazed morsels
        of terrible pleasures valiantly consumed.

We learned to shut up and didn't even
    mention the cobwebs this time
        or the missing moments.

THREW THE VASE

Threw the vase 'cause you breathe
      spitefully calm,
broke the glass dove
      'cause you're a mean pillow—
porcelain cups in the air
      'cause you don't share.
Silver knives go flying,
      you don't care.

If she didn't send these objects
      in a spell,
she'd really get angry
      and break her shell.

TIBETAN HOUSE

They wipe morning tears
from the windows,
busy about the silent, dry house
to gather lost spring greens;

then, still as icebergs, they sit
on velvet cushions,
they transcend—like liquid angels
melting into a mauve night.

I think about the tapping of a gentle stick
on my right shoulder
to remind me of my impure meditation,
my incurable turmoil;

they know I will soon leave,
so they keep their distance.
Oh, the cold showers, the astute
walks in fresh meadows,

white with discipline that pushes me,
to traffic, street curbs,
under rushed, peeved feet
stuck in the darkness like me.

TODD

It was love on our first date,
it was tall and perfect Todd—
or was it
his pale-blue Austin-Healy convertible
(except it was so low and cramped it hurt my legs)?

I'd do anything for Todd and with
(except for actual intercourse),
so infatuated was I with his will
to be a "rich skin doctor," as he put it
(except for the details like
"All you have to do is take the bucks in
with your fists and be quite careful
not to touch the patients")—

and how he promised I'd be part
of his family
(except how "it would be a whole lot better
if my father were a doctor"),
and how great it was to go to Cote Basque
for my birthday.

But meet him there and wait outside
for at least an hour,
knowing it could be worse if it were colder
(except for the first snowflake
that started to fall).

TOO LIGHT FOR DAWN

I left the hospital later than usual
and slept well
thinking of the good times with her
(at my wedding shower
ambitiously opening gifts,
proud, strong).

My lips curl up in this deep sweet sleep—
it's too light to be dawn,
and the ordinary racket's
too invasive now.

The phone rings—my father
is beaten with grief.
"Mommy died!" he cries,
as if it were
his mommy, too.

The funeral will be soon;
hopefully the sun will subside,
and the birds will stop
their inappropriate chorale.

She always loved the summer,
I recall, as I stumble back to bed,
reach for the phone to tell her
about my apprehensions, my stupendous sorrow,
and how much I love her.

ADELE SCHWARTZ

TWO BIRDS ON SIXTH AVENUE

Walking down Sixth Avenue cold and roaring,
hunched over, willful in thought,
the woman stumbled upon two birds
      dropped from mysterious flight,
her pale-deep softness revealed only to those
      two starlings
mildly placed in quiet twigs and grass dry
      ("They will not die.
They'll soar above the Eiffel Tower
      and fly off the roof of the Louvre.")

With worms, meat, milk to be fed by drops,
mulling through the night without stop—
two starlings on top of each other
      as two become one
forcing strength to each other,
      one loose and failing;
      the other took flight to the sweet sun,
      while, amid electrifying clouds,
      the starling flew above a perfumed skyline
over the upright woman whimsically strutting
through the curved streets of Paris.

UNCLE MAX

Uncle Max would take me
to the toy store on Sundays
in his sturdy Packard,
proud as the '40s tunes
he sang on the way.

Smoked Lucky Strikes;
inhaling incessantly
with short coughs and moist laughter
(never could tell the difference),
he'd reiterate his days
with Aunt Fay
in minute detail,
spitting out moments
with fluttered hair
as the car drifted sideways.

He glowed at my innocent hysteria
when I saw the miniature merry-go-round,
little chalk-white people with fixed smiles
on shiny black horses,
sliding up and down to "Lara's Theme"
dull, rusty horses, now rocky, lame,
little broken white folks
with shattered smiles,
the dry, cracked sounds
of the music box playing
"What Now, My Love,"
wearily round and round.

WEEKEND

Are you lingering on the crusted couch?
Salivating on the tongue of possible disasters?
Just out of tousled nightness
I see your oddity evolve with the morning sparrows
      love-hate mutterings
      coffeed small-talk
killing the glamor.

Graying through a weakening day
      of stale perfume
      and overdone makeup,
I advance to the grand TV
      to dance with Fred Astaire.

WHEN I DIE

Will there be sobbing,
   social hobbing,
   vacant stares,
   mundane nodding?

Will there be sighs,
   tons of lies,
   unintentionally broken ties?

Will there be shivers,
   bogus quivers,
will there be armored knights so bold
   to place in stoic silence my last white rose?

There will be minds to taunt!
Finally the stinging haunt:
   "Hey, guys, hey, guys!
Where were you when I was still alive?"

ADELE SCHWARTZ

WHY DON'T YOU LIKE PARTIES?

I don't think of wearing
        anything but jeans,
        always dressing down.
        Why don't you like parties,
        bistros, shows?

Is it the whirling energy of it
        that contrasts your depression,
        or the cost?

You should live with your mother
        if you're so rigid,
        so reclusive in pathetic rituals
        that drive the violent
        sad evil in me,
        the undisturbed deaf patience in you.

Try the joy of being broke,
        living on the edge,
        running on empty—
        out there like James Dean.

It'll get you off the couch,
        to shut the TV,
        hear the music
        across the river—
        you know, the Hustle's hot again!

WILD GEESE REMEMBERED

Wild geese in the midst
of lustered berries and golden fields
remember seasons of ice and take flight.

In glistening warm summers
I, too, feel the chill of winter
in my heart.

In the midst of rivals
and laws that grind,
man does not soar
for his wings are clipped
shorter and shorter.

YOM KIPPUR DAY

Under the critical skies
of a slow-warming autumn,
smells of brewed coffee and frying eggs
are sharpened in a too-silent hallway.

With mouth dry,
dripping faucets a mirage,
midday limbs are weak,
and the mutterings of prayer
cushion an empty hardness
in my stomach.

Smiling, fresh faces enter.
I am sure they didn't fast,
I think, white-eyed and raggedy,
awakening to the *shofar*
intermingling with hurricanes
of pure *l'shana tovah* hugs
and quickening limbs of some
already casting their gray shadows,
embarrassingly too soon,
on this white new year.

Black
Ice

A CAT'S LIFE

My cat's drowning in the tub.
I drag it out,
        dry it, caress it,
        set it free to roam
in circles of uncertainty.

Then magically it turns into a boy,
a boy of nine lives,
whose hands I try to reach
        in the dark,
        my eyes tight shut,
        fearing transformations.

A ROOM AND A MAN

(Impressions of a Painting)

The woman enters the room:
the mysterious differences of northern
and southern exposures,
of August's fiery skies and January's
jeweled colors, carry their reflections.

Shades of dusk in oval lights
fall in mauve beams on the stark wood floor
where once the sun cast only amber streaks.

A man who knows the woman well
is standing alone, his back to her.
He stays still, magnetic,
unchanging—
as the moment's forms
and earthly colors whimsically play.

A WOMAN'S FUNERAL
(A Dream)

It's the darker side of twilight.
The sun is playing with cut-glass windows,
pouring rainbowed forms over her dark pine box,
where hands touch
and eyes shift, avoiding real issues.

A leader sings final dedications, wildly;
then the sobs, the shouts to Jehovah
and his angels,
noises from impatient breaths,
only silent answers.

I look up to see
that everybody's wearing clown costumes
in black and white,
eliminating all the shades of gray there.

ABE OF THE LOWER EAST SIDE

We walked ten flights straight up
the narrow, half-lit stairwell,
resting at each sooty landing.

He stood at the opened door
with laughing eyes,
anxiously waiting for me to find

the newest hidden doll
(always on top of the closet).
His leathered skin

reddened my cheeks, softened
by his moist kisses.
He scuffed about in soft-worn slippers,

as if recovering—never forgot
the shattered homes, store windows broken,
marked with the one word Yid,

the burned books, burned-out shtetls.
He scooped two glasses
of his homemade wine from the tub

and toasted us—*"L'chaim! L'chaim!"*—
with the dignity of noble men,
breathing out the silent peace,

apart yet part of this new melting pot,
objective as a covered wound,
just peddling life.

ALL WRITTEN OUT

1.

I'm all written out—
words dangle unheard;
the assassin in my mind
wipes out all color
and the scent of spring.

Hills groan in a quiet hum,
beauty and beast are one,
the day is long and white
as an ostrich.

2.

A cool sun sheds weak rays upon
discarded paper wads and trash,
evolving as the loveliest collage.

Art muddles through
the opaque clouds somehow.

ANONYMOUS AS DUST

I've gone this far.
My bones and chilled flesh have survived
            nights past castles
like the weeds in their surrounding gardens.

I tread on hot coals,
folding into furious winds still,
sitting on the worlds's edge,
anonymous as dust,
naked as a rock
            under a slippery moon.

AUGUST AFTERNOON

On these hot sidewalks
    I jumped rope,
        played hopscotch;

on these hot sidewalks
    walked with my first date
        the first time that we met.

I stand here now,
    time flickering by
        in little cobalt flames;

raindrops try
    to cool
        the concrete fire.

ADELE SCHWARTZ

TENNIS BALL

When I was in kindergarten,
    I ran out looking
    for my mother.

With her disappearance,
    my life was as brief
    as an Alaskan summer.

In my shame, my classmates
    taunted, "Baby, baby,
    stick your head in gravy."

They threw a tennis ball toward me
    at recess, driving
    to the depths of my dim fears.

It was the biggest ball I'd ever seen.
    My hands couldn't grasp it—
    not yet.

BLACK ICE

1.

Black ice is everywhere,
the skyline warped, jagged.
The sharp, distant cry of a gull
cuts the thin light's silence.
Its dark and beady eyes
take in the world.

A woman in the building across the way
is holding her sick baby;
kissing and touching her warm forehead,
she paces nervously,
phones her husband's office.
"He's not in yet," they say.
"The weather's bad— probably stuck somewhere."

She only wanted to talk
about the baby's fever
as she tells the secretary instead,
"Sounds like she's cutting a tooth."
The response is automatic, indifferent.
"Gotta go—adios!" The secretary
briskly hangs up.

2.

Scents of Jean Naté linger in the tub;
the sheets are unused,
comforter intact,
her pale blue nightgown lies untouched,
unsexual.

Her husband is nursing a beer
in the motel lounge at noon,
thinking it all out (chewing on a toothpick),
trying to find a core of himself
and a good strong sense of how to lie,
but he's about fifty, and that James Dean thing
just doesn't fit.

3.

The haze clears out by half past noon.
The woman then can see the stark skyline
down to the World Trade Center,
can face her rage and deprivation
through the playful whimperings
of the healing child
(the fever's broken).
The woman her husband
was with last night
covers her face
to block the strong sun—
fingers that stroked his cheek
before dawn.
She waters firm and leafless cactuses
that prick her fingers.

BLACK WIDOW

She's the stranger
in the blinded room,
coughing, smoking, and drinking her way
through Rhapsody in Blue.
Gershwin cradles her as a lover might.

Unfamiliar faces just can't miss her
so bizarre in dusty black attire
and frazzled, ink-stained hair.

She knows too well the art of pain
and pain of art,
this alien, this outsider.

They gawk at her
walking the streets,
reciting her poems
(assured of their normalcy, their place).
She peers from her web,
fearing her incomplete self,
awaiting a pulpit.

DOG DAY

I never realized my husband's outrage
over my love of clothes.

I guess he never forgave me for it:
when we split, without a hint,
he burned everything in my closet.

Fifteen years later, I can still smell
the flaunting bonfire of that dog day.

DUSK

There's only static on the kitchen intercom—
    no sing-song cries for me,
        smells of school and play,
           still linger on jackets
       lined up in seasons,
    waiting for some substance, form.

The dripping faucet is no longer irritating—
    it's now the rain sobbing
        deliberately. I'm bare-faced—
          no hint of color
      on lips and cheeks—
    automatically slipping

into a pilled warm-up and wrinkled sneakers,
    the once soft, cozy music of dusk
        exploding into a rocky night,
          whose happy shadows
      play far behind
    thick opaque clouds.

ELEGY

The heart that killed you
is the heart they mourn today—
deceitful organ shrunk
in our deep sleep
(with covers over all our heads).

I dreamt we were feathers
dancing weightlessly,
quills growing heavy, strong.

We wake this day with covers cast aside.
Our world no longer needs its bargaining.

FIRST BORN

In puddles of cold sweat, deep breaths,
soft background voices.
She's ready. She comes out
of the safe, dark socket.
Icicles beat against the misty window,
boasting of a biting storm.
This time the sky's green-black.
This time the snow is not cathartic.

She's handed to me, softer, pinker
than the delicate pastel cloth cuddling her.
Her hand grasps mine unusually tight—
I swore she'd never know of pain or disappointment.

My husbands's relatives arrive like Rumpelstiltskins,
with half-smiles polluting everything.
I scrawl *Beware* on the hospital menu,
thinking this will give me power.

This birth won't be my loss; our hands
are magnets for each other still, and in the end
these fools will know that Nature can't be altered.

FIRST LOVE

I saw him first
in the courtyard
of the Elmwood Apartments:
    his hair sleek, velvet black
    his eyes as blue as his denim jacket
    his firm mouth—breathless.

He'd look down when I passed,
Yet I knew he glanced my way when I left.
Another girl walked by,
    her breasts bigger than mine
    her hair gold streaked by the sun's metallic lights
    he looked at her differently—intensely.

I ran inside, poured bottles of peroxide
through my mousy hair,
stuffed my training bra with tissues
    looked in the mirror and cried.
    Outside, spring breezes whispered:
    Time—in time.

FOUR POSTER

1.

In various shades of pink
the sharp, bright florals
of the paper on the walls
cast dancing shadows 'round her bed.

She slept well on that
early summer morning,
turned-up lips plump, rosy;
fresh-cut grass smells filled the air.

Close to drying out my tears,
she came into the house late afternoon
shimmering of midsummer.
"Your father won't

be coming home again," I muttered.
She said nothing more—
her eyes expressed it all.
She climbed the stairs to her room,

her face growing dry from within,
with each new step, she asked,
"Why are the neighbors here?"

2.

I was too numb to know why really,
ranting at a pace that would soon stop me
from questioning.

Cigarette butts were stashed

in the corners of her bed
where I might not see them,
their pungent scent
seeping through the shut door.

Mostly what I remember that early fall
is the crinkling and fading
of the floral paper sagging prematurely
'round her bed.

I'd study her dresser and pick up
the doll she slept with as a child,
hoping it might bring back happier times.

The yellow of summer gave way
to a stark whiteness—
stoic, calm, new—
the four-poster bed holding her through.

GARLIC

Stay with me all day;
it's okay.
Let the floral-perfumed mouths
back away.

Without you, soups and sauces, too,
would never do.
Holy, unrecognized lump of parchment,
you keep evil spirits back, they say,

strong-odored, knuckled fist
shouting at the quiet, sweeter stuff
that draws, then kills.

ADELE SCHWARTZ

GOOD INTENTIONS

If you'd stayed, I would have worked in fields,
simple in coarse brown skirts,
my fingers swollen under an orange sky,
an earthy love
a token of my earnestness.

Yet you'd beg me to change still,
so my ruthless satin gowns would hang hollow
in twilight evenings,
wanting to swing and swirl in the limelight
as I relented to you,
obedient in your steel shell.

If we were together still,
your icy eyes would turn my blazing heart to ash,
urns of your pleading tears would drown
the last flickerings of my fiery spirit,
and then, with all your good intentions,
you would leave me
but too late.

HIGH RISE

No one really knows true hate
till you wait too long
for the elevator on the 31st floor
after having walked down all those flights
at 4 a.m. for a false alarm.

Paranoia sets in as you're
sure that the doorman you forgot
to tip at Christmas set it off
and kept the elevator stuck
on "L" as well.

The door flies open finally,
telling you to enter now
just as your glove falls down the shaft.
John gets on at 30 and says, "Hi,"
without eye contact or a mutual glance.

"Why is this thing so screwed up
all the time?" he mutters
in a low, pained voice.
At 29 we're ready to kill Carol
who lingers over her kids in a long farewell

before departing.
"What does she care?"
says John. Then on to 28 and Paul,
who's wearing too much aftershave
and mouthwash so the garlic

in last evening's scampi sauce
won't be too obvious. We slither

to the corners of the cab.
We skip the 27, 6, and 5
to 24 and Maggie, who is thrilled

that Carol's there so she can tell her
to be sure to make the book club meeting
in the social room. She's red-faced still
from arguing with her "fucking husband,"
as she puts it on less lucid days

when her wine nail polish is so badly chipped.
Yeah, home free, then, to "L" in hard,
tight mahogany and marble.
John's coffee drips from a one-half open mug
in an almost perfect stream.

I smudge the too clear mirrors
reapplying lipstick, notice dirty looks
from the morning crew, and take
a deep breath past the huddled doormen,
out of this tall trap, head high.

HOW WILL I BE REMEMBERED?

How will I be remembered
a thousand years from now?

An object of strength,
surviving ruins, searching for ideals?

A helpless victim after mundane pleasures—
good, strong, weak, evil?

What does it matter?
What counts is this:

My feet have touched the ground,
neither the black-winged angel nor a risen saint.

ADELE SCHWARTZ

INDIAN SUMMER

My mother and I waded in the drained pool
that late September,
her gray-blue dress reflecting the dull-tired
water of Indian Summer.

She held out her arms and swirled me
in zig-zag loops.
I was delirious with joy. Suddenly she reached
upward in a childlike way,

perhaps recapturing the lost child in her
who rarely played,
she dismantled a bird's nest, scratching
her hands

on an odd, rough branch, then letting go...
I was soaked.
Although the water was quite shallow I knew
I was going to drown.

JET RIDE

The gray sky hangs over everything.
I am far from black-eyed earth,
wishing to forget the things I left below.
I can no longer bear disaster
like the oceans overworked
and hardened shores.

Outside a great white desert lies.
Nothing is distinct or clear up here.
My face is pressed against the hard, cold window,
and I'm yearning to forgive
all that seems so small, so helpless.

As we descend,
all I see are snakes and eels
crawling in dirt,
smearing the earth.

LAST DATE

He said, "Goodnight, moonshine,"
saliva dripping from the corners
of his mouth. "I'll give you
the loins of my labor on a platter
of platinum."

She managed a smile, choking on
a macadamia nut shell
still flavored with licorice liqueur.
He bent to kiss her.
Her lips tightened,

teeth clenched against the juicy droplets
round his mouth. She thought
for awhile, knowing he'd probably
keep his promises,
and how easy life could be;

cleared her throat (a lingering
frigidity preceding a hacking silence)
and faced him with not very much to say,
focusing on the glistening saliva
and faint odor of old gray sweat

on his clothes. She turned away
and opened the door of her cold
unfurnished flat to sleep on hard ideals,
soft seas, star fields, knights, and all that—
dreaming, I think it's called.

LISTS

Watching you in the kitchen, I wonder
why you're always creating lists
(groceries, cards, errands)
in cheerful shades of yellow
like daisies lined up neatly on the fridge.

The words look primitive and large,
like a child's,
maybe to override some monumental voids.

You scratch each word out with deliberate ease,
the way you scratch out our souls.

MARIA

Leaving the Lincoln Tunnel at Eleventh
and 40th, my family noticed
a tenement on its last legs—

sheer pink curtains
blowing from a window toward us
to reveal a lovely, dark-haired woman

dancing in front of a mirror,
holding her newly made dress against her.
She was graceful, delicate—

the poor city's music. We called her
"Maria." My son would call out to her
every time we visited the city.

Years later, driving alone,
I passed Maria's house
(half boarded up),

the sheer pink curtain gone.
A woman with salt-and-pepper hair
and ruddy rounded cheeks

was leaning on the window sill,
her flabby arms supporting loose breasts,
gazing out, thinking of nothing

in particular. Oh, dreams
of Maria breaking, broken, dying,
dead—a human blossom

on a woody stem of tenement furnace smoke
that curls and spurts to form her name
in fuzzy letters rising to nothing.

I pull away and shudder,
sit alone in the theater,
recalling my son to my right, fidgeting,

my daughter on my left
with a finger to her lips
to quiet him,

smells of melted chocolate peppermint
candy, floral-scent shampoo
still lingering in their hair,

plump hands that hold mine.
I curl into the sounds of the orchestra
leaving room for yet another drama.

MONDAY MORNING

The confident, bushy-haired man on the elevator
smiles warmly at Annie.
Do you miss the magic in life? Make haste,
say his eyes.
Intimidated by his thoughts, she stiffens,
yet wants to hold onto him and the moment.
"Bad timing, as usual," she mutters
(when things like this happen).

He's fixed on her watered, weekend eyes
and Monday's weak smile,
without lipstick, smudged glasses,
animal sheddings on her black coat.
She's bent inward, defeated,
even though he asks where she's off to
and about her weekend.

She walks ahead quickly,
without sensation
(only wanting to die),
looks behind—
a last glance—
but maybe, maybe,
another day, another chance.

MOON-COLORED APRIL

That whimsical schoolgirl spring—
      the kind that sprouts shockingly
            bright in Pollyanna gardens—

has made fools of us;
      in moon-colored
         Aprils

where fiber clouds are fixed in a cloth sky
      and thick-rooted trees hunch over
         like old men,

where meandering sparrows plunge
      straight down, strong as eagles,
         and as eagles rise again,

transcending all belief
      in a tarnished, wiser season,
         as they must...

ORPHANS

It was a dusky afternoon
by the time we got to my friend's
deceased grandfather's high-ceilinged apartment
in the Bronx.

The place was wall to wall
with cardboard boxes—
clothing, canned food, toothpaste,
all of that.

We tiptoed over them.
My friend explained
that his grandfather had been given up
as a child

because his family
couldn't afford him—not a decision
taken lightly or easily but executed
nonetheless,

and how this left the child
and then the man
with a legacy of obsessive
behavior.

We gathered the boxes
in the dim space and moved them
to my friend's apartment,
the last bit

of light falling on the rugged,
worn-out forms. He glanced

at the accumulation with a strange
intensity

that complemented sudden outside darkness,
warning me to "never open them."
I lay awake that night
envisioning

my friend's apartment filling up
with cardboard boxes too.
He walked into the bedroom
to adjust

the shades obsessively,
checked his wallet too often
(as usual), and locked the front door,
pulling on it

over and over to be very sure
that it was locked,
till his hands croaked with the pain
that comes

with feeling like an orphan, I suppose.

OUT LOUD

I've become a glutton
for things that eat away at me
back again at the old house.

I sit unobtrusively
by the side street; the setting sun,
familiar smells, nurse memories.

Ginny's veggie garden next door
is in full decor—Italian beans are ripe,
and its scent adds delicately

to the grilled steaks. My heart is hungry.
Ginny gets out of her car.
I move closer, hoping

to smooth out a jagged ending.
Her walk and expression are the same,
her face now drawn; her brow

deeply lined (am I
a part of her tired past?).
She stops and glances my way in her usual squint

as if recognizing something,
then continues
toward the door with nothing on her mind.

The door's ajar, open to traffic;
Hogans are still trying to factor things
out there, a fair-haired cleansing, I suppose.

It's getting cool, and the bright
velvet sod and highly lacquered doors
are dull under a sultry half-moon.

I leave on the dark side
of familiar shadows
fallen, almost immortal.

That flimsy, invisible net still covers
everything there (not letting me in).
This time it's visible.

OVER COFFEE

I've lived without my father
      fourteen years now, wondering still
          about his last moments
          alone,

his once-strong hands reaching out
      (maybe for me).
          I know his soft, unwrinkled face
          was

fixed, unquivering, unrelenting
      to what was waiting
          (maybe too close by)
          and I

too far away to kiss his cheek.
      And I sigh about this
          more times over coffee I forget
          to drink.

PHOTO
(August 1975)

Hair swept up by sea winds,
      they sat together on the jetty,
          sat like that in life's ringings,
her mouth oval, his lips perched,
    for she was singing,
        he was humming, laughter ringing,
humming, singing, sweet
    and fluid voices over the gull's
        harsh one-notes.

She was eight, he three.
      Darkness only at the curled edges, but
        the photo is:
the laughter ringing, humming,
      singing, sandpipers, dunes
        to salt air clinging.

PLEA

The football game and beer is all you do,
fattening the gaps.
I'm out the door,
with twitching, glassy eyes, watching you
toss and turn deep into crevices
of throw pillows.
Earth gingerly drifts
past you, and the solemn, smoky room
is heavy enough to choke and blind all poets.

SECOND STREET

Why should I write about this
       and risk being whiny?
But it's the night before Thanksgiving
       in my first apartment alone.
The only thing resembling domesticity's
       a soggy, mildewed sponge on the sink—
no cutesy Jewish American Princess magnets
       or Luv Ya reminders on this refrigerator.

Trucks rumble by
       (where are the morning songbirds?).
Early commuters slam doors in haste,
       drowning out romantic mutterings
of the couple next door
       still in Scheherezade.
The words I write don't fit today.

I try to fix a lamp
       and an electric shock goes through me.
Yes, I'm still alive;
       figure God must want it that way,
so I take five, listen
       to the morning shrink
who's giving the same advice to everyone
       with just the slightest differences.
Crazy Sue next door knocks meekly
       on my door, swaying back and forth
with sad, dazed eyes,
       and asks if her dress's too tight for
an interview. After four glasses of wine,
       I loosen up and call still-married friends

who hate my state of consciousness, priorities,

how vulnerable I've become.

I unobtrusively hang up on their self-righteous
          inferences, shutting the TV off
because the pompous-ass contestant
          on *Jeopardy* is winning by a landslide.
I look out the window with a heavy heart
          to see a pendant, urban moon
casting a dewy shine on rusty fire escapes
          and shabby figures on splintered benches

in the park across the street—
          a tarnished, golden night.
Newspapers filled with culpable events
          pile up on my doormat,
stay detached behind the door.

SMASH

It was the saddest dog
you ever saw
standing in the cold and dark
of the hall closet.
Smash, neglected, friendless,
waiting for the boy
who loved him so—
the boy away at school
with other interests now.

So I stroked his
stiff and dingy fur,
my heart in my fingers,
sitting with him
growing smaller in the corner,
we obscure as snails,
the wound in his dark, blank eyes
cutting through my wits.
Cold chills soon overtook me
as we curled up, waiting,
shutting out the pain of daylight.

SNOWY DAY

It's crisp and clear;
the streets are empty,
movement only on the glistening icicles.

My eyes are sparkling, playful—
I press my nose against the frigid window
as any child would.

There are no words for this,
no explanations,
only loving this snowy day alone.

STORMY SUNDAY

1.

My kids are somewhere;
they're not picking up.
I guess I called too early
or too late.

The sky is bruised,
stormy, mean, with
serious little flakes.
Whom will it murder today?

Can't watch TV;
I'll close the lights
and look out at the traffic,
maybe spot their car.

2.

God, it's ten and black!
Where are they at?
Stay safe, my babies
(big as you may be)

and then tomorrow—yes,
when all these ghost sounds turn to laughter
weaving through a faint and dying storm.

ADELE SCHWARTZ

SUNSET IS LOVELIER

I think about the end of things,
of loss and death,
maybe too often.

Sunset is lovelier
than sunrise. I have lived
with contradictions and dichotomies,

with contradictions and estrangements,
and with great effort gave
far less than I had hoped.

Sunset's always lovelier
than sunrise, morning smells
of cut grass, bubbling breakfasts,

give false hope—
so I write myself out in a poem
that will be a sunset.

SYNDROME

There's really no positive side of loss:
The husband works keeps the family safe,
fed, content,

yet all those years he stores resentment
without knowing it;
eventually, everything deteriorates,

explodes without knowing it,
until you feel those stones,
building walls,

closing each other out,
pointing fingers,
without knowing it.

TAKE A MOMENT

Away from wires and phones,
"Look—a red pelican
in a field of violets and gold."
It reaches far beyond the clouds,
stretches towards the ocean's silvery algae,
at once a peaceful thing
as still and meditative as an owl,
frivolously swift as peregrines
in young and vital flight.

Stop to feel its music, message, tone—
take a moment to enter this poem.

THE WOMAN, THE ELEVATOR, AND CASHMERE

Staring straight ahead in the brass car,
she faced him and tried to think of something
witty to say (couldn't think of a thing,
just started to feel an illogical hatred toward him).

Getting to the top floor was now a chore—
smells more obvious in that space,
a lonGoday russet stain on his suit;
delicate touches of her gardenia perfume
offset the stale air.

They looked at each other briefly,
keeping appropriate neighborly boundaries.
"Is it getting cooler—do you think I'll need a jacket?"
she asked mindlessly.
"Perhaps—a cashmere sweater will do," he answered
with an underlying pompousness.
"Cashmere," she chuckled.
"I haven't worn that in years."
As if it were passé, like animal fur.
"They don't kill animals for that," he retorted.
"It's costly, though," she went on,
growing near-inaudible.
He glanced most curiously, got off,
and the door slammed shut.
"Cashmere. . .really!" she muttered
and entered the disheveled apartment,
cleared up breakfast dishes and floor crumbs
from last night's pizza.
It was a silvery October night—
the moon sultry, gleaming.
She looked out the paned window:

a couple was bickering;
an old man sat at the kitchen table,
his head in his hands, moaning;
children were jumping rope in the courtyard.
She played her favorite CD and laughed.
"Cashmere. *Really!*"

TOWNSHIP

Sleek cars coated its highways,
      Godiva chocolates,
           riding lessons;

they look at the bony frames and sunk-in,
      crusted faces of peers in Biafra, Bosnia,
           without feeling anything much

and click them away with TV remotes—
      just one of the signs there
           where we left our bones a legend.

WEDDING RING

Was losing it an accident?
      I'd wished to will it to you one day,
          my daughter.
It was a lovely thing in its time
      a dazzling circlet catching the moon's glaze
          glittering always like ripples

in pond water…
      its glow twirled from sight
          one fiery night.

It would not
      have been a simple gift,
          my love.

WHY KILL POETRY?

Why kill poetry,
for it's a dying art—
all fiddle and froth,
cotton flowers around the young,
dreary cobalt dreams of the wiser
filled with neoned monster-angels
camouflaging mom and dad.

Why feel contempt when eyes
dilate and hair stands up on end
to know these agonizing pains again,
kill this melancholy stuff
that so unnerves
those as self-conscious
as a too-full moon that falls too low.

WITH SALLY

Her eyes focus only on the floor.
The garden outside her small room
is pretty but silent.
Her head juts forward—shaking subtly,
as if reprimanding herself.

My aunt is before me
unlike Sally
whose hair is thin, frazzled
lips are naked and dry,
her past my future.

I hold up a photo of her two older sisters.
She's the one in the middle—
perfectly oval-faced with jet black hair,
her presence inconspicuous,
a small frame thrusting toward the camera,
arms out, on her knees,
Al Jolson style.

I study her eyes, her gestures:
not a movement or flinch of recognition.
I open the box of cookies.
Her hand locks on a chocolate one;
she chews methodically
as if in deep thought,
then smiles to be polite.

I lay my hand on her pale puffy fingers.
They quickly grab another cookie
that she swallows whole.

Fallen crumbs below move slowly over acres of life
in a steady flow,
like the ants hidden by the burdens on their backs.

WOUNDED

I've been wounded, split in two—
that's why I don't stop talking
long enough to listen, so they say.

But no one's real, objective,
so I speak at a pace
to smother all the hard words,

stop only to hear
passing angels from their true blue heaven
who find me somehow.

The Fourth Wall

A KNOCK ON THE DOOR

The fatigue of fluorescent lights
cast a gray on her face.
They knew her reluctant, hopeful knock,
yet kept her toying with her necklace,
dislodging the small stones
of the heart-shaped pendant on a stretched welcome
mat (tissue thin),
the chips pelting demonically
on the warped impurities from under it.

She was the same friend, wasn't she,
half-crazed half-brilliant,
maybe less charming without the usual glitter?
She stood there loosely, telling witty stories
minimizing misplaced deeds
mostly forgotten.

They looked at the clock with impatience;
she smiled and lingered, leaving on her own
terms, though—
under shaky willows,
proud dahlias crushed beneath her feet.

A TAP

The day after my mother died
the machine filled up with comforting cliches,
the somber ivory cards stuffed the mailbox.

There was no solace in this, really,
and I was rigid——- unable to get out of bed
even to feed my starving kids.

I felt a loving tap on my shoulder in my gloomy spirit
that pushed me to get going
adhering to her tough maternal ways.
I revealed this to my friends

who assured me it was all in my head.
Now that I'm older—getting closer to her
I know, now, it truly was—all in her soul.

A WARM CUP OF TEA

Coffee always waited for me
on the breakfast table then,
and the danish.
When days are tired and slow, I go back to
Hewes Street,
where I feel the world churning and passing,
getting closer to my lost family.

I walk to the gypsies and find a psychic
who assures me of health, peace, even money.

"What about love?" I say
as she cups her sun-spotted hands to her breast,
till floating letters gradually evolve:
"Missing love?" they read in repetitious phrases
covering the ball.

The sky turns dark and clouds move fast
pushing me to my home congested with distortions
and old wounds,
and you, who throw a weary arm
over my cold shoulder
and hand me a warm cup of tea cluttered with
fated leaves that shape the letters of your name.

AN OLD BLANKET

The stems and petals are indistinct,
muted in gnarled creases that erase
its silky firmness stiff with plucky flowers,
of purples and pinks
fluffy and fit for a queen.

She clutches the last bit of it
tattered
by night's monstrous dreams
and years of tossing in the bacterial
green of a child's heaves——-
churning daily in waves of antiseptic baths.

Now, when the commuter train fails,
when her computer plays dead,
and the night's new video is caught in rewind,
she eyes the soft ridges of the rumpled cloth.

ANGEL AND MAMA

I push Angel's stroller every Monday.
He's the one that got to me at the shelter—
something about his cherubic face, awkward gestures,
sad dark eyes
we go to the bleak park near Crotona Avenue.
and wheel across the hardened stretch of grass
and beds of little stones.
By ten, the cautious sparrows are less frisky
after getting up too early,
and serious pigeons lethargically peck on barren soil
under a weak sun and skimpy rain.

We pass by rows of benches
where slouched souls know
the world conspires against them,
and everybody needs everything
and nothing touches the ground
except for Angel's heavy tears that soften
the crusted soil,
absorbing mournful cries for Mama
that no one can hear.

ADELE SCHWARTZ

AT A SINGLES DANCE

She's one of them now—a single
always considered taboo
in her married years:

Singles dances, chat rooms, support
groups, singles at Club Med.
How did she get here?
Too much pampering, maybe not enough,
 concerned about the kids, not him or me?
The therapist said "don't care about being right,
just be happy—give in." Give in to
 his ego, his girlfriend, the unpaid bills,
the empty bed?

She thinks of her home with the kids:
the smell of popcorn,
the air of spring was like jasmine there,
but in this singles place
the colognes are too sweet and musky
combined with nervous sweat.

The waiter moves about with a wide smile
and reassuring wink,
serving greasy pigs in blankets and weak wine.
He's done this a thousand times
and understands us.
Women check themselves out,
dashing to the powder room,
lining thinned-out lips—
she wonders if the woman next to her is sexier, prettier,
and realizes she is. When the men eye her
she avoids eye contact,
fearful of any hint of rejection.

The pigs are shrinking in their blankets
as an eighty-year-old guy smiles at her, while

she downs her eighth glass of wine moving
away nonchalantly.

The waiter is getting haggard,
his smile turns surly and dull
amid glimmering utensils.

The one guy that's cool
seems to advance toward her
but goes by without even a nod.

The ladies she befriends give up,
discussing rent, value pasta restaurants,
and the 80% sales at Macy's—

During the silent moments, we realize the hard times
and more to come;
never forgetting what is gone.

The surplus of sunlight,
the moon yard that glowed under dusty skies,
familiar fresh smells, the sheen of beaming faces
turned stiff in bone-light—-all she begot

she leaves alone as if adrift
in the darkest night known,
discernible to no one,
and picks up the one glove she still possesses.

CAMELOT

In Camelot I loved JFK
and knew he saw me through the TV
and probably loved me too
in my headband and tie-dyed shirt
in strong communication.

So when he was shot
and Jackie in her bloodstained pink suit,
with matching pill box hat,
jumped on him
I leaped into the TV
to shield her—avoiding what I knew.

Hitting Lee Harvey (realizing he wasn't in it alone)
aware that Ruby knew it all
and after him a stretch of endless falls.

People started to change after that,
the air filled with incense and pungent odors
and through all the firing
tranquility grew
and in the harmony they forgot
about Camelot,
leaving fairy tales where they belong.

CASSANDRA

I've seen her in golden heydays,
whimsical, young and easy in the better stores,
in theaters that play with time,
mingling on white wines,
happy as Times Square.

The sun worked overtime on her small town streets,
with inevitable yellow mornings,
through "loving" in-laws over staying visits.

I've seen her climbing to rooftops—
looking for answers in a green world,
swearing off red meats—
vomiting the carnal blood of her youth.
Crying innocently —her tears overflowing the dirty
rivers of New Jersey.

I've seen her kneeling down in hopeful cathedrals,
in long seconds of short-lived salvations,
crashing to resurrection on the hardened sidewalks.

And then to wake, in the midst
of glassy narcissistic buildings,
demanding therapy and pills
designed for babied baby boomers,

A miraculous wonder woman,
her heart exposed like an iron pendant,
obsessing in the guts of her poetic tomb,
falling out of grace with sooty hands
and artificial empires.

I've seen her always in my dreams
trudging through dingy roads
in a yellowed wedding dress,
smeared with the stains of time,
tossing a bouquet of dead roses toward me.

EDEN REVISITED

A couple alone under the blazing fruit
with nothing to do—only
stopping sometimes to listen to the hissing
advice of the snake.
Eventually Eve handed the fruit
to Adam, wide-eyed and boyish,
who scampered around the garden
noticing his reflection in the water
with delight, arching one eyebrow at Eve
who quickly covered up.

He flared his nostrils and ripped off
the light-weight cloth over her softly rising breasts,
beating his chest—
soon bored and irritated—he ran off madly.

"Come back, Adam,"shouted Eve
"I'm sorry." She blamed herself, of course,
yet sought out the same savvy snake,
then waited, stretched out like a cat, on the
silky velvet grounds.

Adam finally returned,
hoarse and mournful,
disillusioned with this new Empire,
holding judgments, scrutinizing.

Eve, as she basked in the twilight,
wearing a challenging expression and pouty lips,
her eyes downcast, adorned in ruffles and sheer lace,
knowing they were all going to hell, anyway,
as Eden grew cold.

Grandma Eve,
don't fret.
We forgot your stupid move,
hardly mention it.
Your daughters are rich and shrewd,
in suits of gold
that shine on everything we're near
in the gloss of now.

ENLIGHTENMENT

We're on the beach, absorbing
all that the ozone allows.
My body melds in oils of lavender
and—oh, I forgot to mention my lover
caressing my tanned limbs,
our minds swaying in soft waves of wine.

Weathered fishermen walk around in boat after boat,
sweltering and exhausted;
they hobble along the shore, staring—
urging us to be happy once and for all.

FAMILY PHOTO (HUNGARY)

My father's six,
   the youngest of his siblings.
He's dead center,
   frail and awkward

in a peaked cap
   and balloon-like knickers,
eyes cast downward, shy,
   and yet he manages a pixie smile.

His mother's to his right,
   wrapped in a shawl
and long, coarse layers
   covering her laced brown boots.

Her jowls are sunken,
   but her cheeks are prominent
beneath a linen kerchief
   tied under her chin.

She looks far older
   than her forty-three years.
Stiff as soldiers, daughters stand
   at each end, eyes shifted

to her and their baby brother.
   They are startled by the camera.
No one smiles;
   they just stand firmly near

a warped oak table
   under a bare window

that reveals the barrenness
    of old harvests.

The photo sits on glassy tables
    of the younger generations.
I wonder if they feel the slap of poverty,
    or the richness of a simple peasant love.

FLEA MARKETS AND GARAGE SALES

After the separation, she moves into a little place,
away from conventional faces
and unnecessary remarks.

Out of habit, she writes her tender poems,
faking a life she's not yet lived.

She passes through flea markets and garage sales,
caressing objects that were once novel and fresh,
picks up an old lamp for two bucks, a vase for one,
carefully lays them on a battered table,

adopts a cat or two then three;
tutors on the ways of commas, periods, parentheses
with a feminine touch,
controlling all beginnings, pauses, endings,
as she once did with passion—
only, now, enhancing persistence and order,
as if they were substitutes for love.

FORGIVENESS

The damage will not be undone this time—
When his hand reached out to touch
her moist clump of hair in forgiveness.
Cheap words, twisted silence,
inflicted only a furious logic,
souvenirs of black and purple left to be soothed,
she'd show her teeth and hiss, "why do you hate me?"

This time she knew why—
could see his mother's eyes squint at her
through him—she thought.
His face is small, diminutive, pale,
feebly attempting
infinite love.

MOTHER'S FINGERS

In a primal way, I fed them with my fingers.
        Forks and spoons seemed uncaring and cold
        against unarmored mouths with clenched teeth.

My tired hands would astonish onlookers
        who relented to laughter and grimaces.

When startled lips allowed unexpected bits
        of food to seep through,
        and it beat the "all the People in Europe Are
        Starving" routine.

Edible forms and fragrances
        may have been destroyed;
        admittedly, it wasn't an aesthetic exercise;
        but, oh, the results were so exceptionally
        full!

MY BIG BOY

"Be careful on the road,"
Button your coat,
And don't forget to eat fruit,"
I say automatically as my son leaves,
biting my lip at his plea, "I'm 28, Mom—*Pleeeease!*"

When I glimpse through his sinewy muscles and
worked-out limbs,
the moment is suspended in transparency.

I'm his mother —I can see through him
as nobody can
what is his link to things in this strange world?

Oh yes, I forgot he was born on the cusp of the fickle
twins and stubborn bull;
this was enough for him;
I cannot carry him anymore.

OH, ARCHIE

One dark drizzly summer afternoon
 I think of those days
under the covers reading my infinite series
of Archie Andrew's comic books,

hoping to be like blonde Betty—
innocent, guileless, cute
(unlike the crafty vamp Veronica
and her wretched Reggie).
What wonderful theater—large as a child's ego:
Betty and Archie in love without explanation.

Gazing at photos of past beaux,
I realize that they all resembled Archie
in some way, at least initially,

and wonder what happened and why they've gone,
knowing that life did not bring out
the Betty in me
—only the Reggie in them.

OH, WHAT A BEAUTIFUL MORNING

A red blotch crosses her window—
a cardinal fidgeting, its perched weight
mimicking the woman's tune:
"Oh what a beautiful morning
Oh what a beautiful day"
somewhere between its early rounds and
uncomfortable settling,

she smooths out the rumpled morning,
half in scary or splendid dreams,
always with their clear endings and murky plots
that leave a sour taste of life's unending lies.

Oh, stubborn girl, dousing the stench
of last night's omens,
why do you ignore the downward current of the
bloodstained creature,
unremembering the blue streaks of the day before,
drowning out forewarnings.

To think you could create your own bright sunshine,
fill in lonely spaces with the silly feeling
"everything's goin' your way."

PARADOX

My past in this silver frame
 tarnished, with little
hearts engraved,
a steady line of frozen smiles
and gloveless hands rosy on skies
against the ridge of a snow bank,
restraining movement,
fixed eyes follow me,
almost curiously, as if to say
"Don't you remember?"

Small drops stream down my window,
 yet the skyline is brilliant as rubies,
inviting me to scintillating streets so familiar,
admired and frequented in my day,
now,
more enchanting from afar,
a detached and captivating distance.

PROPHECY

Enchanted by logistics of planets
insightful stars,
I discerned the watered Scorpio eclipse, the Leo
sun on my birth date (8/8) in August heat
casting up inevitable conflicts.

Confident Aries came forth as a burning ally
overcompensating to allow for Leo's tough
ascendancy to shine on yet a while.

When I was pregnant with my daughter
an astrologer advised me to be cautious
of deceit and grave disappointment when the child
reached puberty.

I abruptly changed my birthday to 10/9
and carried on——a luckier Libra——
so that soothsayers would let me be.

But Libra's native sense of truth would not
have it:

so came the fire, then the water,
the water, then the fire. . . .

RELATIVES

I think of you
as shadows
lurking in a budding garden,
paralyzing flowers.

You linger there
and over water,
meting conversation out
like mad hatters.

Be loving, temperate;
don't shock me without cause.
Let me burst forth
like a volcano

and live in my web of stars
against the sky's doors.

SAGA

In the midst of their contentment
came a turn of fate.

Day and night had blended in vacant succession;
now she continues, alone, oblivious to change.

When conscious, she moves toward the couch
where they entwined in solitude,
his lead-like fingers conducting her only world.

They sensed the external heat from outside,
drawn to glassy gardens
loosening their warm embrace,

to walk apart, his back toward her;
she watched him pluck the firm and perky blossoms then,
left to shrivel
beneath the feet of their fickle lord, their fierce sun.

SEARCH

The wife and kids are unaware,
just smiling over breakfast,
unwatered plants, bent over, leaning on the bay window,

The TV's blasting,
cartoons are interrupted:
BREAKING NEWS—another train wreck, poor Haiti,
mean China, bold Russia—
"I saw the news today, oh, boy!"

The man of the house shrinks
into the eerie vacuum of his coat—
his slit-like eyes squinting—
he's searching, maybe, for a lost key
or an unpaid parking ticket

in his passage through familiar streets
onto the shore of a different world,
reflecting only on an occasional seagull
or a plane rising into the soft horizon.

His feet sink into the cooling night sand,
his half-open lips around the butt of a cigarette;
smoke circles carelessly evaporate into the blank sky.
He's not crying, really.
His eyes stay red and moist.
There is no going back;
what he left can never be admitted.

SILHOUETTE OF SUMMER

It's another benign afternoon;
I'm slouched on a park bench
      with my pen and pad.
The leaves hang heavy,
abundant with summer's energy,
unremembering the depredations of fall.

A kid from the Bronx,
in an oversized jacket and balloon pants, eyes me.
"Hey, lady, want to buy a dog?"
"I'd like to," I say, and mean it.
The dog's eyes are droopy, sad,
so I back out.
He walks away automatic in rejection
      and drags the leash to someone else.

Hip-hop teens are in their earphones,
Dominican music sputtering from cars,
      staccato style, in perfect choreography.
Hot New York City tee shirts on the stands
      are selling wildly,
tourists cautiously get change,
surveying all angles of the bad Big Apple,
tribal mixtures burst upon their pure ethnicity.

A persistent bee hums by,
buzzing toward and away from an unwanted fence,
to nuzzle a seductive rose
and return more fulfilled and tenacious.

I move and think of somewhere else to go,
throw my leftover lunch to the pigeons
who befriend me, waddling around my feet.

The man beside me is beginning to matter.
"The dog was really cute," I chuckle.
"So was the boy," he says.

I abandon my seat.
"I'm going to make it in this greasy world,"
I mutter.
Years from now, I'll be the silhouette of summer,
the hottest song on everybody's lips.
The bee moves toward my ear,
idle, unfluttering, almost in abeyance,
letting me in on a curious tale.
I turn to another blank page.

STATEMENT

Lovely things do not belong to me:
        the loan was called too soon.
Some are in awe
        of my shattered anguish.

I've learned to hide humiliations
        and my dreams—
to deal with the angers of fate.
        I bestow

all the lush
        rosy moments
on those who know
        only old envy and me.

SUDDEN STORM

Sunday noon—she sits beside him
the broken-in futon holding her in place,
her eyes on a jagged crack on a favorite
terra cotta vase, remembering how it happened.

He stares through her, mesmerized by the flickering
and muted TV sounds.
The vertical structures across the Hudson
generate a clouded sheen,
veiling life's dramas and uncertainties.

She dresses up like a vivid goddess,
grabs the jingling car keys,
adds a spritz of some notorious scent
manufacturing sensations she will soon know.

Voices open every street,
smiles are glorious, moist, dazzling,
her fiery search ends in a sudden August storm.

She returns wet and soggy;
he sits, elbows on his knees,
chin cupped in his hands,
looking past her toward the window,
"Why'd you go out in this awful weather?"
he asks.
Her mouth is half open with alibis.
He turns the volume up and up—full of victorious
shouts for the winning team
that she can't hear
although the storm has died.

THE HOUSE

Did I close its doors,
      knowing I wouldn't return?
           I pass its warm mystery

of long moments, unlimited, whole—
      formed happiness piled up neatly.
           When I first entered, I realized

somehow it was our last stop,
      an ending. It was
           an uncertain structure—

sadly bent, at the foot of a hill,
      slanted to the right
           and barely left.

"A strange settling,"
      the carpenters
           all said.

ADELE SCHWARTZ

THE THIN MOON OF SUMMER

In those last foggy days with him
we'd sit inactively at the dinner table,
reading or watching TV,
while we gulped
our food.

Onto his odd gestures,
jerky movements of his brow;
the thin moon of summer cut through the room.

His distance was gradual, now obvious—
we mocked and made light of his distortions,
as he lingered over dessert,
spooning the last of it, playing with the crumbs,
licking them from the plate,
shouting over our heads
with senseless demands,
adhering to a weakened authority.

In a few days, we were without him,
veiled by a jagged horizon
and unpredictable sky,
around the table, nibbling like crows.

The unhurried season
rushed into an excitable frenzy,
full leaves loosened from their loyal branches,
embarrassingly rusty
against the perched roses, slowly drying—
preserving
their fading scents;
flirtatious bees all seek alternatives.

The chill of fall came upon us prematurely,
the white summer yet outside,
unattainable, unnoticed.

THEY NEVER GUESSED

They never guessed she'd act on a frivolous rage,
her dreamy silence, distanced them—
threw them off during

years of rounded crises that grew so massive
overtaking love and hate.

Numb but peaceful, she watched them gather around
her husband's coppery body,
shining already in cold hell,
same face, no voice—wide-eyed and benign.

A kaleidoscope of fall leaves lifted,
encircling her in commendation—
parched and shriveled garlands around her.

You did the right thing, she thought
the judge would say, as tears moistened her dusty eyes.

Water-soaked wishes—all discord—dead
then the needed music and necessary pain.

TRAIN

I thought you'd kill the past
with love.
When I saw you on the fated train.
I sparkled and shifted into a new style,

feeling lovely, calm in that sensuous interlude
at the rate we were traveling, though the gardens and
decorative stars
diminished too quickly.

Manipulating time, you made your move
and sat next to me—outside the swift window
were deserted streets
irreparable buildings.

"What happened to the lovely gardens?" I asked.
You turned to me
and said, "That was then,"
squeezing my hand, making promises
of blossoms to come,
passing endless deserts begging
for some form of life—
a destination I wished not to imagine.

The train shrieked to an abrupt stop
its doors flung open
to a platform of millions
where you melded
as we became lost to each other.

I remained immobile on the car
and felt it jut backward for awhile
as if undecided.

Then blazing ahead,
it pulled me along,
defenseless, around the torso of this world
'til I saw a caring face
knowing he'd kill the past
with love.

WALKING ON EGGS

I tiptoe over the steamy ghosts of childhood,
with its hearts and spirits lost.
There were the sterile kitchens and austere living
rooms—only to be viewed and then admired.

I see my aunt on the phone, winking and shushing me,
so that other relatives wouldn't know
she was the first we'd visit on a Sunday,
all politics without protocol.

Why did we visit this aunt first?
Was she the nicest, oldest, wisest, or just
the luckiest to grab my father so? . . .

Bickering and feelings hurt over a simple visit
to New Jersey became a sport
and now that it's expired, I miss the passion
behind it (playing favorites, silly pride),
souls thin as shells,
my little feet walking on eggs.

WINTER CARNIVAL

How difficult things are
according to today's women
engaged in sex wars.

In my college years,
girls were just girls,
hardly woman enough
to set on scaring men to death.

I remember the excitement
over an invitation to the winter carnival
at Dartmouth.
My roommate and I gingerly approached
the all-male portals of Hanover, New Hampshire.
We stood out next to all the plain Janes
of the Ivy League
who didn't know how to dress.
We were perfect ornaments
near our dashing jocks.

I almost "went steady" with Ritchie
(my date and president of the only
Jewish fraternity up there).
We'd hold hands and kiss,
coloring the magical ice sculptures.

When he went too far,
I smacked him,
knowing he wouldn't feel much
with a six-pack absorbing his veins.

I spent the rest of my stay
reciting poems

at the frat house,
softening in luminous stillness.

Since I wasn't about to be put out,
Ritchie raced his blue Triumph to the airport
in detached unconsciousness,
placed me on the wrong plane
(headed for L.A.).
I never knew if it was all intentional.

I'm sure that Ritchie probably forgot
the coarse whiteness of my girlishness.
I wonder if he's read
the dark refinement of my poems, lately.

DON'T FLY WITH ME

It's not the thrill of swift ascent
amid the swirling darkness,
jolting up in a vertical lift,
or the sighs when landing, accompanied by applause,
not the theatrical kind,
not like the Pentecostal hands in thanks,
nor the boredom of the frequent flier
who takes it all for granted.

What's unsettling
is the long and steady nothingness in between,
with its bothersome restraints,
the overly friendly voice of the pilot
requesting us to "buckle up,"
because it's going to be a little rough.
The stone-faced flight attendants
starting to play the role of nurses,
no bathrooms, no coffee or muffins,
just when you really need them.

Suspicion heightens, when the man behind you,
surfing on his laptop, is a terrorist for sure!

Who are we to disturb the columns of clouds?
To intrude on Earth's most precious gift, serenity?
How foolish to imagine Mother Nature
will remain backstage,
without unnecessary outbursts:
the scary turbulence,
the unwanted geese,
over a shrinking sea.

FOR OLIVER

He waits for me, a patient gentleman,
perfectly still, till I complete
the last phase of getting ready,
down to the red lines on my lips.

Just a slight wagging of his tail
gets me to move on,
so he can investigate each blade of grass,
each leaf on a stem,
linger over a mound of dirt,
alert to what lies beneath,
exchange a knowing glance,
as if I, too, have his instinctive gifts.

His butterscotch fur gleams in daylight,
walking briskly, turning every which way
to notice everything,
occasionally looking up
to make sure I'm still there.

Love object on the river walk,
the high school girls sigh,
woman with dachshund praises his intelligence,
the spiritual with soft, godly eyes,
recognize his gentle little soul;
even the joggers rushing by
remark, "He's the good guy here."

When I read my poems
or sing a Rogers and Hammerstein tune,
his eyes are attentive in admiration;
there's no need to plead for just one more minute
or close the kitchen door, so he won't leave me.

HOMAGE TO ALLEN GINSBERG

I'm writing this poem because I woke up
from a sweaty nightmare,
old and abandoned,
in a nursing home, drenched in urine.

I'm writing this poem because my cousin threw
tomato sauce
on my lovely white dress
because I was writing this poem.

I'm writing this poem, because my family
gets together only at funerals.
I'm writing this poem to stop eating
at three-thirty a.m.
I'm writing this poem because I can't sing or dance.

I'm writing this poem because my mother
loved poems.
I'm writing this poem because my father
hated them.
I'm writing this poem because I can't watch
It's a Wonderful Life for the fortieth time.

I'm writing this poem because I hate computers.
I'm writing this poem because I'm sad.
I'm writing this poem because I'm happy.
I'm writing this poem because I need it for class.
I'm writing this poem because I may never write
another one again—

HUCKLEBERRY FRIEND

You're dark and gone,
yet we still live in the web you've spun,
oh, how we planned and created,
created and planned,
over and over.

But those were the days of ice storms,
spirals unwinding.
It was easy to follow you from there to here,
even through the twisted maze,
deliberately set up.

Did you know that I found my way out?
Old Huckleberry friend,
wouldn't it be like you to know why I bothered?
And like me to know if I didn't?

I'M RUNNING LATE

I left a chunk of myself behind
in a nurturing, sunlit room —
warm, lazy,
'til shock set in one day.

So what is left of me
pushes ahead and much too fast,
yet, I'm usually late
and always for a very important date.

Have I become the rabbit at the hatter's party?
I hit the pedal, zooming off to somewhere,
I'm running late and I'm so lost.

I stop someone who gawks at me with innocent eyes,
I ask for directions—he doesn't speak English.
I stop a character type, a slinky man
with a loose plaid shirt over faded jeans,
but he's from out of town and has no clue
regarding my destination.

I sit for a while under a wasted sundown
and know that the attractive woman walking briskly
will give me detailed directions that will surely mess
me up.

Getting out of the car,
exhausted and tight, like old garters,
I take five,
watching scrambling little feet
stampeding toward the ice cream truck,
pleading for change.

An elderly couple
sits across from me,
mellow, silent, holding onto what's left of peace
in their folded hands.

I've lost the child in me
and I'm not ready to recline in powdered parks!
Oh, God, I'm wasting precious time here
and there's so much more to do,
the flies are growing weak
waiting for me—
the plural moments will not stop.

ADELE SCHWARTZ

LUNCH WITH MY MOTHER

In the local coffee shop,
my mother rested against the vinyl
of the corner booth.
We idly picked at the invisible crumbs of Danish.

That day, her floral black and white dress
lay against her chest,
a crease above the crooked scar
that had replaced soft roundness.

I studied her in unfamiliar ways:
the nervous tugging of her neckline,
puzzled eyes fixed onto me.
She gave her all, a constant overflow, I thought,
but now, I'm just someone she used to know.

I tried to remind her of a humorous time,
when my daughter paraded around in my
high-heeled shoes,
the heavy air required a change,
I was hoping for her playful grin. . . .

Leaning forward, she weakly sipped iced tea,
intently squeezing lemon slices into it,
over and over again.

MRS. ANDREOLA'S BACKYARD

Her tomatoes basked in the sun,
relishing the coolness of rain,
aligned on a firm vine,
steady, even,
among chaotic ferns and weeds.

Mrs. Andreola held back healthy stems,
cutting only what was withered, dead.
Behind, near the two-story old brown house,
I sat slumped in my stroller—
a tiny mouth turned down,
my spotted, measled face thrust back
against the wrinkled plastic pillow.

Mrs. Andreola, a martyred widow in black,
at my side, as strong and willful as Mother Teresa,
murmured sweet Italian phrases
that I never understood—
pressing her soft lips on my sweltering forehead,
the warmth of me rushing to her heart—

"*Mangia, mangia,*" she would say, tempting me
with the thinnest slices of a glistening tomato,
"Good for you—eat, eat!"
Oh, to make my way back to her yard,
so crisp and so predictable,
to know the sounds of early summer:
laughing at grasshoppers,
the steady rhythm of a broom
sweeping a spotless kitchen floor,
the clicking of her huge black clock.

ADELE SCHWARTZ

MY FATHER ATE DINNER

My father ate dinner on a portable tray
in front of the TV.
He'd go on about how good the meal was
and how he especially liked the pot roast.

He'd chew the meat, yet never swallow it,
I guess he was a vegetarian, of sorts;
he'd watch the news,
while sopping up some gravy with bread pieces,
inhaling an unfiltered Lucky Strike
and downing his coffee.

My mother and I sat at the kitchen table,
there was nothing much to say,
we'd just nibble away,
viewing the colorful array
of greens and reds on the plate.

I'd go into my room,
turn on the TV to watch *Father Knows Best*,
the Anderson family, holding hands,
saying grace at the dinner table
before ever touching a utensil.
Later, Mr. Anderson would sit on the floral wing
chair,
the youngest on his lap,
the rest gathered around to listen
to his end-of-the-day story.

I'd gaze at the TV in an hypnotic stupor,
glaring intently
as if I could empower the screen to open up
and let me in.

NO TIME TO CHANGE

I'm rushing past the closing cemetery gates,
summer's giving out, under the steel sky
of a premature fall.

Still in jogging shorts, guilty about
my incessant need to run,
with a drawn face, my eyes fall sadly
on the faithfully still stones of Mom and Dad.

The granite is more bleached and sacred now,
smells of pine and salt from stagnant tears.
I kneel to place two pebbles on their names,
can hear them click, weighty in the pensive quiet.

I know my mother's thinking
that I'm coming down with something;
her uncomfortable stirring worries my father,
who urges me to eat more,
eying my anorexic ankles one last time.

NOVEMBER 7, 2005

Shock ran through me, when my sister died.
My niece told everyone, then me.
Why didn't she call me first? I thought.
God only knows.

I don't hold grudges and besides,
the girl had problems,
so the anger melded into empathy,
the horror of it brought the stoic out in me.

Friends' trembling voices going on and on:
"You're being so strong, handling it well."
A piercing retort, I would think:
Were there accusations, too,
of insufficient sisterly affection?

At the funeral, I exclaimed,
"You know, she always bought me
little gifts after work,"
pleasant moments over the years were scarce.

I weathered empty days without her,
intentions left hanging that couldn't be,
no good-byes, no apologies,
just some spirited smiling photographs of us,
in lovely frames.

OLD FORT LEE

Under an enraged red sky
stood the marble hi-rise,
gray smog overhead, an empty skyline,
only white clouds over a sad, tired sea.

Wars of the co-op with silly rules
and bogus penalties,
neighbors scrutinizing cars outside the white lines,
off-scheduled deliveries, always behind—
to live and have to die there,
can fate be so unkind?

Now, resting at the water's edge,
open and free,
the light of Manhattan
glittering over me,
I forget the plastic faces,
the vexations of old Fort Lee.

ADELE SCHWARTZ

OUR LADY MACBETH

Around the bountiful kitchen table,
serious issues were discussed,
usually when I was almost in the depths of sleep.
My ears drew bits of conversation in,
then curling up like a curious puppy,
I would listen to the worried words of concern.

The dilemma of my sister's
hand-washing ritual came up,
my mother painfully explained how Doris —
a near-genius and my sister's closest friend —
bit her nails and chewed on pencil erasers;
she turned to my father, who offered no solace,
and my sympathies went unnoticed.

My sister's listless eyes would look
toward the stainless basin filled with oily water,
her meditative river,
twisting and turning her young wrinkled hands,
fingers on fire.

What were her hands to touch or not to touch?
What did they pull apart or idly hold together?
What imagined dealings in her palms
to rinse incessantly and wring,
doubled over at the sink,
in fiendish prayer,
turning the furious white foam pitch, pitch black?

POOR

Your jean pockets bulge with crinkled bills,
held tight by a dirty rubber band.
You gawk at statements from the bank,
in fear of next year,
ignoring an annoying present.

Don't you notice the tattered threads
under your suit cuffs,
their blackness with a grimy sheen from wear?

Maybe Dickens had the solution
I'll become the ghost of Christmas future,
scare you, so you'll hurl your bills into the air
everywhere
like a whimsical flower girl
tossing rose petals.

SUDDEN MOMENTS

I want to tell of sudden moments
when silky darkness smooths the blinding glitz of day.

Only when I hear the Earth move,
closing up what's known,

making harsh squeaking noises
as it slowly enters a scraping future,

the worries of the world
replaced by soothing dreams of those nearby,

and I alert with a friendly little flame
that keeps away all those still up to see

who might destroy the mystery for me
that sometimes hands me a gift of words.

THE FOURTH WALL

The old house sits slanted to the left;
the grayness of this day exaggerates
the dirty snow.
My children are snow angels—
limbs puffy and flaying,
little spacemen in pastel snowsuits,
one glove under a loose branch,
a misplaced boot just beside it.

My presence is better than absence, I think—if you
know true pain.
My spine stretches itself into a sigh.

Hoping not to miss the cherished moments,
a dark-haired woman steps out the door
onto the blue portico lined
with dried-up Halloween pumpkins
and a shriveled spider man mask.
She is frail—nervously calls for her child,
interrupting the imagined scene.
Who is she? What is she doing in my home?
Imposing on my unclaimed eternity,
I sit catatonic and erect—
like a condemned structure waiting to be saved,
a devastation that history condones, a heroic survivor.

The sun is lowering in the lonely west,
leaving my hands cold and sluggish.
I drive away as usual—reluctant, sober.
The car wavers over the white lines,
as if fighting the predictable course.
I'll be back again, maybe in early spring
with its sporadic ice clods and dark greenery
and persistent impatiens.

THE SMOKERS' ROOM

After attempting to bite
the last of a Reese's chocolate square,
he focused on the Marlboro Lights
on the window sill,
the New York skyline appearing uneven,
vague, above the small and dusty window.

I sat beside his propped-up bed,
his tobacco-stained, abnormally long fingers,
out of proportion,
grabbing a loose cigarette with unexpected strength,
and forcing new enthusiasm, we shared the Yankees'
win.

Between his muffled coughs, he pleaded over and over
to be taken to the smokers' room.
I lifted him and wheeled him to the place
where the scent was strangely inviting.

In the long silence of the nursing home,
the frail all held their cigarettes, cool and casual,
as if the place was a dark, mysterious bistro,
gazing at the gray circles of smoke they could not see.

WHY I STOPPED WRITING POETRY: PART ONE

Words would burst from a heavenly space
on the pillow.
Slits of paper on the cold hardwood floor
cling to the legs of my bed.

Specific words,
unfinished,
idiosyncratic. . . .

The sensitive felt pain,
my stronger friends stared up at the ceiling
making sure to feel nothing.

I've said it all already,
why go on and on bothering everyone?
I'm tired now and it's time
for Larry King to do the work—

Whiffs of my small children in their deep sleep,
curled up like pretzels . . .

Here I go again. . . .

WHY I STOPPED WRITING POETRY:
PART TWO

You tell me you hate poetry,
the self-indulgence,
the undeserved passion of it. . . .

The days of seeing you off to school,
squeaky clean, in mind and attire,
beaming at your report card,
shielding you from the sufferings here,
are no longer my life's work.

You tell me that you don't get
how I could even think of such frivolity,
when you're fighting a bad cold
that will probably result in bronchitis.

And how almost everyone you know
might have a serious ailment,
while the poisonous smoke
of your cigarette
creates a colorless dome
over anti-oxidant oatmeal and blueberries,
that by some chance
or good luck will save you.

Be temperate, my little girl,
the torments of a hellish summer are over,
yet we are still at risk, confused by demons
offering destructive edibles.

If only we, together,
could have cast off all the spells
of an unnecessary suburb,

spells that pushed me on that plane,
falling far away from you. . . .

ADELE SCHWARTZ

ZAIDY'S DOLLS

When visiting my Zaidy on Sunday afternoons,
I would reach high for the newest hidden doll,
always in the same place.

He'd help me down from the wobbly stool
to kiss my cheeks, sopping wet,
gazing at the painted wooden face
of my latest treasure, always named Kathy.

I'd caress her, burp her, feed and bathe her,
singing to her accepting stillness and stony lids,
mechanically shut.

I knew Zaidy was nearby,
as I sniffed the fermenting wine from the tub
on his stained, rough hands.
He'd stumble toward me, scuffling
in his leather slippers.
"You're going to be a good *mamala* one day," he'd say.

I wonder if he knows how I fulfilled his prophecy,
remembering my sleeping children,
held in their delicate love blankets,
lullabied and made whole.

Now, as I move backwards in dusky winter,
everything is gone;
my heart continues to beat patiently,
waiting to be complete again.

I doze on and off
in front of the dying fireplace flames,
sure that what I thought was true
is still there.

THE HOARDERS

"He wasn't crazy really, just a bit eccentric,"
said my friend, slowly opening the door
to his deceased father's apartment of thirty years,
tucked in a corner of the Bronx.

"He was just a little boy from Russia
when his mother had to give him up—
too poor to keep him."

One would weep to see a place so strange,
a maze of boxes sat, soggy, sad,
from gray wall to gray wall,
from high ceiling to battered parquet floors—
all living room furniture pushed to the side—
the boxes packed with new pants, shirts, clocks, canned food,
cigarettes, cigarette lighters—
everything he needed for a rainy day.

I took a deep breath and I left—
I'd just noticed that the packaged wine glasses
given to him last year
were still sealed.

On top of that, were other countless unopened packages
from years back.
The couch and chairs were secondary there—
they seemed to edge their way to the wall,
each time I visited.
My friend sat on the floor,
hunched over in his suffering.

THE HOUSE ON OAK STREET

Jane was squeezed into a room
with three crazed women,
beds without sheets—without pillows,
smudged boots, itchy pilled coats,
sticky scarves clumped at the edge of the mattress.

No sleep there—constant wet snores
rising to an orchestrated crescendo,
sleepless feet calloused,
dirty underwear, spots of urine,
clods of vomit.

Jane knew the thin hopes
of her roommates:

Annie, a diamond in the rough,
pretty, sexy,
clear-eyed,
why was she there?

She'd sneak out to strip in the park,
dragged back by the police.

Lisa's father was a big deal somewhere;
her done-up mother, somewhere else.
Lisa, would rock back and forth most of the day,
a diagnosed schizophrenic.
Her face was thoughtful, reliable at times—
even tried to get a part-time job,
probably to please her dad.

Catatonic Pat was the real challenge there,
frozen in dirty looks,

except for occasional outbursts,
mindlessly shouting at Jane,
"Everyone here hates you—
you'll never get out, *bitch!*"

Jane would take her rough exits—
walk up and down unfamiliar streets,
around corners,
staring at store windows,
longing for that dress, those shoes,
make-up—
to dress up,
to go to a fancy restaurant,
to a play,
maybe even meet a guy.

She couldn't go back,
to that house of pranks,
beetles placed on her bed,
cigarette holes in her already shoddy clothes,
and Annie who would crawl into her bed
at 3 am to push her off.

Jane would sit on a bench,
thinking and thinking,
wondering why it was so hard to die,
how her life had become a mudslide.

An unexpected beating rain stings
as she finds a safe niche
in front of the courthouse
across the way,
hunched under the tarnished bronze figure
of a woman nonchalantly holding
the cold, unbalanced
Scales of Justice.

ADELE SCHWARTZ

MESSAGE TO MY DAUGHTER

I did what I could—my very best,
stumbled out of bed
to the small white attic window,
steered you safely into the school yard,
on rainy days, stretched over you
with a huge black umbrella,
even though your alert brown eyes
told me to know my place,
and why couldn't I be like Mrs. Miller next door?

I did what I could—my very best,
I call you now to tell you I'm alone, lonely,
on this balmy summer evening.

You tell me I'm too sensitive, childish—
and that you can't help me,
 because "I'm not your mother,
and what if I lived in California?"

THE BLACKBOARD MONITOR

With certainty and ease,
my little classmates were building
rainbowed towers
with wooden blocks.

My thundering eyes
could only focus on the tightly-shut window,
where my mother could be seen,
expecting this scenario 'til the end of the day.

Eventually escaping her patience,
I'd flee out of the room
hoping that I had looked in the wrong direction,
gawking at the empty space,
the thrust of its vacancy pushing me down.

Without turning back,
I clumsily entered the classroom,
tired, ashamed.

The morning sun
had moved away from the window;
the darker afternoon
left me shuddering over her disappearance.

My stomach churned,
as my searching eyes
more vehemently continued
this depraved hunt for my mother.

Just yesterday, Mrs. Herman, my teacher,
had given me the honor
of becoming the new blackboard monitor—

the glacier of tasks—
what could be more rewarding
than to wipe away cloudy scribblings?

"You're a strange little girl," she said,
creating chaotic laughter among my friends,
giving away the special job to my classmate, Joyce,
who reluctantly accepted the assignment,
obediently approaching the blackboard
to erase the teacher's firmly formed
alphabet letters of the day.

THE EPIDEMIC

In the rusty gold
    of a heat wave,
        the possums were dying in the yard;

pungent florals
    and sweltering grass
        provided an appropriate setting

for their final resting place.
    They were aligned on their sides,
        the sapphire glow of their eyes

still lingering,
    forefeet pressed against their breasts,
        cuddled in their own blood

like oversized fetuses.
    White foam surrounds their mouths
        (almost in a smile), as if

something jovial
    occurred in their last moments—
        maybe approached by something

thought to be helpful,
    safe: They lie
        frozen in that hope.

ADELE SCHWARTZ

A LOST POEM

Out of nowhere the white morning
shed its brightness on an empty page,
reminding me of a lost poem:
my best one—the one that said it all.

I check the stiff bookshelves
to search for a neglected stained
page innocently squeezed between
immovable books—

then chaotically dart off to the sly
half-opened bureau drawers;
shuffling through meaningless trinkets,
my hands fall limp.

Oh, yes, the loyal window sill
never let me down.
Surely it will show up—obvious
near the neatly stacked blank paper—

but it was last seen
on the stove;
could it have drifted into the old back pipe

now in charcoaled ashes
over a beloved place?

Destiny

A FALL

Took a walk,
my dog's leash a perfect fit,
no need for adjustments;
my hands forcing a tight grip.

Entered a store—
the door suddenly opened,
fell on my back.

I lay clown-like,
my feet to the sky,
my head a gilled trout,
Mexican beans juggling about.

There I lay,
fished at last onto a stretcher,
snug as a bug
under warm blankets—
a substitute for love?

Wondered if I'd ever get a clean slate,
to sit under the last bit of sun,
the failing heat on my face,
to hear the steady static of singing birds,
every detail in place.

A POETRY READING II

Worse than root canal,
a wordless space hangs between me and them,
like looking through a dusty window,
past thoughts of dated photos—
where did they go,
self-exiled from all they knew?

Powerless now,
strapped to cell phones, computers,
buried in prose,
fantasizing what's to come,

I'm never wiser from lessons done,
my life, the poetry,
burnt pages of a larger book,
but the poems are mere events,
just fiction.

I am only a voice,
deliberate, cool, detached.

But God, what will I wear?

EXIT I AND II

I

On those days, dim, misty,
visions unclear,
your words (intense, firm),
my thoughts.

Your thoughts depleted my means—
lack of fortune became my art,
my art, my voice,
my voice, my weapon.

II

What if I told you to leave?
If I went to your room,
those familiar scents faded;
I could never stop looking at the cherished photo
of that trip to Venice,
now a short dream—small and meaningless.

If telling you to leave was the worst thing I ever did,
why do I open the window,
after another harried night,
to a day that's a bouquet of light?

HERR HARRY

I had a friend who admired the Nazis.
He showed me his endless collection
of Third Reich memorabilia:
storm trooper boots, hats, jackets,
and varied Nazi arm bands.

He hated Wall Street, the theater, the Garment Center
and BMWs (which I thought was strange).

He tried to be a good friend:
when I was consumed by despair,
he'd give me detailed instructions
on how to end it all in my car:
attach a pipe to the exhaust and make sure
the doors and windows are tightly shut.

He was outraged when I didn't get it right.

His Jean Harlow-type daughter
was his pride and joy;
she took me to a great Chinese restaurant
for my birthday.
I drove.

When we hit the highway,
she began to panic and sweat.
She said she feared driving on highways
and over bridges, she went on about how traffic
and driving over water were like being in a war.
I didn't get that.

When she got home, she said she felt dirty,
ran to the bathroom like a bat out of hell,

and jumped into the tub.

I heard the running water,
splashing sighs of relief.

LEGACY

Life advances by seconds—
loose ends, unresolved quandaries:
flowers colorless, the grass coarse and jaundiced
where your soul hovers over crowded voices.

In no hurry to leave,
it looks down on eyes pinched shut,
skeletal hands growing distant, strange.

Once your comfort zone,
your flesh and bones
are stitched now into the Earth's blanket.

The wild sky accepts what's left,
rising, rising to the truth,
deeds, done or not,
subject to thousands of verdicts
no one will ever know.

The moss on your stone
protects and softens your name.
Does anyone remember the days you spent
healing a sick sparrow?

MY DESTINY

Hovering over an irrational ocean,
bright lantern in hand, always,
bloated nets filled with fish,
you stare at the sunlit water,
mesmerized by its harshness,
its rumbling and roaring.

The turbulence threatens my destiny.
Now, with a glad madness
you tell me to "take grip of my wits"—
my loving paddler of a swift sea,
keeping us afloat always.
My savior.
My heavy anchor.

OCCUPY

You on the streets,
your stirrings throwing weight,
weightlessly,

the cops, the cops—
upside down, inside out,
pulling at all elements.

Blankets, coffee, tobacco on lips,
speckled signs, crumpled papers—

everyone else on the other side:
     tall, straight, squeaky clean,
     their measuring eyes glance
     through blank windows.

They don't hear
     just listen to
     the thin voices,
     their conscience,
     their families,
     their auto insurance,
     their auto-immune,
     their meds,

their chanting,
over and over—
they, whom the Earth welcomed so.

SANDPIPER BEFORE A HURRICANE

She stands erect and astute,
the turbulent sky pulling at her feet.

Her pace quickens
to the speed of sound
(by now, she knows how lightning can strike twice,
occasionally hops sideways
to let a worn-out seagull pass.

The crowd thins out,
"Go, girl, go!" they say,
thinking, *Better her than me*,
glancing at a battered beach umbrella
and lost sandals.

Her eyes, quick and beady,
cut through the chaos,
contemplating the quiet of dusk.

She rises and falls
against the folds of a warning wind.

And when the hurricane
harasses the sea,
when the current has lost control,
her glistening feathers frazzled,
broken twigs in her beak stay rooted,
unwavering above the tugging sand.

The crowd thins out;
they flutter like frivolous butterflies,
delicate and unsteady.

SLAVES

The slaves were set free.

They walked through the Red Sea
quite leisurely,
for they were above mortal deeds.

The slaves within us,
misplaced bad seeds,
must dissipate this Passover,
for you and for me.

SUMMER IS LONG GONE

The summer is long gone,
        somewhere under the snow,
not just another season,
        it's something different,
        something half-dead.

"Where are you?"
        I said over and over.
Your closet's empty,
        no trace of you.
My hands trembled so,
        I tried to hide them,
        tried not to let the kids in on it—
        they were too young—not ready, never were.

The frivolous domesticity
        and its Pollyannaish tasks
        a Currier and Ives.
I struggled to make a home
        we did not loathe,
to know how to undo what was done,
to remake a new art.

Our flesh and souls
        won't know each other again.

ADELE SCHWARTZ

TO WOODY ALLEN ON MY BIRTHDAY

Lost my car keys—I forgot to put them
on the hallway table —
        and when I find them I'll forget I did.

In the muddy mess of a spiteful sunny morning,
                I trash my lottery tickets (a sore spot).

Usually, I'm terrible about remembering dreams,
but last night, as I lay in a herky-jerky sleep,
I was encircled by whiners and complainers
who pointed fingers at me, pleased that I was pissed.

The only one that seemed to be on my side said,
"You're too hard on yourself,"
                knowing I really must be harder than hard.

On this day, I'm tired, moody,
knowing the alternatives are worse.

So, Woody, I've chosen you as my confidante
on this special day —
hoping you don't find this weird.

I'm always at the wrong place at the wrong time.
One day I lucked out —

I saw you at a restaurant on Second Avenue;
you caught a glimpse of me,
then quickly half-turned toward the door,
as if you had something to hide.

I knew, then, you mirrored segments of my life
(without my knowledge):

Gautama, an Indian philosopher, 5th century BC, said:
"All is empty; there is no self."

I've been:
the whimsical Annie Hall,
the hysterical Vickie suffering in Barcelona,
the unlucky, honest Melinda,
the lucky, unscrupulous Melinda,
the frightened robot, fearing perfection
and enormous produce,
The Purple Rose of Cairo—am I not?

I ask one favor of you on this day, just one—
I haven't got much to look forward to;
I'm no less passionate, arrogant, fragile
and can still write of love, pain, truth, and lust—

Could you have that 1920s bronze Peugeot
take me far away from New Jersey?

Hemingway, F. Scott, even Zelda,
are waiting for me—
and my low-waisted flapper dress
has been hanging loosely for days.

There will be no other night like this.
Dear Gertrude Stein is feverishly
turning the pages of my new book;
never will I forget the look on her.

ADELE SCHWARTZ

FINE-TOOTH COMB

When I came back
from summer camp (three weeks prematurely)
I'd just developed breasts
or got too fat from all that starch
(no one knew the difference),
strangely enough, I missed my father
more than my mother,
dreamt he'd died,
Did he miss me that much?
I pretendeed I couldn't swim
or throw balls
so I'd get
kicked out,
stopped showering
(couldn't fathom
standing naked
among my bunkmates).
What got me home
was lice,
lovely little friends
crawling on my scalp,
Oh the warmth of that fine-tooth comb
lovingly gliding through my hair.

Steffie

In memory of my daughter Stefanie Ann

All she had to give me: her sweet soul
   kind words, soft touch,
the snowman she so cherished (that read "for Mommy")
   from small pebbles,
colorful pictures she drew as a child
   signed by Stefanie—written in steady, even print:
crimson stars, taupe clouds, against a golden beaming sun
   stick figures of Daddy, Mommy, Greg, and *me Steffie*
    (aligned in size).

All she left me:
   smiling photos, shimmering trinkets,
    cotton candy scents
     and darling Annabella
My gut is empty,
   shattered leaf,
drifting through lost days
   except for the peaceful walks
    with Oliver and Annabella
     that keep me walking.

HOW AWKWARD TO SPEAK

How awkward to speak to her
her whereabouts unknown
yet know she hears my pleas.

Just the other day
she massaged my knotted back

laughed at my crazy family's
quirks and my humorous take on them

just yesterday pouted her lips
wondering if the new deep-wine lipstick
was a bit much for work.

Did she stumble into a fog
so thick she couldn't find her way back
Even unable to say good-bye

or did she find a clear horizon
where life and death and time
all flow on like a quiet stream?

I go on living the impossible,
a crumbling diamond,
still ocean,
cool sun at noon in August,

unable to cry.

THE STARS FLICKER

The stars flicker,
sympathetic yet helpless,
chatting—
when I'm gone are sharp knives

Van Gogh's pain,
positive
(why would he inflict bodily harm?)—
wisdom, genius, creativity,
maybe so.

My pain
is a different thing:
the best in me drifting away,

studying my slanted pen
still, cool,
even under the dazzling sun
on my untouchable desk.

STEFFIE'S LOOKING DOWN

Steffie's looking down on me (I'm told)
watching me watch her sweet Italian greyhound
(Annabella),
my eyes moist red as I pass her home,
watching me livid as the jerk at the market cuts in front
with endless produce—
does she think I'm crazy when I ask the salesperson
if the navy dress would complement her hazel eyes
and if she's a small or petite,
clutching this gift close to my chest.

Steffie's watching me (I know)
in the midst of an eternal light soft as a winter sun
under pastel clouds
surrounded by clusters of stars guarding her
outside a room of gold

the niche of happiness in me,
now gone,
will not return
till the awaited sleep,
darkness upstaging the overrated bright day,
no doubt her usual warm welcome:
hands on hips,
laughing eyes,
tapping feet impatient,
like a mother and lost child.

ADELE SCHWARTZ

NO LONGER THE NEED TO ARGUE

No longer the need to argue
about the inarguable.
Just wouldn't do—
you're ethereal now,

rid of the impurities of this world,
this fickle place you cherished so.

My insufferable suffering will not weaken me—
it will not punish,
will gladly expedite our reunion.

Annabella and I will soon
follow your path—
that long journey will eradicate
the endless boredom and loneliness.

I ache for your soul—my soul.

IN MY DREAMS

In my dreams
I called you over and over.
How could you have thought I'd forget?

In my dreams,
TV blasting: *It's midnight—do you know*
where your children are?
The night raced on in bluish gray
bits of the past flickering like a kaleidoscope
I used to inch around—as if you never knew,
this crucial duty unattainable.

I wait
till you pick up
so I can scold you,
"Everyone is worried!"
Overworked tongues shattered
by now. . . .
but to hear your laughter
then silly giggling over your crazy concerned mother
is worth this dream
over and over.

ADELE SCHWARTZ

HOW SAD FOR SUMMER TO END

How sad for summer to end this way—
firm flowers loose, scentless, sunspots on bent petals
facing the sky,
forgetting girlish days.

The fickle August stars
hide behind a cloud or two
this odd season,
a sleek and colorful new friend
whose beauty is corrupt, collapsing
(the bees seek nectar,
buzzing crazily around in their despair;
the fresh smell of cut grass
turns sour, musky).

One can see it on the face
of a gloating moon
stealing the last of daylight,
expiring too soon.

STEFFIE

The serene, happy beginning:
Her tiny hand grasping mine
with an unusual strength—
yes, we would need each other in this life.
The gut of her expanding in me each day—
she was my sun to warm the cold misty mornings,
the cool breeze to soften the heat of noon,
the brightness that blanketed the darkness
with dancing gold and silver stars.
Maybe I pampered her too much.
She could have been selfish, spoiled,
but only grew strong, giving, and wise,
an old soul; I would think,
Was I the child?
Her sweet face,
petite and tender neck,
her perfectly arched little feet
that I caressed
from the beginning, to no end.

STEFFIE AND ME

I wanted this child more than any lover,
to have known the bosomed contentment
together

under colorful skies
(the golden array of fall,
the bland dirty whiteness of winter,
the soft baby blues and pinks of spring,
the blinding hot crimson of summer)
together,

fighting strong winds,
then the drops of soft rain
soothing our weary souls,

stepping through the moist grass
on our morning rush
to school,
glancing at the last rays of sun
just before dusk,
her heart-shaped face looking up at me.

Did she know that these familiar things
would not last too long,
and did I,

somehow, aware of our fate,
only together?

THE SURVIVOR

Morley's chains tie me up,
robotic, melancholy, empty—
daily chores accomplished
"going through the motions."

Constant loss of keys, cash, cells—
a mystery taken by an unknown force,
liquids spilling,
the anti-Midas touch.

My shriveled heart
loads up on
heinous chemicals,
steams down hazy roads,
heavy clouds on the way.

Nothing is as it was.

BELOW THE EARTH

Below the earth lies the little pine coffin,
the Star of David just below her name—
looks like the one
I fastened on her eighth birthday.

Mounds of foliage soften the supposed ending:
the curve of her lip when pleased,
her half smile when in doubt,
the tiny scar just above her right eye
(only obvious when she swept
her golden bangs to the side),
the way she held a pen.

How can I allow her to stay in that setting,
let go till "time heals,"
this child who held my hand like an anchor,
who studied my eyes
before she knew of sun and sky?

If I can't hold her once more
I must go to her,
the only mother she knew.

LOVED THE HOLIDAYS

Loved the holidays,
especially Thanksgiving:

new scarf, boots, lipstick
(maybe a deeper shade of plum?),
looking for kitchen gadgets—
the wonder blender, coffee grinders,
fancy fruit slicers—
these domestic things Steffie relished.

Miss the urgent calls from Trader Joe's
deciding which dessert would do,
the raspberry walnut tart
always the winner,
flourless chocolate cake
a good second.

I carefully place
packages in back
of my green SUV,
drive to her house;
the fireplace is flickering still—
an eternal flame perhaps?

The clutter
under my arm is slipping.
I notice a group of birds pecking at
the perfect alignment of crumbs;

the flourless chocolate cake crushes
the raspberry tart as usual.

SUNDAY

The birdsong's more mellow:
Are they praying?

Not a usual day—
hardly any cars and wobbling trucks
under my window on River Road.

The elevator door flies open
in a heartheat.
No need to tap my feet,
wondering why it's stuck on 11,
knowing that someone is hoarding it.

I study the churchgoers
in their squeaky-clean attire
and their angelic faces
thinking they will go to heaven,

get ready for the gym—
the weekday crowd
is sleeping in, so there will be
no wait for the ellipticals

(I'm a Sunday gym rat, I suppose,
knowing that my body
is not eternal, and all this is meaningless).

No, Sunday's not an ordinary day:
The quiet leisure is uncomfortable,
the calmness doesn't
overcome my need for anti-depressants.

There's time on my shaky hands

to glare at my children's photos,
flat and still in wooden frames,

to phone them
relentlessly—
until someone picks up,
asks if I going to be around
on this clear October day.

Stories

ABOUT HIM

I LOVED HIM more than life itself. Now I hate him. I wish he'd shoot himself—suffer, then die. I dream of ways that he would be in great pain. I *love* to dream of horrible things that could happen to him." The shrink looked at her over his glasses. She went on, "Oh, I could never do it, doctor. . . . It's not that he may or may not have fallen out of love with me. Oh, no, not at all. It's the way he *tricked* me." The shrink started to close his eyes. His glasses were on the tip of his nose. One shoe was half off, and his big toe was teasingly swaying back and forth. She made a yawning sound, tried to create a clearly audible *shock*.

Dr. Gold jumped up. "Yes, Mrs. Selden—what are you thinking now?"

"I'm thinking about my shitty karma—that's what I'm thinking about. I must have been a serial murderer in my other life." Dr. Gold's eyes were half closed. He started to breathe more heavily and deeply. Corinne went on anyway. "I don't mean a Jeffrey Dahmer type, really—I don't think I'd be capable of that sort of thing. What I meant was—"

The doctor was in a deep sleep again. "Dr. Gold!" she shouted. "What's wrong with you? Do you—do you have narcolepsy or something? My life's shit, shit, shit! It's so undignified. I can't go on like this . . . . Do you hear me, Dr. G.?"

But Dr. Gold seemed to be solidly asleep again. She went on anyway. His glasses were on a slant, and he forced a sigh and looked at her without any expression. "Remember my friend Priscilla that I hate? She was screwing around with *everybody*, and her husband kissed her ass. It's not that she was particularly attractive or even bright. I know she went to a good school, but that's because she had pull. The woman had no heart. Why do things like this happen, Dr. Gold?"

He sat up in a still-erect manner. "Well, Mrs. Selden. . . time's up! We're going to have to discuss it next week."

Corinne grabbed her purse and ran out, flew by the secretary, and shouted. "That man is incompetent—please cancel me for next week, and the week after, and the one after that."

She was happy to be at the diner. She ordered lemon meringue pie and hazelnut coffee, happy not to have to delve into her humiliating past, and wondered about her kids. She thought she'd call them after she finished eating.

But she thought again and realized she couldn't. Her daughter was starting to talk to her like a used car salesman, and her son was a living *StarWars*. No, no she couldn't call them, not then. She went to the rest room instead, looked in the mirror, carefully applied her lipstick. It didn't go on the way it used to—her lips had been dry and thinner the last several years. She hadn't noticed. The liner went too far over her natural line. She thought she looked like Bette Davis. Priscilla: The last time she'd seen her, Priscilla had a gel implant of some kind in her lips. They looked great, thought Corinne, except that, when she touched them, they'd felt like an unfrozen ice pack. The thought of doing that to herself would have to wait anyway, since she couldn't afford it.

Corinne looked at her checkbook register. It was overdrawn, probably because of the unnecessary dental visit she'd paid on a Sunday to a dentist who had charged two hundred bucks just to glue a laminate. She went to the pay phone anyway, called Oribe's, and figured she'd worry about the money later. She had to do *something* special, and it had to be now. The old Corinne Selden had to live again.

On her way, she passed a boutique and saw a lovely black silk dress with a matching jacket. She knew she couldn't buy it but went in anyway.

The salesgirls looked her up and down. She was wearing an old suit. It was a good suit—conservative, blue, and practical. The skirt was too short, and the cuffs on the jacket were slightly frayed. Corinne pointed to the black dress and asked if she could try it on.

They examined her again. "You're about a size 4, aren't you?" The other salesgirl looked at her backside and thought a 6 would be better.

"Could I try them both?" Corinne asked.

"Of course," said the taller of the two women, who brought both sizes.

Corinne went into the dressing room and tried the 4 first. It fit perfectly. She came out to show the salesgirls. "You look great!" they said.

"It's divine," said one of the customers. Corinne hadn't felt that special for years. "You look like a model," the customer went on. When Corinne looked at the price tag, the print was small and she thought she was misreading it.

"How much is it?" she asked.

"It's five hundred," the salesgirls said in unison.

Corinne returned to the dressing room and took off the dress, her eyes filling with tears. She muttered, "With all my problems, I needed this," came out of the dressing room, and handed the dress to the tall salesgirl.

"Don't tell me you're not going to get this," the girl called out.

Corinne was terribly embarrassed. "Oh, not at all," she said evenly. I-I just want to show it to my daughter. We share clothes, and she has to like it as well. Could you hold it for a couple of days?"

The salesgirls looked at each other as if they knew the truth. Making her exit, Corinne tripped on a step and landed head first on the sidewalk.

There was a copy of *New York* magazine right beside where she had fallen. Into cosmic things lately, she took that as a sign, picked it up, and walked to the park, where she slumped on a bench and opened the magazine to the personals. She felt as if she was constantly holding back tears.

She noticed the first ad that caught her eye under the title MAN SEEKING WOMAN: *Successful businessman seeks woman in her late 40s to mid 50s, between 5'3" to 5'5", blond and perky (nonsmoker, tennis player, vegetarian preferred).*

She started to laugh out loud. People passing looked at her, but she was too upset to care. "How *primal*—how *demoralizing!*" she called out.

They turned around again. She thought of going back with Rick— anything would be better than this. "Yes, anything!" she agreed.

When she got home, Corinne plopped herself on the sofa, grabbed the Cool Whip from the freezer—it was her fix—and spooned the stuff into her mouth till it was gone.

The phone rang. "Hi, there," he said. "What's happening?"

It was her new neighbor. She tried to be neighborly but couldn't date him—he was too young and immature. Attempted to keep it cool but friendly. It wasn't working out, though—he was misinterpreting her neighborly ways. "I'm really dead, Phil," she sighed. "Maybe I'll see you at the diner for breakfast, but I really have to get to sleep soon."

He hung up quickly. She was sure he was going down the list.

She put on the TV and caught the last moments of *ER*. She wished she could meet someone like Dr. Green—sensitive, caring, bright. She opened the personals again and picked up on another ad: NO PARTICULAR REQUIREMENTS, *Just someone who wants to share a good life.*

This got to her. She was happy that there was a telephone number instead of a box. She picked up the phone and dialed, hand shaking, glad the line was busy. She'd call back—she had to. It was her duty to be happy again. She'd gone to a Kabbalah lecture awhile back where people stressed positive attitudes and how they naturally flowed into the souls of one's children.

Determined to turn things around, she called again, and he picked up. "Hi. Robert here," he said.

The sound of his voice was appealing to her. "Hello," she said nervously—"I'm calling in response to your ad in *New York* magazine?" Upset with herself about being so robot-like, she lowered the TV and saw Dr. Green while listening to Robert's voice. She pictured him like Dr. Green and was ecstatic. She could tell by his voice—he was just the type of guy she needed, and was worried if she'd fit the bill.

"I'm watching *ER*," she said hesitantly. "I really don't watch TV that much," she went on, just in case he was an intellectual who never put on a TV. "I just love Anthony Edward's Dr. Green. The thing about the character is that he has soul. I've been into Kabbalah and other metaphysical things lately, and I can just pick up on people like that."

Robert was silent just a bit too long, she thought. The pause worried her. Then suddenly he added, "That's great. I'd love to get into those things one day. I get too caught up with work, though."

She wondered what he did but certainly would never ask. If he didn't volunteer, she definitely would not ask. She didn't care either; she only hoped that it was decent work. He quickly said, "I'm an architect, and it's been hellish lately." He went on to explain, "I'm not your typical *Architectural Digest* type guy. I plan roads and bridges in third world countries," he added with pride.

Corinne was thrilled; he had to have soul, too. "That must be totally gratifying," she exclaimed.

Robert went on, "It gets to be a bitch," he sighed. "You know, all work and no glamor—but yes, yes, it is gratifying. At this point, I wouldn't have it any other way."

Corinne was growing more confident. "We're going to have a lot to talk about, Robert—I was a teacher, but I'm taking courses in paleontology. I have just a few more courses, and I've applied to the Museum of Natural History. It seems promising," she added with great enthusiasm.

He sounded thrilled. "That's really unusual. You're right—there's lots to talk about, and I can't wait to see you."

She called her daughter excitedly. She couldn't wait to tell her. "Hi, Julie, guess what!"

"Look, Mom, I really can't hear that stuff now—I have eczema all over my body, my boss is the anti-Christ, and I broke up with David. Call me later, okay?" She hung up before Corinne could get a word in.

Corinne then phoned Josh, her son, and got his machine: "Hi, you know the drill—so, at the tone. . . ."

She left a message anyway: "Hi, Joshy. Mommy wants to tell you something great—*call* me." She thought about the message afterwards and wished she hadn't said "Joshy" and "Mommy": If someone was there, it would embarrass him. She also realized he'd probably avoid getting back to her for a while. He was turned off by "maternal mush," as he had put it since the divorce.

Robert called her back almost immediately. "Hi, Corinne. What's going on Thursday—are you free?"

She studied her face in the mirror, noticed deep circles under her eyes . "Well, I have to go to a course early in the evening," she sputtered, "but I could meet you about nine."

"Great!" he said enthusiastically. "We're on."

Corinne broke into a deep sweat, was in fact unable to remember the last time she'd felt so nervous. She thought about the dress—needed *something* to feel more confident—but dismissed the idea when she remembered the price.

But she had something similar! She ran to her closet. The thing wasn't nearly as chic, but it would have to do. Maybe some new lipstick or earrings would help out. It was already Tuesday, and she didn't have enough time to pull herself together. She called her closest friend. "Renee," she pleaded, "please *listen* to me for a change. I have a *date*, and I'm stuck—do you remember that black dress I wore to Jonathan's bar mitzvah? Do you think it's still in style?"

There was a long pause before Renee laughed. "Cor, that was five *years* ago. *Go* for it! Get something more *in*."

Corinne went on about the price of decent clothes. She thought of asking to borrow the money but couldn't. Renee didn't offer either. "But you're resourceful kid—you'll find a way! *Ciao, ciao!*"

Corinne grew enraged. Renee had always left her hanging like that. As she hung up, she muttered, "Thinks I'm a friggin' magician."

Thursday night at nine, Corinne was waiting in the lobby of St. Regis. Robert had told her they would meet at the bar, but she wanted to see if she could spot him first.

She gave up eventually and went to the ladies room to check herself out just one more time. The old dress was okay, but she looked drained by anticipation. She combed her hair, peeked in her compact to check out her backside—the dress was a bit loose around the hips, took a deep breath, and returned to the bar.

There was a man sitting alone there, talking to the bartender. He had a wide, warm smile. She knew it was him. He was wearing a gray glen-plaid suit and a solid crimson tie. His sandy-colored hair Looked like Jack Kennedy's. Yes, that was Robert, and he was more than she'd hoped he would be. She moved toward him; he immediately noticed her, approached, said her name, took her hand. . . . Her heart was palpitating, and she thought she would faint.

As they entered the dining room, she remembered a scene from Noel Coward's *Still Life*. Corinne hadn't felt that way in years. The color in her cheeks was high, her eyes bright, that moist feeling in them gone. After the sommelier left and Robert offered a toast, then studied the label on the bottle, she brought the wine glass to her lips and slowly sipped the Merlot. She hadn't smoked for ages, but she needed one now. They were on the table, in a crystal glass, and she couldn't resist. She tried unobtrusively to light it, but the matches kept going out. She hoped he wouldn't notice and light it for her, since her hands were shaking. When he did, she knew he had noticed the trembling. She waited for him to say "relax," "calm down," or "what's the problem?" but he didn't say anything, which instantly reassured her, so she could notice the glittering chandeliers and the lovely china on the tables. The leaves outside were shimmering; she knew that there wouldn't be too many evenings like that.

Robert stared at her. "So where do we begin?" he chuckled. "Should I say, 'Where have you been all my life?' or would 'What are you doing for the rest of your life?' be better?"

They both started to laugh, and she quickly downed a second glass of wine and stopped focusing. Her head began to spin, and it became hard to keep the conversation going in a way she had hoped, and then she was angry at herself for drinking so quickly and thought how she had ruined it and how she was slurring her words . She wasn't even sure of what she was talking about. She went on and on anyway.

"Listen," he said, "let's finish the bottle and start eating."

She began to hear Robert clearly again after coffee: "You? You could never kill—you're not the type."

Oh, thought Corinne—had she started to talk about *him*? Oh, no— not about Ricky again. How could she do that now? She could hear her heart beating. How dumb to dump her stuff like that in less than an hour. She heard the noises in the restaurant, but she couldn't move. She had to go to the rest room but was afraid to leave, figuring that if she left the table Robert would probably disappear, probably even stick her with the bill.

The dining room was almost empty. She searched his expression for approval. He took her hand and squeezed it. God, she thought, it's a miracle, a miracle, he actually likes me. The room was getting dim. "Excuse me," she said with renewed confidence. Strolling off to the ladies room, she turned back just to make doubly sure, saw he wasn't leaving, and called back, "Could you order a chocolate mousse, please?"

APRONS

AMY WAS AT THE LAKE, the first inclement day that August. The ground was damp and soft after a hot summer. She was pressing her feet into the soil and then the heavy, stagnant lake water. She was peering beyond the white house, on the mountain that she had adored since she was a child, at the rowboat moving slowly away from her.

"Gary!" she called out anxiously. "I'm sorry—please come back!" He didn't hear her, or at least didn't appear to.

They had been married for almost four years and the humdrum difficulties of those years together were more than apparent. She tried again. "Come on, Gary. Don't bust me!"

Gary was reclining in the boat, holding his chin in his hand and his forehead and jaw were crinkling with pain. He'd tried, he really had, he thought, but it was just not going to work out.

Amy went back to the calico blanket, the lovely finger sandwiches and freshly-made potato salad just waiting. She took a delicate bite of the tuna sandwich and dozed off, remembering the picnic when she was seven and all the formidable preparations.

Carol, Amy's mom, had been quite nervous about the event—the first time the family had been together for months. Harris, Amy's dad, had been working into the evenings for some time then, and she'd hardly gotten to see him. It just wasn't the way it had been when she was a child. She remembered the drawn look on her mother's face, as she scrubbed the pots with SOS pads, floral-print apron smeared with jam that blended with the colors so that it wasn't noticeable. Amy had tried wiping the jam stains off before her dad came home.

"You don't have to do that," her mother said. "It'll be okay." But Amy knew Harris and was trying to prevent hurtful words from him.

Finally, Harris had appeared. He had seemed calmer than usual and Amy glowed at the possibility that it would, as her mother had said, be okay. Carol had saved the SOS pads in paper towels.

"Mommy likes to save things," Amy had said to Harris.

"Yeah, I know," he'd barked in disgust, turned to the finger sandwiches and said, "Jesus, Carol, you're so *dated*. These things are from the '50's."

Carol, feeling inadequate and deeply hurt, had exclaimed in pathetic disappointment, "I thought you liked them."

"I thought we were going to barbecue—there are tons of pits at the lake. Or did the price of hot dogs go up this week?"

"There's no time to argue, Harris. Let's get going."

Amy had done her usual twilight sleep in the station wagon. The constant bickering during the intermittent hard words had made her do so. When they had arrived, she'd run out of the car and open the new purple kite, soaring with its movements, relieving the tension she had endured on the ride. She'd finally sat down alone on the picnic blanket and indulged in the finger sandwiches. Amy had thought they were so special and couldn't grasp her father's disapproval of them.

He, meanwhile, had immediately rented a row boat and paddled his way to the middle of the lake. She'd noticed the defined muscles in his arms. He had been using weights lately. She often giggled at his tightened jaw as he gripped the weights so seriously. She would laugh at the strange sounds he made then. She wished her mom would exercise as well, since she was losing her girlish figure.

Carol had come over and poured a glass of milk for Amy, who was about to drink it, when she heard her father impulsively call out, "Carol. Come over here. I've gotta talk to you."

Carol had run to the boat. He had been standing at the sandy edge of the land. "Carol," he'd practically shouted, "I'm leaving. This time, I mean it."

Amy'd spilled the glass of milk, saturating her new clothes. Carol was soon reassuring her that it would be okay, but the girl had felt saddened by the grief that always lurked whenever her mom and dad were together.

Carol had held her, rocking her back and forth, as she had done many times when Amy was an infant and the girl had fallen into a deep sleep.

When she woke up, her mother's face had been neon red. Amy'd thought she'd heard strange sounds during her nap. Carol was holding the girl's hand—squeezing so tightly that it hurt. She wiped the blood on the apron near the picnic basket and hid her hand from Amy.

"What's the matter, Mommy?"

Carol could not look at her daughter's inquisitive face. "Amy, darling, something very bad happened."

"What is it, Mommy—where's Daddy?"

"There was an accident, sweetheart. Daddy was upset—h-he got out of control, and the boat tipped over, and I couldn't help him … Amy, *stay* with me. Don't look. The police are here, and they're taking care of everything."

Amy shrieked, "*No!* No, Mommy, this isn't *true!* I want to see Daddy. I'll make him better." She had run to her father's bloated body and flung herself on top of it, then ran to her mother and started to hit her. "Mommy, *why? Why* couldn't you help him? *Why,* Mommy?"

Amy sat up, staring out toward her husband. "Gary!" she shouted. "Get off the boat! Hurry! Please! Please!"

He started to row back quickly. He'd never seen her so upset. "Gary, darling," she had whispered when he came up to her, "I love you and I know I'm too hard on you." She flung her arms around him and touched his cheeks. "Give me another chance."

He ran his fingers down her tightened lips. "Amy, I'll *always* be here," he jested. "Do with me what you will."

Amy looked at the swaying rowboat and called out, "You know, Daddy, you could always come back. Gary would love to meet you."

She lay on her stomach and pleaded with Gary just to "sit still and not go anywhere." She envisioned her mom (who had recently passed away) and her dad walking hand in hand toward the elegant white house on the hill above the dark lake.

They were laughing as Harris held Amy in his strong arms. Amy's legs were limp and thickly crusted with dark crimson blood. Her eyes were wildly cheerful, staring only at her father—she knew then, as she did now, that she was the culprit—the sharp thorn that kept them together and forever apart and that her absence would have saved them. This thought was there always and had recently become much stronger. Her mind whirled as she glared at Gary and gently picked up the knife lying on the sticky floral apron. She knew she would always be a monkey-on-his-back and yet could not live without him.

"Gary, look at that beautiful white house out there." He turned toward it, his back hunched over slightly. She picked up the knife, her face hot and moist and her body slimy as an eel. Her shrieks echoed toward the hill. "Gary, my darling," she said, delirious with joy, "we're going to meet Daddy."

DEAD OF WINTER

HER COUGH WAS TIGHT and hard—not the usual type that's loose and phlegmy. "I don't think I should go to school tomorrow," she said. It was about two a.m. She had awakened in a puddle of sweat, her flannel nightgown spotted with bright red blood.

"Oh, come on," he said, looking at her without any particular expression. He never really slept well and was quite casual about her conversing at that hour.

"I feel like I'm burning up —do I feel warm?" she asked.

He looked at her vacantly and tried to be convincing: "You just started there—you can't not-show-up so soon. And that principal is tough ..."

He went on and on and she stopped listening. She'd become quite good at turning him off. She got out of bed and went to the medicine chest to see if she could find some cough remedy. There was some red, syrupy liquid in a sticky bottle with a faded label. She wondered if it was okay, but drank it anyway. She went back to bed, moved further away from him and curled up. She pulled the blanket over her head and started hacking away again.

"Come on," he said. "Stop making a racket. You gotta get up soon!" He broke into a half-grin, slunk over and touched her forehead. "You know, babe, you're getting to be a hypochondriac in your old age. You feel cool as a cucumber."

Fumbling for her navy pantsuit, she broke out into a cold sweat again. There was a deep burning inside her and she started to fill up with hatred—a calm hatred this time, not the usual shouting bouts and throwing of things. She was proud of herself. Her physical weakness gave her a strange inner strength. She felt in control.

When she was dressed, she looked out the window. She felt cooler, and the uplifting morning light and glittering snow made everything seem less dark—less serious. She started to feel weak again, but sipped some leftover coffee and was soon on her way.

It was 8:10, only a few minutes later than usual, but it made a big difference in the traffic. She sat patiently in the car and felt knocked out, which was not typical at that time of day.

She felt tense about being late. There was another teacher waiting for her in the classroom. Mrs. Arnold looked annoyed. "We really do try to make it here on time," she sighed. "We're not running a country club." Eve noticed Mrs. Arnold staring at the old engagement ring from her first marriage. She turned it around so that the stone would not be visible. It was a lovely piece—the only thing she had left of that twenty-two-year-old connection. Eve never took it off, although she realized people reached certain conclusions when they saw the stone.

"Well, have a nice day." Eve coughed quietly and noticed that the blood in the Kleenex was darker than it had been during the night. Mrs. Arnold lingered in the classroom. She looked out of place in the school. Her hair was shocking red, and her skirt was far too short. She was quite terse and consistently chewed gum.

Eve took her seat at the worn-out desk and struggled to open the warped drawer, so she could give out a safety ditto usually reserved for subs. The students were onto any of her vulnerabilities. It was a Special Ed school and the kids, who were classified as emotionally disturbed, seemed to be more instinctive and street-wise than the mainstream students.

They picked up on Eve's weariness and as she handed out the math dittos, they started up. They crumpled the dittos and put their chairs in a circle. Tim looked into her soggy red eyes. "Hey, teach." He went on in his slurred way, "This is sub stuff. We're gonna play cards—this isn't Jersey, you know."

Most of the kids had criminal records, but Eve liked teaching in that environment. The kids were usually workable and if she showed some concern, they were more than responsive. But, there were the more difficult days. She started to write the assignment from the math text they were on, but sat down again, feeling light-headed and weak. Though she wanted to call the office on the intercom, she didn't want to draw further attention to herself, since she'd arrived so late.

Ray, the most sensitive boy in the class, seemed concerned. "Miss Mann, are you okay? You look yellowish or somethin'." When Eve didn't respond, he went back to playing cards with a half-frown that he hid from the other kids.

Eve looked up. Everything went gray. Then there was nothing.

SHE WOKE UP IN the ER. A gentle nurse was taking blood. "What happened?" Eve asked.

"You passed out, sweetie. You're gonna be all right—don't worry." The nurse put her hand on Eve's shoulder. We think you have pneumonia, but it's viral and everything is going to be just fine."

Eve thought of calling Bob, but decided against it—she didn't want to alarm her kids—and she dozed off.

When she woke up, she was shivering more than ever. Her entire body was hot. She thought about the past few years of her life and figured that her immune system had had it. She remembered the marital home. She pictured the kids in front of the fireplace, lying on their stomachs, roasting marshmallows and coloring. She'd felt comforted on those snow days, when they were home and there was nowhere to go. She smelled the veggie soup and salmon croquettes that she prepared on those days. She wished that, if she did die, she could spend just a few more hours like that.

She remembered the dog running around in circles, when her husband pulled up and the mild, strange scent on his clothes. She had known it wasn't her perfume but had dismissed those thoughts.

The door to her room was pushed open by the nurse and two doctors. They drew more blood. She wanted it to end. The doctor wrote something on the clipboard attached to the bed.

"What's going on?" Eve asked.

"We have to wait a couple of hours. Be patient," said the caring nurse. She was petite and dark-haired, like Eve, and seemed to have insight about things going on in Eve's life. She smelled of a floral fragrance similar to Eve's. Eve was glad she was her nurse, rather than the tall, heavy-set RN on the other side of the room. She wanted to pour out her troubles, but leaned over for the remote and put on the TV.

She thought again of calling Bob, but she knew how he was when bothered at work. She picked up the hospital phone and called the daily horoscope.

Suddenly, Bob walked into the pale green room wearing a fixed smile. She wished he hadn't shown up so soon. She didn't smile back, answering him with one-word replies. If only he didn't push her so much. She knew that was what had put her there.

Dr. Porter entered the room with a confident air. He was fine-featured and stately. He looked as if he knew everything about Eve. His eyes were shrewd and clear. Bob turned toward him, wide-eyed, concerned. "She really got herself good and sick this time," he sighed. "I told her not to wear that flimsy thing in the dead of winter." She hoped he felt guilty for once. It was better than nothing.

"What a tan, Doc—where have you been?"

Dr. Porter smiled broadly. "Hawaii ... it was fantastic." Eve felt a pang of envy. She'd always wanted to go to Hawaii. She couldn't remember the last time she'd basked in the sun or taken a vacation.

Dr. Porter's tan was more obvious, as he stood near Eve with her chalky face. He jotted something quickly on the chart again. "We're going to change your meds," he said.

She swallowed two large tablets. She felt lighter, and the tightness in her chest let up a bit within the hour. Bob bent over to kiss her. His aftershave seemed stronger than usual, and she felt nauseous.

She slumped into the folded pillows after he left, relieved that he was gone. While he was visiting, a woman, breathing heavily and deeply, had been rolled off a stretcher onto the other bed. The woman had silver-gray hair and a porcelain complexion, and she reminded Eve of a Barbie doll. The nurse mentioned that she'd swallowed "a bunch of pills." She went on about how the woman was going through some hard times and how this was the last straw. Eve wished she would wake up. Maybe she could help her—maybe they could help each other.

She heard her muttering. The words were unclear, but Eve was sure that the woman was trying to say, "I'm tired of people leaving me."

Eve sprang from her bed and sat in the chair near the woman's bed. She straightened out the wilted flowers on the night table. When the woman stirred, Eve pushed her moist hair away from her forehead and hummed a tune that she'd sung to her kids, when they were sick. The woman appeared to be less restless.

Eve dozed off and soon dreamed about buying a new car. She pays the salesman in cash. There's cash flowing out of her wallet. She can buy anything. She's bounced back. She doesn't need anyone to help her. She gets into the car and drives quickly down a road with huge red neon arrows. The further she goes, the warmer it gets. "Summer's where I'm going," she laughs.

She woke up smiling, until she realized where she was. She wished she had more time on her side, she needed a break, she took a deep breath. She was determined to make it—to stand on her own two feet.

Her roommate was tossing and turning. Eve wondered if she'd ever get up. There was so much to tell her. She pulled the blanket over her shoulders and turned toward the window. The sun was bright and too strong for the end of January. Things were never really the way they looked outside, she thought. She wished the sun could penetrate the frosty window. The outside world seemed like a movie set, exaggerated, synthetic, and unattainable.

DRUMSTICK

REGAN ARRIVED at Mr. Vicone's office about noon. He was a plump man in his late thirties, and his full lips curled up in a sly way when he spoke. He was constantly manipulating his pipe, which drew more attention to the lips.

He began by complaining to her about being a public attorney. "I have three kids. I can't hack it on this salary."

She didn't get why he was complaining to her—he was well aware of her grave situation and her inability to help him. She figured it was a rationalization, a guilt thing, since he was being lazy about her case. One minute he'd listen to her attentively, then turn around and look at the window, just staring , hearing nothing. She anxiously handed him the list he had told her he needed for the court. He sucked feverishly on his pipe and told her to see Gladys Kurtz, the new public attorney.

She entered Gladys's office with a half-smile, but the stone-faced woman with black horn rims didn't smile back. "Mrs. Martin," she said firmly, "you'd better sit down—we have some serious issues to discuss."

Regan, who didn't like her tone, squirmed into her seat. Gladys leaned a bit closer. "Well, I don't quite know how to say this Regan, but there's no chance of any compensation on lost property. Mr. Martin is broke. He can't even pay his debts. The chances are slim that you'll even get alimony."

Regan sat there stunned. Gladys went on, "Some are winners in this game, but most are losers. Join the club, lady."

Regan went on, as if she hadn't heard a thing. "B-but, what about all my *things?*"

"Accept it, Regan. You know what to do." Regan doubled up. Her stomach spasms were growing more frequent. "It's all a lie—he's not broke. He's a successful lawyer! . . . I don't know what to do," she whimpered. "I haven't worked for twenty years." She doubled up again and cried out, "This is the worst day!"

Gladys rose, adjusting the pleated skirt over her full hips, and led her client to the door. Regan was still clutching the wrinkled list of losses, hoping it might still have some merit. She went to the phone and started dialing all the numbers that came to her. There were no answers. She finally realized she was alone.

Since the apartment was cold when she got back—a problem she'd had for as long as she lived there—she phoned the janitor about the heat before opening a can of tuna.

But she looked at it, unable to eat. The thought of suicide returned—more methodical and strategic this time. She had already eliminated pills and alcohol. Her roommate at college had tried them, but instead of dying, she had gotten terribly sick. Regan remembered a suggestion given to her by a neo-Nazi acquaintance. He thought a pool pipe attached to the exhaust and then placed through the driver's window of the car would be a sure-fire thing. She knew she'd be capable of that—all she had to do was close the garage doors.

She dressed quickly. At the pool store, the salesman looked at her inquisitively and she worried that he wouldn't sell her the pipe. When she paid for it, he looked straight into her eyes.

She threw the pipe into the car, afraid to stop moving. She had to go through with it, without hesitation. She had tried to sit in her car with the motor going once before, but it hadn't worked. And, since she knew it might take a while even with the pool pipe, she went into the kitchen to get a book. The thought of what she planned to do, so peaceful and so final, comforted her.

Regan heard a loud knock on the garage door that wouldn't stop. Finally, she got out of the car and took the pipe off the exhaust. "Regan, it's Barb," said her next-door neighbor. "Are you okay?"

"I'm fine!" Regan shouted back, having decided not to open the garage door and reattached the pipe before heading to the kitchen for a granola bar and settling into the car again.

As she started the engine, she heard some cars outside and noticed flashing red lights through the garage windows. "Oh, no!" she whimpered. "It's the cops! Nosy Barb can't mind her own business!" The pounding on the garage doors wouldn't let up.

Feeling defeated, she dragged herself out of the car again and opened the doors.

"Are you okay, ma'am?" said the cuter of the two officers standing there.

"I'm terrific," Regan retorted, and smiled at him almost flirtatiously.

The other officer, older, sour and suspicious, muttered, "What's that?"

"Oh," Regan explained, "it's a pool pipe. I'm cleaning it out. It's filled with gook."

"Are you sure everything's okay?" the cute cop asked again.

"I'm terrific," Regan retorted with exagerrated cheerfulness.

The other officer, older and suspicious, muttered, "What's that?"

Regan convinced him that all was well, and they finally left. The cute cop winked at her before he departed.

Having given up on suicide for the day, Regan returned to the apartment and phoned her neo-Nazi acquaintance, whose name was Peter. She reprimanded him and explained the circumstances and how his technique hadn't worked. He seemed disappointed as well.

At the end of her rope, Regan went back to Mr. Vicone with the list, figuring she had nothing to lose. She had put on the shortest tightest skirt she could find, hoping he'd act more attentive. She sat in front of his desk and swung her long shapely legs at him.

Mr. Vicone didn't appear to notice. "Look, Regan," he said, a bit more sympathetically than ever, "You really have to get on with your life. You're smart and even somewhat attractive. You could get a very fine job."

But Regan had tried that, in vain—she didn't have the necessary background to help her family in any substantial way. He suggested she phone the builder, a Mr. Van Dyke, who had bought her home at the foreclosure and who had all her possessions in storage. She quickly called. When the secretary told Van Dyke who was on the line, though, Regan heard a click. "Please help me, Mr. Vicone!" she shouted feverishly. "I won't accept this snow job." "Perhaps you should see a doctor," he re-torted. "You may need medication." His lips were curled up more than ever. She took out her worn list of losses, looked at him tearfully, and left in silence, her hips swaying back and forth in an exaggerated fashion.

She drove directly to the marital home. The weeds were high, the grass yellow, dying. She remembered when her family had moved in. The lawn had been a deep blue-green then. She could smell the flowers surrounding the home, and hear the kids' laughter in the family room. An old neighbor was straining to see who was in the car. Regan pulled away quickly.

When she entered her apartment, she felt forlorn and chilled; her clothes lay everywhere. There was an old futon standing along a wall. The pine wall unit on the opposite wall was still unpainted. She noticed her kids' photos on the sill, their eyes following her like the Mona Lisa's. She knew they were aware of everything.

The solitude of dinner had always weighed heavily on her. She looked forward to returning to court the next day. The list of losses rested on the kids' photos. She knew the truth had to surface. Possibly the new judge would see through all the deceit.

She opened the fridge to examine the week's leftovers, most of which were moldy. She grabbed a still moist and fairly edible turkey drumstick, sat in the kitchenette and listened attentively to the ticking of the clock. The clouds outside were banking against the hills. She nib-bled ferociously at the drumstick, far into the bone.

GOLDIE

W HEN WE left New Jersey to live in Brook-
lyn, my parents rented a spacious apart-
ment in an old-fashioned, well-kept
building in a still respectable neighborhood. The building stood eight
stories high, yet had a lovely brass elevator—unusual for an apartment
complex in Brooklyn. When nothing was going on, I'd invite the kids
from other buildings, who didn't have an elevator in their place. We'd
push the buttons wildly, bent over with laughter, jutting up and down
the floors. Tennis, riding and camps were for rich kids. I'd see them
when my folks took me to Central Park. I didn't envy them—I just knew
they were different from us. Staring them down became a thing to do
and, of course, they stared back. This emphasized the distinction and
created ultimate hostility on both sides.

My mother suggested I had an "attitude problem" and thought I had
a shaky understanding of reality. I was thrilled, though, not to have to
wear their gawky pleated skirts and matching knee socks in saddle shoes.
My mother commented on their good taste and style. I was thankful for
my less-coordinated tight pedal pushers and iridescent windbreakers. At
times, she tried to buy me plaid, pleated attire, but I fought her on this
matter to the bitter end. I just wanted to fit in with the kids in my neigh-
borhood.

It was a time in my life when anything different or unusual both
upset and intrigued me. I guess that's why Goldie took on an importance
in my life. My mother had become quite friendly with our downstairs
neighbor, Anna, a tall, plain woman who never wore makeup. Goldie,
Anna's daughter, hardly left the house and rarely left her room. When
my mother visited, I usually went along to try to catch a glimpse of

Goldie. Once, I saw her through the crack of her bedroom door. She was sitting on the edge of her bed with her head bent over stiff, lead-like arms. She caught me watching, though, and slammed the door shut. I was amazed at her distinctive, chiseled features and slender body. She was a refined version of her mother, I thought. "Don't look, it's not polite," my Mom said, as if I had been viewing a freak.

Visiting at Anna's was, in any case, a chilling experience. Her place was dull, Spartan—no pictures on the walls, no knickknacks. The doilies on the sofa only emphasized the soiled spots. And Anna offered home-baked oatmeal cookies I could never eat—I had this thing about eating in homes that weren't crispy clean.

Strangely enough, the only room that seemed cheerful was Goldie's, with its southern exposure. Sometimes, I caught her lying on her bed, taking in the rays from the yard, as if she were at the beach.

My mother often discussed the situation downstairs. She felt dismay over the plight of Anna, who would not leave her daughter for long periods and therefore had no obvious means of support. For some reason, it made my Dad feel uncomfortable enough to walk away, when Mom brought up the subject. My sister enjoyed intellectualizing about Goldie. "Jesus H. Christ, that girl is going to die young," she cried out. "She's not crazy—she just needs to fix herself up and meet some guys. That'll do it."

My mother shushed her quickly, hoping Anna hadn't heard anything and offered, by way of reprimand, "If you had a heart, Carol, you'd go down there and help her out—you're all talk," she said, shaking her head and flipping her hand at her in disgust.

I took it upon myself to heed those words and save the day. I had a sure-fire plan. I'd get some nice clothes from Carol's closet and bring them to Goldie. Then, we'd go to a movie. I figured she would appreciate a dark, quiet place the first time out.

When Anna left, I lugged over the bag of my sister's clothes and knocked on their door, hoping Goldie would open it. When nothing happened, I retreated to the back courtyard, brushing against the *sukkah* on my way. (The *sukkah* was a four-walled structure with a roof of tree branches, built for the autumn holiday of *Sukkos*). It hadn't been taken down after the holidays and I was pleased with that. It served as a play-house for the kids in the building. I sat in it to contemplate my next move.

Moving to the fire escape, I spotted Goldie's room and climbed up the hot metal steps, as cautiously as an alley cat. Soon, I was right outside her bedroom window, absorbing the residual warmth and smells of sum-mer. It was a Saturday and almost everyone on the block was in syna-gogue. This made it easier—no one would call me down. I held the bag of clothes with one hand and laid the other on the sill.

Goldie's radio was playing her favorite, Doris Day's "Buttons and Bows." I was lucky. I saw that she was still in her bedroom. Just then, the half-opened window slammed down on my hand. As I shrieked in pain, Goldie appeared at the window. Her pale face jutted out in anguish and her eyes blinked uncomfortably at the sun, like a bat's eyes at high noon. "*Help* me!" I shouted feverishly.

"I-I can't!" she muttered.

"You have to!" I shrilled. "I'm going to faint."

Though she observed me falling to one side, she continued to walk around her room in circles, wringing her hands. Suddenly, though, she jumped onto the fire escape and threw me onto her back. She was shud-dering like a frightened animal, too, which made me feel I was on a horse.

Soon, she was pounding on the door to my apartment. My mother just stood there, still and shocked, to see Goldie with me. My hand was examined briefly. Everyone concluded it wasn't broken, since I could move my fingers. My mother hovered over Goldie with a constant smile.

I took Goldie into Carol's room, imagining she'd like hers more than mine, since they were about the same age. She glanced at Carol's clothes and makeup scattered on the bed and touched one of her lipsticks—I took it upon myself to give her one shiny cylinder that contained a glim-mering coral tip. She sat near the mirror on the night table and awk-wardly put it on. "You look gorgeous," I sighed as she turned toward me with her lovely smile.

Carol trotted in, holding her portable radio. She was wearing bright orange lipstick and short shorts. Jumpy as a fish at the end of a pole,

Goldie looked at her. "Hi, Carol," she said with lowered eyes.

My sister, who had concluded that her theory of Goldie's sanity was right on target, since she knew her name, sat down next to her and showed her some photos. One of them had been taken at a local park. "*That's* the *park!*" Goldie blurted out.

"What—what park?" my sister and I said simultaneously.

"That's the last place I was," she cried out. Goldie went on to tell us about how her father had taken her to that park as a child. He had said he was going away for a long time and left her there. She'd been lost for several hours until the police came to take her home, wet and shivering uncontrollably. I guess Anna was too embarrassed to mention the incident to my mother. That's the way things were then.

I went back to the *sukkah*, leaving Goldie with my sister. The white sun of dusk had created a halo over the building. When I looked up at my sister's window, I saw Goldie's arms moving about expressively, light as feathers. The lamp on the night table was casting a golden aura around her long, delicate frame. Her teal blue eyes seemed to be penetrating the walls of the *sukkah*. "I love you, Goldie," I called out, listening to the echoes of the angels who had helped me help her.

GRAY VASES

G AIL SAT next to me in high school biology. She was a smart kid. I'd ask her a million questions. I knew most of the answers, but Gail was flawless in her work. Her brown hair was tied back in two braids, like the hair on a Dutch doll and parted in the middle, clean, away from her face. She looked like her work. She always smelled of Ivory soap.

Gail was a loner, for the most part. She'd get involved in some activities, but soon dropped them. Her mind seemed to wander. She was prophetic in many ways. Sometimes it was scary. I remember when she predicted an accident and refused to go on the school trip. The bus was rear-ended and we never made it to the circus. I thought she was part of some weird cult, but that was just a fleeting thought—Gail was just a bit ahead of most of us. She was a kind-hearted girl from a nice Irish Catholic family. Her unique ways were mildly obvious, but they were what intrigued me about her.

One day, she whispered excitedly, "Guess what, Jane, my mom is pregnant! I'm going to be a sister." Her eyes were shining, and that sadness was totally gone.

I was somewhat taken aback. I wondered how I'd feel if my mother got pregnant then. I was eighteen and the youngest. It would have been embarrassing to me. "Great," I said.

"That's super."

"Promise not to tell anyone," she went on. "Not yet."

This secret created a new closeness. I visited her home after school. Mrs. Tighe was thin, with salt-and-pepper hair. She had grayish circles under her eyes. The swell of her stomach just didn't fit. She was sitting on a floral wing chair, knitting rapidly, as she spoke to me. Gail and her mother were going over the inverted cable stitch on the small, pale yellow sweater. "This is for the new baby," she said. "I don't know the sex. I want it to be a surprise."

Gail's dad was home. He seemed to be home a lot. Whenever I called Gail, he'd pick up. He came out of his bedroom after a while. "Hi, kid. It's hard to believe you girls are seniors." He ran his fingers through his thick reddish hair, as if he'd just awakened. He wore oversized jeans and work boots. I wondered what he did. Gail never talked about it. He sat at the kitchen table and drank some tea. Mrs. T. brought some biscuits to him. "These are great," he said, as he concentrated on the taste. "You outdid yourself." He squeezed her shoulders. Mrs. T. smiled and walked away with a slight hunch. He turned to me with a wide smile. "So, where are you going to college?" There were crumbs all over his clothes.

"I think I'd like to go to Skidmore," I said.

He grinned. "Fancy, schmancy."

I turned away, uneasy about his remark and went on, "A lot of international kids go there—I think I'd really like it."

We went into Gail's room. It was filled with patchwork pillows and covers. I knew my mother would think it was too quaint. I thought it was homey, cozy. Gail's books were lined up neatly on the sill, in perfect order. Her homework was stacked according to subject. I admired her organizational qualities and started to feel guilty about my neglected homework.

The sun was getting weaker and the leaves were falling more rapidly in rusty clumps. I started to leave before it got darker. I looked at Mrs. T. and told her I'd be back soon. I felt obligated to do so. Gail was in the background, biting her thumbnail. I waved. "See you later." I reluctantly opened the front door.

There was an unusual chill in the air for early October. I walked home with a heavy heart, though I didn't know why I felt that way. Maybe it was envy. If my mother were pregnant, I might feel closer to her. I didn't really think that was it, but there was something.

When I got home, I was happy to see my mother puttering cheerfully around the kitchen. She looked fresh and energetic. The oven smelled of roast beef. I was happy with things, just as they were. She and I exchanged glances.

"Why are you looking at me that way?" she asked. I was imagining how she would look pregnant—I shrugged off the thought and went into my room. The house looked more attractive to me than ever.

I walked home with Gail a few days later. She told me to wait, went into her mother's bedroom and came out with a painting. "Ta-da! Isn't this super?" she boasted. "My mom's an artist."

I was surprised. I'd never thought of Mrs. Tighe as an arty person. I guess the knitting and patchwork had thrown me off. The painting was different. It had huge pastel flowers, whose delicate form was being pulled down by oddly shaped gray vases.

Mrs. T. walked in. "Do you like it? Impressionism—that's how I paint. I studied at the Art Students League for years." The look on Gail's face was proud, which seemed strange—she was acting like a mother or older sister. I realized that Mrs. T. was Gail's main concern. I suppose she didn't need the kids at school that much. Since I usually avoided being with my mother, I felt guilty. I thought maybe we'd go to a movie together over the weekend, but quickly dismissed the idea. My mother would suspect that I was up to something.

Gail was late to class. When she finally got there, she looked flushed. She said her mother was bleeding and that the doctor was concerned. She was leaving school early. I felt great sympathy for her. We were both seniors in high school. I was concerned about the prom, clothes and college. I thought her karma had some dark shadows. "I'll be over later," I said.

I decided to go shopping with a friend instead and never made it to Gail's. Frankly, I felt I needed a break from the Tighes. I tried to call later that evening, but no one was home. Gail was absent from school the next day. When I got home, my mother, her face blanched, told me to sit down.

"Mrs. Tighe passed away last night," she said in a whisper. She held me close to her. I rested on her soft shoulder, unable to move away. When I finally sank onto the seat, I spotted the small replica of Mrs. Tighe's painting. She'd given it to me that last time. "It's the gray vases in their life," I kept saying.

"What are you talking about?" asked my mother.

I kept staring at the delicate flowers and the harshness of the vases—the downward force of the floral patterns. Impressionism, that's what she called it, I thought. "She called the painting 'April'—that's what she was going to name the baby, if it was a girl." I suddenly thought of the baby for the first time. "Did the baby—?"

She stopped me and shook her head. So the baby was dead, too.

I started toward the phone to speak to Gail. I couldn't pick up the receiver. "How can I speak to her now?" I asked myself. They'd needed me and I'd gone shopping. I burst into tears. My mother mumbled some comforting words I couldn't comprehend.

I ran to Gail's house and knocked feverishly. She opened the door—her eyes swollen, her porcelain face spotted and red. When I tried to touch her, she quickly pulled away. She seemed reluctant. I finally grabbed her and realized she was trembling. "I kept bugging her about having a baby," she said in a distant voice. "I was sick of being an only child … she was too weak, too *sick* for this!" she cried out. "She did it for me! I was so *selfish*!"

"It was a fluke, Gail, "I said. "She was fine—she could've easily had the baby. It's not *your* fault … *stop* it!" I shouted.

Mr. Tighe opened the door to his room. I could smell the tobacco; the ashtray was filled with butts, the room disheveled. "She's gone," he said. His eyes were heavy, dark. "She's gone. We'll have to live without her now." He moved around aimlessly.

Gail sat stiffly in the chair that Mrs. Tighe had used most often. There was a crucifix above it. I'd never seen one in a home and never noticed it at the Tighes' till then. It was creepy to see a man nailed to a cross. It added to the sadness and morbidity.

The pale yellow sweater was lying folded over the original April painting. I picked it up and held it close to my chest. I walked toward the door, still holding the sweater and quietly left. I felt helpless to do or say anything. When I looked back and saw Gail, her head was on her arms and she was weeping and again moaning, "She was too weak for this, Dad—just too weak!"

I was fearful about the wake. I'd never been to one. I couldn't imagine viewing a dead body—especially Mrs. Tighe's. There was an extraordinary quantity of flowers at the funeral home, the pungent scents adding to the discomfort. I followed the other guests toward the coffin. I didn't want to look, but did it out of respect.

She looked like a young girl. Her hair was loose and soft around her pale, frail shoulders. Her hands, folded on her stomach, looked much smaller than I remembered. I quickly moved away. Gail and Mr. Tighe were in the reception room. They were much calmer than I thought possible. My mother, who was walking behind me, whispered that it was shock. Gail was not responsive and Mr. Tighe looked dazed. He groped for my name.

I felt Gail's deep pain. Her anger created a more mature look. She seemed stronger than before. Her behavior toward Mr. Tighe was almost authoritative. I knew she'd bounce back. Though she probably would never be the same Gail I knew, she'd be okay, maybe even better.

My mother, at the door of the funeral home, looked at me sympathetically. "You'd probably better go home now," she said. "You haven't eaten all day."

I was thinking of Mom in a different way. I'd never considered her tentativeness here. I recalled Gail's words to me: *"My mother's dead. You can't know what it's like."* She had been right—I couldn't.

On the way home, I thought of Gail, wondered what would happen to her. She was smarter than her dad. She was strong. She would help him get through it. But the hard turn of events would destroy her innocent girlishness.

I thought of the time I'd looked over at Sandy Gorlyn's spelling test. I had been desperate. I'd blanked out on a word. The more I stretched over, the higher Sandy had barricaded her desk with books. Gail had looked at me impishly and started to giggle—innocent young laughter.

I wondered if she'd ever laugh like that again. I knew her adolescent years were over. I could tell by her look. It was happening already. I recalled the story of a cousin who'd lost her mother when she was sixteen. It had become impossible for her to have a normal relationship with men. Having been robbed of the most important role model in her life, she had never married or had kids and was lonely and depressed always. I prayed this would, by some luck, never happen to Gail.

My mother made hot chocolate and moved the steaming cup directly in front of me. I stirred it with my finger and licked the foamy topping, unable to swallow anything. She tried to convince me that everything happens for a reason. She went on, "I'm not saying it's *pleasant*—but it's in God's hands, and there is a reason for it."

I shouted, "A reason? Come on, Mom—how could there possibly be a reason for this?" I pushed the hot chocolate to the side.

She rose and started to clean it up. The kitchen was filled with the soft light of fall, and it streaked over her. She was, I realized, getting older. I'd never seen it before. Her arms were loose and fleshier. The firmness of her neck was starting to sag. Her eyes seemed to be set more deeply than I had realized.

Suddenly, she laid her head on top of the table, her face resting on her arms. We talked about the Tighes till early morning. We spoke of the talented, lovely Mrs. Tighe, of Mr. Tighe, concerned about his helplessness, but mostly we talked of Gail's future.

My mother, looking drained, fell into a deep sleep on the kitchen table. I wondered how much time she had and started to worry about her health, her aging. But, she was here now. I knew how lucky I was to still have her. There was a chill in the early morning air, so I draped the green throw over her shoulders. I knew she'd be with me for a time. She couldn't die—no, no, my mother would never die on me like that.

LIFE IS GOOD

THE THIRD session at mental health services in my designated county. At this point, I'm devastated about human nature. Why am I here? The psychiatric social worker is clearly visionless. To think, that a respected establishment can allow a mere social worker to take on the role of a shrink—and charge more. How worthless to pour out my guts and get inane conclusions like, "Why do you come here to vent?" Am I there to entertain? Is this the hour to be comedic? This place is another of society's sick jokes. I'd rather be stuck half frozen on Mt. Everest. After three months on anti-depressants, I felt as if I were in some weird bubble—distant, zombie-like. Clearly it was better to feel the pain.

I've been through one of the worst divorces imaginable. My kids suffered from an unscrupulous legal system. My ex, a divorce attorney, set me up. Down to the last day, he coiled around me like a snake. I, with my trusting nature, was unaware of his outrageous schemes.

It became obvious only when he forced foreclosure on our marital home and left. He took every last item, down to his tennis racket. My friends stopped by from time to time, observed my constant state of hysteria and advised me to "pick up the pieces." "So what? Get a life! So what?" After twenty-three years, there was no chance in hell for me to get anything back. My ex was every judge's buddy.

Everyone I knew and respected had trouble thinking clearly about my mess. They just couldn't be perceptive or objective. I knew *exactly* what was happening. It was another "Rosemary's Baby." I was either surrounded by demons or only happened to know the least lucid and caring of people. Bureaucracies destroyed it all. Yet, all along, I survived the nightmares of the legal system, thankful in the end that I still had mental clarity. Why everyone crawled into the woodwork will always shock me.

For instance, I was visiting my hypochondriacal niece in the hospital and picked up the phone when it rang. The sound of my voice led to mumbling and a snicker, "Shit, it's fucking Linda." They might have been upset that I wasn't the patient.

During the lonely days, I'd visit my cousins on the upper east side of Manhattan. It was awkward trying to chill out on their stiff contemporary couch. The bookshelves were filled with books on vegans, veggies and how to live to be over a hundred, because life was good. There were also several coffee-table books on the rich and famous. They would sit on the other side of the room, as if I were an odd and unusual artifact.

The most wicked one of the cousin clan, Irene, was intolerable. Maybe she once envied my charmed life. We were at an Irish pub having lunch, when Irene suddenly screamed at me, "Look, lady, get it together like everyone else. If you can't function, work at MacDonald's." I started a conversation with a lovely couple from Ireland. Irene freaked out yet again. "When you're with me, don't start yapping with other people." I glanced at them from the corner of my eye, noticing sympathetic looks. Irene proceeded to throw French salad dressing on my stark white linen dress. I threatened to call the police, but the sympathetic woman next to me made me see reason. When she left the place, Irene slid into a cab and that was the last time I saw her. The younger of the two Irish women took me to the restroom and tried, in vain, to get the stains out. "She has the devil in her eyes," she said with a heavy brogue.

"But, she's my cousin," I said, as if that gave her the right to act like a crazy lady.

"Stay away from her," shouted the concerned bartender.

I left, forlorn and embarrassed.

I drove to my daughter's house. When I rang the bell, a slim, tall young man about her age opened the door. He looked down, as if he had something to hide or was just not ready to meet me. "Hi, I'm Janie's mom," I murmured softly. He seemed sensitive and vulnerable, so I tried to be as unassuming as possible.

"Janie will be back soon," he said, stunned. "She really isn't going to be in the mood for company."

"Company?" I said curtly. "I'm her *mother*—didn't you hear me?"

"This is my first time here," he whispered, as if letting me in on a secret plot. "We met on Match.com. This is the second time we've been together." He cleaned his oversized, black-rimmed glasses and considered again, as if the picture of me had become clearer. I was upset that my daughter could be attracted to such an oddball.

Janie arrived about half an hour later. She entered the hallway with a shocked expression. She was wearing a blue velour warm-up suit and Ugg boots, which hung loosely on her petite frame. "What are *you* doing here?" she said with a nervous giggle.

"Janie, you have to hear what happened to me with Irene—don't give me a hard time. I have had the worst of days."

She ignored my state of dismay and guided me to the bathroom. She grabbed a cigarette, lit up and inhaled deeply. "Look, Mommy dearest," she whined. She always referred that way to me when she was pissed. "Look, Mom, I was depressed one day and met him on a suicide website."

She sank onto the tile floor with the oversized boots under her butt, looking up at me like a sad kitten, her light-brown hair falling loosely over her shoulders. I thought she was putting me on, just because I'd come unannounced. But when I looked out the door and saw Ricky's face gawking at the floor, I knew it was true.

"He ... he's just had a bad day, like me—he's fine," she said, trying to be persuasive.

Well, this was the perfect time to read a poem, I thought. "You know, I didn't catch your name, with all the confusion," I said innocently, after we returned to the living room. "Richard. But everyone calls me Ricky."

I read one poem. As he listened attentively, he eyed my daughter as if he thought I would be a good candidate for their website.

Annabella, my daughter's Italian greyhound, was under his feet. He looked at her with a half-smile, but didn't actually seem to notice the frail dog.

"That wasn't a good poem," I exclaimed. "I'll read another."

"Stop, Mom, we're not in the mood for poetry!"

"But the others aren't like that one," I insisted. I got the message, though, and closed the book. They both slouched on the sofa. Janie rested her head on his shoulder. Ricky looked weak and drained. Had it really been just a couple of bad days for both of them? I pushed her silky bangs away from her moist forehead and gently wiped a leftover bit of food from her face. I got a blanket from the bedroom and covered her. There was nothing left to do. I tiptoed out the door.

The half moon was pale, hardly noticeable. The clouds were still and peaceful, except for one or two that seemed to want my attention.

OH, THAT FOLIAGE

THAT NOVEMBER just before Thanksgiving break, my roommate Shirley Perkins and I hung out in our room much later than usual. Even though it was still early November, the snow wouldn't let up. "I can't take the cold and snow here," I said. Shirley was from Buffalo, so she was used to ghastly, biting winters. She had that Nordic look, so it fit her tolerance of cold weather.

Homesickness was an embarrassment and curse that freshman year at Syracuse U. It was difficult for me to get used to the ambiance of such a school. Some of the girls in my dorm were quintessential metropolitan area JAPs. The desperation to enter a sorority was just another pressured thing to deal with. Yet I didn't get why I was homesick. I called my mother every day begging her to let me transfer to a school closer to home. This was odd, since I'd been one of the few kids in overnight camp that never missed home. Why was it happening now?

At first, Shirley thought I was sophisticated, "cool," as she put it. I was from the city, so she admired my sense of style. "You really know how to pull yourself together," she often said. That boosted my ego. What a letdown for her to think I was just a big baby.

Shirley was a brilliant student, on a full scholarship. She never studied—just blasted classical music almost every day. By comparison, I had to study or flunk out. I'd go down to the boiler room to avoid Mozart's greatest works.

That November day, though, there was no need to pick up a book. We were getting ready to go home. The classical music was louder than ever. Shirley was slumped against the pillow, her legs stretched out. A wicked and sinful stench filled the room. She was holding onto a joint.

"Shirl," I said, fearful and shocked, "it's really too early to start."

"It's never too early or too late," she told me. "Come on, Delly," this was an endearing way of getting me to do something, "just take a drag. You'll forget your silly homesickness."

Life is short, and I told myself I had nothing to lose, but my sister had told me that weed could cause brain defects. You could give birth to sick babies.

"It's really not a big deal," Shirley went on, "Everyone does it—I bet your crazy homesickness will leave you forever."

I would never have thought Shirley was into pot. She was clean-cut and appeared totally bookwormish. She dressed like a little girl at Catholic school—always in a plaid pleated skirt and knee socks. As a devout Catholic, I wondered if she had ever discussed this with her priest. Novels of Hemingway and Fitzgerald covered the huge blotter on her desk.

I figured she was smarter than my sister, so I gave in. Shirley's lips were full and demon-red against the small wrinkled joint. She quickly handed it to me. I awkwardly placed it in my mouth and took a deep breath, and then another. It burned and tasted disgustingly bitter. "Come *on*, Delly, you've got to inhale and hold before you breath out," she insisted. It was as if she was a scuba diving instructor. It didn't work for me. Nothing was happening. I just felt like vomiting. I continued to follow her very specific instructions. "Yeah, right," I was suddenly doubled over with laughter. I looked at Shirley with a crazed giggle. Her eyes sparkled as I glided across the room. "Bye, Mommy, bye, World—you're off my back," I cackled.

Our door was unintentionally ajar. "Well, *looky-looky* at the Newton cookie," I slurred.

Shirley just sat on her bed and didn't say a thing. She didn't have to.

In strutted Priscilla Fox, from "snootin' Newton," as she called her upscale town in Massachusetts. She smelled of Joy, Jean Patou's most expensive scent. Everyone could smell her from miles away. One couldn't miss her long bleached-blonde hair. I opened the door just a bit more. Shirley was slumped on her pillow, hands folded in her lap, hiding the weed. Priscilla wasn't exactly her cup of tea, either.

"Hi, Prissy," I called out crazily. "You know you never returned my favorite periwinkle blue sweater set."

She told me that she had fallen in love with it and was nervous about her first date with Stewy. Stewy was a Sammy, the most flashy, vociferous fraternity on campus. From Great Neck, he was the poster boy for Sammy. Yes, they were the Syracuse soul mates.

"Look, you Newton bitch, if you don't give it back to me in an hour, I'm calling the police." At this point, I was flushed and shouting. "MY dad broke his ass to get my things," I said, almost in tears. I looked at Shirley. She was at peace and smiling. I knew she was proud of me.

Priscilla proceeded to knock on Trudy the housemother's door. She backed away, knowing it was all in vain. Trudy wasn't about to make waves. She was a lesbian and always stared at us in the shower. We all knew why Trudy wanted the job. Priscilla glared at me. I glared back and slammed the door.

"We are out of here, Shirl," I said nervously. "Do you think we'll get suspended?" She stood with her arms folded, like an Indian wood figure in front of a cigar store.

"Who cares? I really hate it here," she mumbled, looking for candy.

"Yeah, I really hate it, too." I started the giggling thing. "All the Stewys up here are obnoxious and flashed out. I should have gone to B.U. I could've been hanging out with Harvard guys—what a waste."

Shirley slowly moved toward her phonograph and put on Gershwin's "An American in Paris."

We floated around like Isabella Duncan dancers. Shirley looked like an angel—her small upturned nose and rounded blue eyes were striking, as she twirled and twirled into oblivion. I slid toward her nightstand, took a piece of chocolate, then another and then another, till I finished the box. I replaced "An American in Paris" with "West Side Story." I pulled off my Syracuse sweatshirt and matching warm-ups, grabbed my lacy beige nightgown and tossed it on. It was powerful and magical. The fantasy began: "I feel pretty, oh, so pretty, that the city should give me a key." We were sweating and red, so Shirl opened the window. The reflection of the silvery snow cut through the curtains. Shirley was coming down and didn't acknowledge my Natalie Wood portrayal. She gazed at me in a pedantic manner. Nevertheless, I went on: "See that pretty girl in that mirror there." The music enveloped the room—probably the entire dorm.

Oh, oh! Priscilla again. She pushed the door open. I swept up to her powdered face. "You guys a-a-a-re in deep shit," she articulated in her exaggerated Boston accent.

"Bug off, bitch." I was loose, uninhibited. I just eyed her long blonde hair-do. Prissy inhaled the pungent odor in the room and gawked at my chocolate-covered face. She closed the door slowly, oddly enough in a protective way. She really had nowhere to go with her shocked observations. Nothing could harm me, anyway. I was Queen of the World.

Shirl fell into the folds of her wrinkled sheet, encrusted with cookie crumbs and candy wrappers. The ecstatic state began to lessen for me as well. The sharp green joint was just a grayish dust on our shag carpet. I sat on the floor next to Shirley's bed. I was back on Earth, yet no longer had any feelings of homesickness. Shirl's firm, rounded face looked saggy and sad. A small wooden crucifix of Jesus over the bed looked down on her. I noticed a crumpled card held tightly in her hand. My head felt heavy. It was as if little sticks had been caught in my brain. I feebly pulled the card out of her hand, tried to smooth it out so that the words were clear. Shirley had been rejected by the sorority she'd so wanted to be part of. Her genius eyes were half opened. She looked beat up and depressed. This place wasn't for us.

I saw a small, ivory-colored envelope appear under the door. My name was written in calligraphy. I ripped it open. Wow, I'd gotten into SDT, the best Jewish sorority house at Syracuse! I examined Shirley's devastated face, the sinking sun moved to the far left and over the mounds of snow and disappeared. My ivory acceptance card, that always arrived a week after pledging, had a small rip. I continued to tear it up, leaving the scattered pieces to fall to the floor under Shirley and Jesus.

POLLY AND WINSTON

Y DISTANT NEIGHBOR, Polly, a stocky, round-faced woman, who always dressed in a long beige raincoat and scotch plaid boots, would glance at me from time to time. Her white hair was softly parted, perfectly straight against her clear ashen complexion. She would stand stiffly against the black gate of her apartment, waiting for Winston, her dog, to do his thing. I loved seeing Winston. He was a fourteen-year-old boxer, who had taken on Polly's expressions and gait. He walked slowly and cautiously with his master, as if clearing the way to protect her from any upcoming problem. The only time I saw Polly smile or act cheerfully was when she was having some sort of communication with Winston.

She seemed lost and sad most every time I saw her. I suppose life had taken its toll and there was nothing for her to hide by then. I felt an enormous sense of sympathy for her, though I knew nothing about her. I was twenty and had been just married, when I moved into the garden apartment across the street from Polly and Winston. She was the first person I had seen, as I watched the moving men carrying in my furniture. She pretended not to notice anything going on around her. I believed she was in her late sixties or early seventies. The number didn't much matter—she was just an old woman, I thought.

Getting to know Doug as a husband, rather than just a boyfriend, was difficult for me. I was fearful that I had made a mistake. The things I loved about him somewhat vanished after the first few months we were together. He was unpredictable. There were moments when he was the affectionate and caring Doug. In a heartbeat, he became an out-of-control Godzilla. There was nothing in particular that set him off. It wasn't as if we had arguments. It was the insignificant things that set him off.

The first incident was the time some of the food in the fridge became green and moldy. I had not yet become the best of housekeepers, I admit. But, he used to think it was cute and girlish. When his friends would tease me about my whimsical behavior, he found it humorous. Could it be that my stately six-foot, perfectly groomed husband was a fraud? The next clash was even worse. We were going to a family wedding, when I noticed an obvious stain on his jacket. I pleaded with him to change. This battle went on for hours. His long atlas-type arms remained stiff. His huge hands and long fingers rested on his hips. I ran to the bathroom and locked the door, not knowing what to expect.

"I'm not going to be embarrassed in front of my family." I whimpered.

When I entered the living room, pieces of my cherished Hummel collection were scattered about. Staring at the ceiling from my bed was the only thing I could handle. He opened the door gently and became the old Doug. He now appeared professional and sane, with his expensive wire-rimmed glasses that hid the strangeness in his hazel eyes. After a few deep breaths, I figured that a new marriage just needed time.

Maybe that's why I focused so on Polly. She and her dog got to me in some strange way. I felt her tenderness, when she held Winston's leash in her soft, chubby hands. The simple wedding band she proudly wore was overshadowed by an impressive pear-shaped diamond ring. It seemed to brighten her face when she raised her hand over Winston to get him to do a trick or to move more quickly.

One day, she nodded to me in a deliberate way, as if she wanted to say something important. Her clear blue eyes were piercing, stunning; their glow seemed to look right through me, as if she knew about everything in my life. I wanted to say hello and pet darling Winston, but felt uncomfortable approaching her. She seemed to value her privacy, yet I knew she, too, might have been feeling some awkwardness. Our introduction, therefore, never took place.

When I passed her apartment, I smelled chocolate chip cookies in the oven. I caught a clear glimpse of a photo on the wall. A distinguished, handsome man was holding a beautiful child. The warmth of the cookies and photos of loved ones were a relief. It was comforting to know that she was part of a beautiful family. At the same time, it was upsetting to realize that there was no one ever around.

I didn't see them during that dark, cold winter. As I was sitting in my bedroom and watching the wind drive the melting snow, I heard police cars pull up in front of Polly's apartment. One of the officers was holding Winston. The dingy-haired dog was howling, crying and bloody. I thought he noticed me looking out the window. Polly had died and no one had known about it for several days.

I ran down the stairs to try to comfort Winston, but the officer wouldn't allow me to touch his crouched body. He told me that the poor dog had had no choice but to nibble on Polly's remains. How could such an unwavering love end like that?

I went back to my apartment in shock and disbelief with hands clenched. I felt my wedding ring pressing into my finger. I twisted it until it came off, wishing never to put it on again.

If only Polly could have been a part of my life, then.

TEMPORARY

EMMA INTENTIONALLY got a job near her son's house. He was staying temporarily with his father. She and her husband were separated and she was not in a position to support her son, Josh, though the court had promised that, when she got back on her feet, Josh would be allowed to live with her again. She was numbed out over this, but after years of trying, she was too overwhelmed to do anything.

Since she knew Josh got out of school early on Fridays, she took a late lunch on those days. It felt like a crap game: sometimes she'd get to be with him and at others, she didn't luck out.

But today would be one of the lucky ones. She felt it in her bones. The air was crisp and clean as it often was that November. Something cathartic and pure filled the afternoon and she was going to cash in on it. She hadn't seen Josh for a couple of weeks and a visit was due. There were no cars in the driveway, for which she was thankful, so Josh would be there without her husband, just him and no one else.

She pulled into the driveway and noticed his bike. It was on its side, rusty with a missing tire. Emma shook her head sadly, taking the condition of his bike as a sign: her son was not living as she had hoped.

It was just before Thanksgiving and she inhaled the savory aromas emanating from other apartments. She knew how Josh had been warned about her visits and how he would probably not allow Emma to enter the apartment, unless it had been set up beforehand.

She looked at the mirror on the visor and quickly applied lipstick and blush, since she wanted look as cheerful as possible. She grabbed the gift beside her, purchased weeks before, with the intention of seeing him. The ribbon had lost its perky curl and the wrapping was faded from its stay in the car. She knew he'd like it, though. Having sensed her anxiety about the purchase, the salesman at the store had assured her that the video was perfect for an eleven-year-old. "Don't worry, Miss, the kid is going to go bonkers over this—it's hot!" he had said, and patted her on the shoulder, expressing an unusual concern. She'd figured she was acting like a lunatic, so she had quickly terminated the transaction. The video salesman had kept looking her way as she left, as if he wanted to say something uplifting.

When Emma got out of the car, she looked up at the apartment. She was taking a chance, without the necessary protocol. But she was the boy's mother; it was ridiculous and sick to go through all that. It just wasn't natural. If she planned the visits, it was worse. Her husband would sit there, on a wing chair in front of the TV and look at his watch. He would even do a countdown. Josh would look his way in disturbed concern. "Em," Donny would call out when she got comfortable in her son's room. "Em!" he'd call again, "you'd better start wrapping up, you've got about ten more minutes!" At times like that, her head started to swirl with hate and she wished she had the courage to go out and shoot Donny.

Emma went up the stairs to the apartment but hesitated on the second floor landing and instead peered through the living room window of the apartment to catch a glimpse of Josh. He was sitting solemnly in front of his computer. She knew it was his only friend and wondered how much time he spent alone. Her eyes misted over. She remembered how he'd been before the separation—a bubbly kid, always upbeat and peppy. She knew he needed a mother and that he was starving for her.

They were both stuck—prisoners of the system—and helpless.

When she lamented about the situation to her lawyer and friends, they had assured her that the situation was just temporary. But she was losing hope that her son would ever live with her again. She couldn't compete with Donny. She would never be able to give the boy the material things his father could.

Her hands were clammy as she knocked on the door. She saw Josh pull the ivory lace drapes aside. He looked down and saw her car. "The poor kid is on guard," she muttered.

He opened the door and stood in the center to block the entrance.

His hands were on his hips and his expression was hard and strained. She acted calm, nonchalantly handing him the gift. He didn't reach out or even look at it.

"Hi, honey," she said effusively. "You're really going to love this— the guy at the video store said it was the *best one*."

He hesitantly took the gift and stepped aside. She sighed a deep breath of relief.

"God, Mom, your skirt is really short." His father was doing a great job, she thought. "Yup, his father," she muttered to herself.

"Well ..." he hesitated. "I guess you *could* come in for a while, but you can't stay long," he added robotically.

She swallowed hard. His eyes seemed as hard as marbles. Still, trying to keep things light, she went inside.

The apartment smelled of garbage. When she entered the kitchen she saw six bags of it piled up in the corner and her heart grew heavy. She turned around and watched Josh open his gift, ripping off the festive paper, covered with golden leaves. He hid a slight smile. Her heart started to beat quickly. Everything grew brighter, she thought, seeing his old self starting to seep through.

"It's great," he said.

"Well? Try it!" she exclaimed, glowing with her words.

"OK," he said cheerfully, then caught himself and looked at the clock. "You're going to have to leave soon, he said automatically. "My father gets home about now."

She might have fought this a while back, when things were different. But she had learned to relent and be thankful for any time with the boy, who eventually forgot about the time and went into his room to use the new video.

She clutched her hands as if in prayer and wandered around the apartment, as if it were hers, too. She opened the fridge and just stood there, staring at the food, realizing it was her way of becoming familiar with Josh again. She reached for the red wine, grabbed a glass from the cabinet, and poured. She sipped it fiercely, glaring at everything in the cupboard—all the packaged cereals and canned stuff. She went back to the fridge, absently took a bite of an apple and threw the rest in her purse. She also took some pears, grapes, and frozen veggies. She thought she was entitled, at least, to that.

In her husband's room, she spotted his girlfriend's sheer, frilly black nightgown tossed on a chair. She picked it up and brought it close to her widened nostrils. The odor of cigarettes nauseated her. She opened the drawer of the night table. In it, lay old movie tickets, a few unsmoked joints. Picturing activities involving these objects, she sat on the bed and wrapped the comforter around her chilled body, convinced that Josh could no longer live with Donny. She kicked the night table and turned toward the bathroom.

"Mom!" Josh suddenly shouted. "Where are you? What are you doing?" He was looking for her. "He's coming home soon!"

"So what?" Emma called back. "He—he's the one who tore up our family," she added in an undertone, recalling the time Donny tossed her out and stumbled out of the bedroom. She stopped in the bathroom and flushed the toilet. Even this unpleasantness created an attachment to the boy, who by then was shouting at her uncontrollably.

Later, sitting in her car, she watched the stream of traffic making its slow way home. She watched the cars go by, one by one. She had never thought that she could envy traffic.

THAT SUMMER, JEFFREY

T HAT SUMMER, Jeffrey was the only living crea-
ture to fifteen-year-old Gwen. She had been
sent down the shore to be with her aunt and
uncle, since her parents were convinced she was in a whirlwind of melan-
choly and gloom. Nobody in the family wanted to bring up the "inci-
dent," but Gwen would talk about it from time to time. It was as if she
didn't really want anyone to forget.

"God, it was only a fifty-cent eyeliner pencil," she whimpered un-
easily. "Everyone made such a big deal about it." She fidgeted with the
tortoise-shell hair clip that swept up the gleaming chestnut hair at the
sides of her flawless, heart-shaped face. Her voice started to deteriorate
to a plea. "Mom and Dad shopped at that drugstore for *centuries*, and
Mr. Nagel, who knows my whole entire family, totally freaked out over
a crummy little *pencil*."

Her Aunt Ruth and Uncle Dave were trying hard to act nonchalantly.
They were simple, honest-to-the-bone (as her mother put it) people who
had probably risen above the lower middle class by sticking to all rules
and their accompanying programs.

Gwen's dad always cited their no-brainer *modus vivendi*—which al-
ways hurt Gwen, who was fond of them in her own detached, whimsical
way.

Gwen went on about the incident, noticing slight disapproving
glances shooting back and forth between them, as if she'd been watching
a game of ping-pong. Determined, though, to tell the rest of her story
regardless of the discomfort, she stammered on. "He actually called the
police. I w-would've been really pissed, but one of the cops was gor-
geous."

Her attempt to lighten the mood didn't work. Aunt Ruth started to fill the teapot, as she always did when things got out of hand. Gwen's tone became more sullen. She started to sweat and shoved the falling wisps of her hair back in place. "The judge was an okay guy," she said. She talked of him reminiscently. "'Young lady,' he said, 'this is not the w-way to begin womanhood.'" He'd sentenced her to one year of therapy.

Stammering, yet more assertive and calm, she finished her story. "Anyway, I saw this corny shrink who'd mostly yawn and then pass out for the rest of the session. He said I was a classic example of an adolescent in need of extraordinary attention." She crossed her legs in exaggerated seductiveness and grabbed one of Uncle Phil's Salems, pretending to inhale and exhale without lighting up. She slid her oversized black sunglasses over her bangs. "Look, you don't have to be Freud to figure that out. H-he was such a. . .*nerd*."

Gwen felt more comfortable away from home, more independent and savvy with Aunt Ruth and Uncle Phil. Their ways, compared to her parents', were relaxing and allowed her to feel in control. She was pleased at the recent obvious roundness of her unripe breasts and overjoyed with her hourglass waist and definitive curves.

She was glad she'd met Bonnie, the kid next door. Bonnie was a year younger than Gwen but ahead of her in maturity. She had curly blond hair and amber eyes.

Gwen thought she was a strange amalgam. Bonnie constantly complimented her and told her she looked exactly like Natalie Wood. Gwen thought she was being overly nice, since the only resemblance lay in the color of her hair and eyes. Bonnie was airy and innocent, yet she felt a sadness in Gwen.

"Gwen, I have a *great* idea!" shouted Bonnie when she saw her the following morning. Her fair skin reddened with excitement as she put her arm around Gwen's shoulder. "There's this place called Mike and Lou's. All the kids that are cool hang there, and the jumbo hot dogs are great."

Gwen backed away—although she felt a great deal of affection toward Bonnie, she wasn't up to socializing.

"Oh come on," said Bonnie, "it'll be so much fun, and the *cool* kids hang there, and besides, the jumbo franks are *awesome*."

"Okay," said Gwen reluctantly, "but I'll only stay for an hour."

Yet Gwen was more excited about the upcoming evening than she imagined she could be. She ran to the bathroom mirror, beheld herself, and felt dreadful. "*Ugh*," she gasped. "My face is a mess, and I left all my good stuff at home."

She washed her face fiercely, hoping that some recent eruptions would disappear. She opened Aunt Sue's cabinet, hoping to find something that would help, found Lionel's Instant Magic Masque and was thrilled, felt guilty about going through Aunt Sue's things without permission—but there was so little time to get herself together, so she carried through with her intentions despite these misgivings. She grabbed the bath salts, and poured the entire bottle in the bath water, and submerged herself in the soothing tub, tingling from the effects of the masque.

Her face was glowing when she emerged, and she grabbed her oldest and most form-fitting jeans and jumped into them. They had long since become part of her body.

She chose the brown summer velour top that Aunt Sue had given her for her birthday. Her black faille wedged sandals completed an unintentionally avant garde look. She had an unusual flair for sophistication, for a fifteen-year-old.

When Gwen had completed these preparations, she felt truly relaxed and happy for the first time since "the incident." Aunt Sue felt uplifted when she saw the happiness on that exquisite face. "You look like Marilyn Monroe in those jeans," she said. Gwen blushed.

The doorbell rang; it was Bonnie, excitedly twenty minutes early. When she threw her arm warmly around Gwen's shoulder, though, Gwen backed away—although she felt a great deal of affection toward sweet Bonnie, she wasn't ready for physical contacts. She was hesitant about going out. "I'm not really sure—"

"Oh, come on," said Bonnie, seeing which way the wind might start to blow. "Please?"

"All right," said Gwen reluctantly, "but I'll only stay for about an hour." At this, Bonnie hugged her. "Great! Great, great!"

Bonnie's father drove them to Mike & Lou's. He was bald and quite overweight. She thought of her father and his obsessiveness about being in shape. Gwen thought it immature that, at his age, he'd go to the gym every day and indulge in weights with the young guys as if he were a contemporary.

Bonnie sat in back of the car and noticed Mr. Chase (Bonnie's father) looking at her a little too frequently. He wore gray-tinted glasses, which annoyed Gwen. She became overwhelmed by his relentless questions about her family—like what her dad did and what kind of car he drove. Gwen felt worse about his nosiness because she knew it embarrassed Bonnie terribly, so she answered politely.

When they got to Mike & Lou's, Gwen started to feel uneasy. There were thousands of kids in clusters there, and they could barely make it to the enticing hot dog grill. They were determined, though, to trudge through the crowd. Gwen felt as if someone were staring at her. She had a great sixth sense about being watched. She looked back and noticed a sexy smile and perfectly aligned teeth. It can't be him, she thought, stopped short, and tapped Bonnie to ask if she knew the guy.

"Oh, that's Jeff," Bonnie said. "The male JAP." She laughed carelessly. "He lives in that big white southern-type mansion on Ocean Road. Forget him—he's a real snot."

But Gwen couldn't stop looking, which was quite unusual for her. She was always so aloof. Finally, she walked up to him in her most sensual manner, which was new for her too, and she shocked herself. "Hi, Jeff here," he said, as humorously as she could ever have imagined. Gwen laughed so hysterically, her mascara blackened her eyes. "And you are— you are Bat Woman," he went on, chuckling over the smudges.

They walked away from the crowd. Gwen moved a bit closer to him and caught the scent of Polo. He looked at her dubiously. She felt tipsy, weak. "God, you're a *knockout*," he said. "Did you know that?"

Gwen thought for a while. She knew most people thought she was pretty. . .but not a knockout. "No, actually, I never did." She smiled innocently.

"Well, you sure as hell are," he said. She followed him as he paced ahead of her. She noticed the neatly tucked glen plaid shirt and his perfectly pressed off-white Polo slacks and soft Italian sandals. He must be a clothes nut, she thought. It was something she'd never liked in men. She preferred guys who dressed sloppily, more played down; but this fit Jeff, and it worked. It just went with him in a beautiful, natural way.

"Do you want to get something to eat?" he asked in a caring way. He had just gotten his license. "I don't mean booze, don't worry."

She sat stiffly in his new fern-green Volkswagen. Nothing was said for several minutes. Finally, Gwen broke the strange silence. "Do you like tennis?

"It's okay," he answered. "I'm good at it—B team at the club. Skiing is my thing these days." He broke out in a quirky grin, as if embarrassed by his answer. "I have a bumper sticker that says *I'd Rather Be Skiing.*" He forced a laugh.

"That's great," said Gwen. "I love to ski." She hated it, and the thought of being cold. "But I'm so stuck in dancing lessons—modern ballet—so I don't really have time for sports." She hoped that would be a good excuse for any future invitation to ski.

They stopped at Manny's Water Cove and split a pizza. She looked at his teal-blue eyes that stood out so against his olive skin and knew she had met her Waterloo. He was everything she'd ever dreamed about. His strong yet delicate hands, his drop-dead smile, and deep dimples so perfectly symmetrical. . . God, she thought he even has a cleft in his chin (something she'd always admired).

"I love looking at you," she said before turning away in disbelief of what had flown out of her mouth with such spontaneity. He blushed and said, "Ditto," and they both laughed again at his choice of words. When they stopped, Gwen wanted him to hold her, to envelop her and never stop. He looked down sadly and held her hand.

They drove back to Mike & Lou's to look for Bonnie, who was involved with an old friend from home. She seemed very content, so Gwen did not interrupt her but let it be. She walked back to Jeff, who was waiting patiently in his car. They decided he would take her back to her aunt and uncle's. Gwen was thrilled not to have to go through any further interrogations with Bonnie's dad.

When they got there, Jeff said he'd had a tough day, and that he would call her. Gwen turned toward the house with her eyes on the white cotton tie-back curtains. Her mother always criticized Aunt Sue's taste. Gwen felt embarrassed about the appearance, hoping that Jeff wouldn't notice. "Well, Madame," he said, sweeping his hand like a Victorian chevalier, "the evening has come to outstanding finale, so, *au revoir.*"

Gwen laughed hysterically at his exaggerated gestures and moved toward him. He jumped away and joked again, "My fairy godmother will turn me into a, uh, a. . ." He couldn't keep up the forced humor, jumped into his car, and with pain and honesty said, "I'll call you. . . ."

Gwen ran into Aunt Sue's gushing tears. She saw her sitting faithfully on the stairwell, waiting. "He didn't even *try* to kiss me—he, he didn't even *try!* " she moaned, and wept. Aunt Ruth tried to soothe her by suggesting that he'd acted out of respect, and that she'd have been thrilled if it'd been her.

Gwen completely disregarded this notion and went on as if she hadn't heard a thing. "Oh God," she moaned again, "I know he was bored. I'm, I'm boring, and I looked like a jerk." She crunched over, holding her arms stiffly. Her red, distorted face reminded Aunt Sue of when Gwen had been a baby bent over with stomach spasms.

Exhausted with grief, Gwen fell at last into a deep sleep, breathing heavily.

Jeff, meanwhile, had dragged himself into his car and cupped his chin in his hands. Brow creased in despair, he looked much older than his eighteen years. I shouldn't have egged her on, he said to himself silently, with flooding, watered eyes. I can't do this phony *scene* anymore.

He kicked the dashboard and zoomed off. Soon he was sitting in front of his beautiful southern-style summer mansion. He thought of his mom and dad and how they loved him . They had been at endless odds lately. He constantly overheard his mother discussing Paul's midlife crisis. He noticed an obvious and very recent lack of affection. The warmth was clearly gone from his home. His sister, Emily, tried to stay away as much as possible, which had added to the deterioration of the nucleus of his life. There was no one to speak to—he felt too distant and hostile toward his dad. Marla, his mom, was inundated with problems, and Emily was so bitchy and selfish that the thought of confiding in her was inconceivable.

He felt sorry for Emily since he knew she felt the dilemmas and pressures of family problems as he did. Finally, Jeff forced himself out of his car to face his dad.

Paul was just getting in as well, and Jeff smelled alcohol on his breath. He slapped Jeff on the shoulder in jest. "How's it going?" he asked, trying to keep his balance.

"I-I was just getting in," said Jeff.

"Did you get any?" His father glared at him with a newly devilish, horny look, salivating at the corners of his mouth.

Jeff felt ill, his stomach sour. He marched off toward his bedroom. He had decorated it with bold navy and gray stripes on the wall. The border on the top was patterned in *fleurs de lis* in the same colors. There was an oversized wing chair, in a soft wine suede, in the corner. There were french doors off his room that led to an enclosed garden filled with exotic plants. Jeff was diligent in caring for them. Copies of *Gentlemen's Quarterly, National Geographic,* and *Architectural Digest* lay neatly aligned on an oak table next to a wicker chair in the corner of the garden. "That's not like my room when I was his age," commented his father frequently. He would take off his finely framed wire glasses and clean them nervously when he got into this spiel about Jeff's bedroom. "He should have pictures of broads all over the walls, not that silly wallpaper." Marla preferred to emphasize Jeff's creativity. Jeff would be driven out of sight during these confrontations.

He jumped into bed and pulled the wine-colored comforter over his head. His eyes swelled; all he could think about was Gwen, and he wished things were different.

At 9:30 Saturday morning, the phone rang as if out of place. Marla ran breathlessly to it, thinking it was Judy, her die-hard confidante. She could hardly contain her words about Charley's behavior the night before.

She was surprised to hear a soft young voice nervously ask if Jeff was in. In a sing-song voice ripe with forced happiness, she almost screeched, "Jeff! It's a girl, and she sounds like an angel!"

Jeff seized the extension phone on the antique marble-topped de-milune table near his bed. "Hi," he said in a voice more reserved than usual.

"Hi, hi," said Gwen, still feeling shaky. "It's an outrageous day," she added with forced confidence, "and I thought we'd play some tennis." She was looking out at a summer scene yellow enough to be Currier & Ives, and she was still unable to fathom that she'd had the guts to phone him.

"Great," he said. "We could use the clay courts at the club. . . . Wow, that's super —is 12:30 okay? You rule!"

When he picked her up, Jeff looked as if he'd walked out of *GQ*, dressed in white shorts and a coordinating shirt, his legs tanned and per-fectly modeled. "God, you look great," said Gwen as she looked down at her denim cut-offs and old Keds. She wished she'd thought of some-thing other than tennis; at least, she told herself, it'd gotten them to-gether.

At the club she felt a coolness. She couldn't identify with the mem-bers and thought they were "pompous assholes," as she put it.

He didn't respond, just looked down. "My dad's showing up soon," he said. "You'd better get your sweater on—he's horny as hell lately."

Paul was more than pleased to meet Gwen. He winked in total ap-proval at his son. Jeff knew it was not his happiness that really mattered, but the usual show and what Paul's friends would think. He watched Gwen obediently put on her sweater and felt a momentary sensation that he had never experienced, but it left quickly.

Jeff's mother put her hand over his eyes from behind; she was playful around Jeff and felt an inner warmth and identification with him she could not feel with her daughter. She kissed him affectionately. "Um-um—you're absolutely the most delicious!"

Jeff wiped the kiss from his cheek, self-conscious about doing it (but he always had, especially when he had been much younger) and sorry that he'd done it just then, since his feelings toward his mother had changed in a positive way. He introduced her to Gwen, who could see where the boy got his looks. Marla had a glowing, clear olive complexion and lovely blue eyes. Her frame was delicate and animated by a pixie spirit. She stood five feet three inches tall.

"Would you guys join us for dinner at the club?" she asked.

The thought of being with Jeff at an evening function was over-whelmingly enticing to Gwen.

"Okay," Jeff said moodily. Gwen went into a state of panic trying to figure out how she would lay her hands on her only sensational evening dress.

They went back to Aunt Ruth's. Ruth and Jeff got along very well, which soothed Gwen in the midst of her dilemma. But Jeff started to fidget, and Gwen, worried that he was losing his patience, ran to the phone and whined breathlessly to her mother, as she always did when she knew she might not get the help she needed, "I *desperately* need my prom dress."

"Which one?" asked her mother, a woman of formidable composure. She was named Elizabeth. "We bought three, dear."

"Oh, you know, Mom. The one I *wore*—the white chintz strapless . . .oh, come on, Mom, the one you hated because it was too played down."

"How would you like me to get it to you?"

"Maybe Daddy will drive down?"

"Fred!" Elizabeth shouted, and the sound came out of Gwen's ear-piece and went right through her bones. "Can you drive me down to Ruth's? Gwen needs her dress."

"Are you *kidding?*" her husband barked back. "It's the only day I have to relax, and I'm watching the game. You can't be *serious.*"

After much muffled bickering, they agreed to drive the dress down to Gwen.

Gwen slammed the phone down and turned hunched over to Ruth. "They're unreal!" she exclaimed in a fury, but was relieved to know she would have her favorite dress.

Gwen and Jeff sat at a large round table set up to perfection, layered in mauve and raspberry, the centerpiece a lovely high crystal vase with unusual orchids and yellow roses in a halo of baby's breath. Gwen had never been surrounded by such elegance and beauty. Self-conscious since all eyes were on her, she looked stunning and dreadfully chic for someone her age. Her face and perfectly formed shoulders were lightly sun kissed and framed by soft, shiny auburn hair.

Jeff noted that she was a work of art but made no physical contact. This disappointed Gwen greatly. In her discomfort, she asked him if he cared to go out on the veranda. He gladly agreed. "I know you're feeling weird. They're jealous 'cause I just broke up with Maggie, their precious spoiled daughter, and they're giving you the evil eye."

It was dry and balmy on the brick veranda, and the stars shone bright on them. Gwen loved his concern and caring, having thought she didn't matter and this was proof enough. She wanted to hold him as she had before, but something stopped her. "I love you, Jeff," she said unflinchingly, coaxing him to hold her.

He looked at her with an awkward stare, his eyes fixed on her body, and he reached out very deliberately to touch her hair. He turned back toward his parents and their friends on the dance floor, his fists suddenly clenched as if in pain. He bit his lip as if his insides were going to blow up and called out, "*Why?* Why the fuck did this happen to *me?*" He seized Gwen and held her tightly, kissed her on her forehead, then abruptly pushed her away.

Gwen, breathless, gasped, "What's wrong? What is it?"

"I'm gay!" he shrieked. "*Got* it?"

She couldn't speak or pick her head up. Her eyes filled with tears as thick as blood. "What are you *talking* about? No! It's not *true*. The way you looked at me, you—you even got *excited* when I moved close to you! I-I felt it in my bones. You *flirted!* You're *crazy*—you're j-just trying to bust your parents. I know that happens when families get mixed up. You're not really going to hurt *them*, Jeff . It's not a punishment to anyone but you and me!"

He ran to the lot to sit in his car. Gwen ran after him recklessly. "No, no no *no!*" he screamed at her when she reached him, his voice almost feral, like a cornered animal's. It brought her to a sudden halt. "You're in denial like them," he added in exasperation. "I told them I thought I was gay when I was fifteen. They never heard me. 'Oh, Jeff,' she said, 'but you're sexy, so creative and softly macho.' And my father with his when-I-was-seventeen shit. . . . You're just like them, Gwen.

You can't accept it. I love you more than anything, but I can't be *with* you. Get it? Do you *get* it?' It's *sick*. I'm a perverted *sickie*, okay?"

"No. No, Jeff, it's not true—you're just going through something. I know it. I've been to therapy. I know a lot about these things, Jeff. I have problems too, and I think crazy things too."

Out of the blue, he started to kid around again. "These are the facts—nothing but the facts." He turned away, bent and drawn. She reached for him again, knowing she would never feel this way about anyone ever. He seemed exhausted and limp in her arms. "I'm going to UCLA," he murmured at last. "I'll be leaving in about two weeks." He rested his head on her breast and added in a barely audible whisper, "I'm sorry, so sorry. Always love me, Gwen. Always love me."

She left and called Bonnie just to talk to someone. She never mentioned anything to her about Jeff. Two weeks later, she told Bonnie she was going to the airport to see him off.

When she got there, she was like an explosive force. She banged her knee into a cart without feeling any pain, since she was too full of purpose to feel any. Approaching the counter, she saw Jeff lounging there. He seemed more frail than she remembered. She crept closer so he wouldn't notice her, in case she decided to back out. He was with a friend who had perfectly modeled short blond hair. They were both wearing fitted Lycra shirts with jeans. The friend looked a little older, very theatrical. Jeff was gazing at him with an obedient love, as if he were an older brother. Strangely enough, the passion she recognized when he was with her seemed to be absent.

She turned away, thinking only of how he had so easily touched her heart and so spontaneously evoked the laughter in her the way no one ever had. She turned as if spinning, light-headed. She entered the gift shop and picked up some gum and two magazines. One had an article on family problems and the adolescent male; the other magazine had a cover piece entitled "Life in the Nunnery." She left without paying, clutching the magazines to her chest, in a state of willed unconsciousness. She ran out to the observation deck in a daze and, to her surprise, saw Emily there, Jeff's sister, crying, out of control, "What did they do to you, Jeffy? What did they do? My little brother." She went on as if Jeff knew she was there. Gwen looked up in time to see the jet rise into the clouds. An enraged wind slapped her cheeks.

THE LEASE

THE HEAVY SUMMER storm wouldn't let up. Ali tossed about and wound up on his side of the bed.

He'd call her by their daughter Julie's name. He'd get lost when driving to the usual places. She was sure he was losing it and knew it had started with his heart attack. No one had believed it when it happened. He'd only been thirty-nine and the picture of health. He'd had this way of speaking ever since, became disconnected and uncommunicative. He was not the same man she married,

She thought of a sci-fi movie she had seen years before, about aliens who cloned people and substituted the imitation for the real person. Ali was beginning to think that was what had happened to Stu.

She finally dragged herself out of bed and turned toward the guest room with heavy steps. He was snoring loudly and mumbling in his sleep. They hadn't slept together for two years. As if driven by an outer force, she automatically placed her hand in the back pocket of his neatly folded jeans. She found his wallet and a legal-sized document that read LEASE.

She opened his wallet and found a new Platinum American Express card. She'd thought that was unusual, since all the credit cards had expired. He complained about his overdue bills. He told her that things were getting bad and that he couldn't get any credit.

She went down to the kitchen and shakily poured water into the teapot. She held the lease loosely, casually. Realizing he'd gotten more involved in real estate law since the heart attack, she assumed it was a client's document.

She glanced around the newly decorated kitchen, pleased with the results. The chairs surrounding the table were bleached rattan. The table was Spanish glass over a custom-made bamboo pedestal. The plants in the bay window had been carefully arranged, enormous and rare. The ambiance they created was jungle-like and sultry. Ali was happy, for the moment, to be a wife and mother, but there was an underlying emptiness and insecurity in her life. Sipping chamomile tea, she glanced at the lease and her heart started to palpitate. His name was on it—along with the name of a woman and her child. She started to shiver in shock and ran up to the guest room.

The lightning outside was illuminating the walls. He was sleeping and still mumbling.

She shouted, "Stu, wake up! What the hell is this?" She waved the crumpled document in front of his face. "You *bastard!* You're leaving us, aren't you? It says August 20 and it's July 18!"

Stu rubbed his eyes and looked at her blankly. He was hardly awake. "What are you talking about?"

Ali shoved the lease closer to his face, as if to smother him with it.

"Okay, okay," he said, yielding pathetically. "Look, I've been seeing this woman for kicks. That's it. She threatened to blab this thing we had all over town, if I didn't leave you."

Ali started to cry and then laugh hysterically.

"*Stop* that!" he screamed. "It's a farce. I-I just made up a lease to shut her up."

Ali doubled over at the edge of his bed and sobbed. "How are you going to get *out* of this—she'll *kill* you."

"Don't worry," he quickly assured her, acting more even. "Don't worry," he repeated in a paternal way. "I'll take care of it."

Suddenly, he became impatient. "Really, Ali, you must have suspected *something!*" He looked disapprovingly at the mirror above the dresser. "Well … I've been coming home in the middle of the *night* lately. What did you *think* I was doing?" He stared at her and sighed. "God, Ali, you never even mentioned a *thing* about that."

She put up her fists and cried out, "You *sleazebag*. You piece of *shit!* I'll *kill* you!"

She stormed out of the guest room. The thunder was getting louder and she hoped the noises might prevent the kids from hearing anything. She ran down the hallway to check on them.

Her daughter was sleeping peacefully. The room had just been decorated and the smell of fresh paint was still noticeable. The child was tightly clutching her favorite doll, Sasha. The fresh smells reminded Ali of the beginning of things—hardly the end. Her son seemed happy in his dreams and looked so grown up in his new campaign-style bunk bed—she wondered what would happen to them if the family fell apart. She knew she couldn't handle it all alone.

She stormed back to the guest room, bathrobe falling off her shoulders. Her nightgown was sheer, and he stared at her body as she ran in. She grabbed the blanket and covered herself. He was sitting still at the edge of the bed, eying her disgustedly. He got up and started walking around in circles.

"Are you sure that lease is just a gimmick?" she called out.

Stu continued to stare expressionlessly. "*Answer* me!" she cried out. "*Say* something!" She grabbed the lease from the night table and started out toward the kids' rooms.

He pulled her back. She looked him straight in the face. His eyes seemed like slits behind his glasses. He reminded her of an eel.

Without eye contact, he said evenly, "Just give me the lease!"

Ali was exasperated. "Why the hell do you care, if it's only a phony?"

He continued in a monotone, "Julie, I-I mean, Ali, hand it over to me." He forced her fingers open and pulled it out of her hands.

She ran down to the kitchen, grabbed the phone book and flew through the yellow pages. There was nothing under "Attorneys," so she quickly flipped through till she found the right section—*Lawyers–Family—Domestic*. Her hands were trembling, her cheeks damp and flushed, as she picked up the phone and then went to the utensil drawer. She pulled out the largest knife she could find. Her eyes were red slits. She ran up to Stu's room and rested on the landing before she entered.

The thought of divorce had brought back a childhood memory. Sally, her next-door neighbor, slim, attractive, a survivor of the Holocaust, had been going through a divorce. The desperate knock on the door had been hers. She had sat over coffee for hours and cried about her husband to Ali's mother, who said, when she left, "Poor thing. Like Auschwitz wasn't enough, she had to marry a bastard like him." Sally had smoked constantly and had spoken of Hilda, the other woman. She'd put out one cigarette and immediately light up another. The husband had fallen in love with Hilda in Accounts Payable—they'd sat next to each other at work. According to Sally, it had been inevitable, because Hilda was not only aggressive, but "very sexy."

Ali had not thought of her since then or of how her eyes watered up when Sally left, a broken woman. She had looked at her mother tearfully then and had sworn that, if it ever happened to her, she would kill her husband.

She heard her son mumble something in his sleep. It was an uncomfortable sound. "I'll be right in," she whispered. She knelt at the side of his bed and murmured, "Don't worry, sweetie—everything will be fine. Mommy is going to take charge. We'll be just fine without him." She rose to an exaggerated erectness and stared at her son wildly, as she closed the door, her narrowed eyes filling with tears, as they had when Sally left.

Stu was sleeping as if he had passed out. It was that kind of sleep. She stood above him with the phone in one hand and the knife in the other. She just stood there, frozen in place. The thunder stopped. She heard the steady sound of soft rain.

THE MAGENTA DRESS

MARA HAD just started to teach at Haverhill High. Having graduated early, she'd entered her new career at twenty. She looked younger than most of the students and her petite frame and whimsical manner added to her youthful aura.

The kids knew she was a novice, though, and took advantage. In addition, she had been assigned to teach the business students, the ones who were not college material. They were sensitive about it and had pegged her as a preppie at first sight.

She knew how they felt and tried to play down the college thing, tried to be caring and sweet, to be their friend—but once the mass attacks of paper wads started coming on a daily basis, she recognized the need for drastic change.

She stopped smiling and became strict and robotic, though she could never come off as mean, only standoffish. This approach didn't help much. Her classes reacted to her in a predictably negative fashion, turning to more devious measures, like sticking gum on her seat or singing "Ding, dong, the witch is dead," in the corridors, as they passed her classroom.

Soon, Mara could barely drive home at the end of the day. She started to plop into bed and skip dinner. She knew it was futile to speak to Paul, who was usually distant. He would listen to her complaints about school, but hardly react. So she soon stopped talking about her frustrations at Haverhill. It was truly a tough year—her first of marriage and of teaching.

This gnawed at her. She awoke refreshed, in a more positive frame of mind, but things started to drag her down shortly after lunch. Somehow, though, an extraordinary inner strength kept her going.

One day, Mara's sister gave her one of her old dresses—a magenta shirtwaist silk shantung, with covered buttons down the front. It was one of the few things the sister had ever given her, so it had special meaning—maybe a renewed closeness, as in their childhood. Their lives seemed so different. The sister had never worked or gone to college. She was a pro listener to radio talk shows and knew all the latest trivia.

Mara admired this type of thing, since she didn't have time for talk shows. She had just married and her life was busier than ever. She wished she could spend more time with Joan, who never initiated any ideas for things they could do together, preferring to be home with her husband and the radio. That was about all she needed. Mara wished her sister could be more lovable—more sociable.

She woke up feeling refreshed and as clean as the newly washed blackboard she had left behind the day before. She put on the magenta dress. It wasn't her style, but it was perfect for teaching.

Her classes went well. She entered her seventh period with more of a professional sense than ever. She was getting over the hump of her first year. It was a Business English and Typing class combined and the kids were typing away peacefully. But the eyes of one of the students looked rather glossy and strange. She checked the seating chart. Second row, fourth seat: Karen Solis.

She looked up, suddenly, only to see the girl flailing and jutting her limbs. She tried to get to her before she fell off the chair. Some of the kids were astounded. Others started to giggle. One of the boys, laughingly, said. "What *weirdos* in this school!" Ryan, the boy sitting next to him, retorted, "Look, four eyes, I'll punch you out if you don't shut up."

Mara reached Karen too late. Frustrated that no one had forewarned her that the girl was an epileptic, she remembered the tongue must be compressed when a seizure occurs. She ran back to the desk and found a flat stick. She laid the stick on the child's tongue in a loose, shaky way. As she was doing so, the adjustable typing chair slammed down on her finger. The pain was excruciating and her eyes watered up automatically.

Louise ran up to her and whispered, "God, Mrs. Stein, I think your finger is broken. I'll get the nurse." She dashed out of the room. Mara, meanwhile, was doing a great job of holding back her tears. She continued to keep a stiff upper lip. She tried do what she could for Karen. After using the stick, she continued wiping the girl's forehead until her jerking movements subsided. When Karen's eyes slowly opened, they looked soft and normal.

The students were out of the room by then. Mara hadn't heard the bell or even noticed them leave. Finally, the principal, Mr. Foreman, and the school nurse entered the classroom in a most apologetic manner. "I'm so sorry, Mrs. Stein," he said. "We should have noted that Karen is an epileptic. It was a terrible oversight." He bent down to help the girl without noticing Mara's swollen finger.

Mrs. Damon, the school nurse, however, looked right at Mara with her kind, soft blue eyes. "Mara, dear, your finger is a mess. I think it's fractured." She suggested that Mara leave to get an x-ray.

While Mara was in the Emergency Room, she noticed the forlorn faces on all the patients. This made her feel comfortable—as if she was where she belonged. A young woman with a baby sat next to her to share her sorrows. "You look like I feel," said the woman. "Missy is *constantly* getting low-grade fevers and sore throats. She'll probably need a tonsillectomy soon ... Jesus, what happened to your *finger?*"

Mara didn't want to talk about it and instead inquired about Missy. Five minutes later, though, she ran to the rest room and started to cry hysterically. It wasn't about her finger, really. It was just another thing, another bad sign.

When she got home, about two in the afternoon, she crawled into bed, as she usually did after school and sobbed her way into the evening. Paul was used to this and sometimes didn't even wake her for dinner. Suddenly, he sat up. "Mara, what the hell *happened* to you?" he gasped, noticing the cast on her finger.

"I broke it in school," she said flatly, without going into the details. She heard him asking questions, as she slipped into a deep sleep. When she awoke, she ran into the bathroom, extremely nauseated. She tried to throw up, but couldn't and, since she had missed her periods for a few months, she knew why. She had always wanted to be a mother, but lately had her doubts—the world no longer seemed a good place to her, at least not the type of world to raise a child in. She immediately became secretive about these thoughts. Paul was not aware of her pregnancy either.

When Mara had stayed out of school for a week, he decided to take a couple of days off as well. He was a law clerk for a white shoe firm on Wall Street. The senior partner was a "stiff old WASP," as Paul put it. He knew he didn't have half a chance of joining the firm, because he was Jewish and he couldn't wait for the clerkship to end.

Paul spent most of his time off skimming through law journals, searching for a position after his apprenticeship. He ran his hands through his hair and his eyebrows twitched sporadically. When Mara noticed the rough, scaly eczema on his hands, she was sure that the stress of clerking at Vanderwall and Smith had caused it. "I can't *take* it there anymore," Paul complained.

She also noticed that he had grayed some, since the clerkship. She thought it looked sophisticated and distinguished, even found his state of stress appealing, though she couldn't understand why. The misery of his clerkship had, it seemed, created a depth he'd previously lacked. She felt a pang of sympathy for him now, a feeling that she hadn't had for years. She thought she might break the news about her pregnancy, but she couldn't—not yet. Instead, she suggested they get out for the day, pleaded with him to stop going through the journals. The snow was falling lightly and the streets looked like mounds of clouds.

"Paul," she said emphatically, "let's go to Rockefeller Center—we haven't seen the tree or the ice skaters for ages. Come on, Paul, get dressed." It was two-thirty in the afternoon and he was still in his robe, hunched over the wrinkled periodicals.

"Why don't you go without me?" he moaned. She looked at his face closely, discovering a strange emptiness in his expression and decided, instead, to roast the frozen turkey Paul's mother had given them a while back. She thought that would cheer him up.

It did. He soon felt more comfortable being home and he seemed more relaxed than he had been for some time. They spoke of their first Thanksgiving together. "You've come a long way with your cooking," Paul commented, as he scratched his arms. He put his hand on her shoulders and bent down to kiss her head. They finished off the bottle of zinfandel, sat on the sofa and fell asleep on each other's shoulders. When Mara got up at three a.m., she was glad she had decided to cook.

The couple of days passed quickly. Soon, Mara was ready to return to school. Her energy was high the first day back at Haverhill. She spent more time on her makeup and hair. "Do I look okay?" she asked, holding in her stomach.

"You look fine," Paul said, as his eyes quickly passed over the slight bulge, thinking nothing of it. "Might have put on a few pounds being home, though" he chuckled.

The staff seemed warmer than usual. Mr. Thompson, the gym teacher, patted Mara on the back. "How you feelin', kid?" he asked with paternal concern.

"Fantastic," she replied enthusiastically.

"We got some great Famous Amos chips—why don't you go over there?" He pointed to the teachers' coffee klatch area. "Go ahead, put some meat on those bones!"

Mara turned toward the table, but a wave of nausea overcame her as she smelled the cookies. Instead, she went to the rest room and looked in the mirror. "God, I look *ghastly*," she muttered. Her face seemed so much thinner than it had a few months before. "I thought I was supposed to look *fatter*." When she spoke about her pregnancy to some teachers, though, she began to feel comforted. Otherwise, the day went smoothly. She hoped that Karen wouldn't have a seizure in seventh period and her prayer was answered. All ended on a peaceful note.

On the way home, however, she had an attack of chills and when she entered the apartment, she saw Paul sleeping, sitting up, on the couch. At 3:30 in the afternoon, he was still in his pajamas. He noticed the worried look on her face, when he finally awoke.

"I've got two more months at Vanderwall, Mar," he sighed. "I'm going back Wednesday, but I'm going to take it good and easy—they're never going to hire this Jew boy. Why break my ass?"

The TV was flickering on mute. Mara thought she would mention the pregnancy to cheer him up—but, maybe, she told herself, the added responsibility would do more harm than good. She smoothed out his moist, ruffled hair, kissed his forehead, and crawled into bed. She heard him call out about breaking news on CNN. "Mar, you've got to see this," he pleaded. She tried to get up, but her legs felt like lead pipes. His voice faded out as she fell into a deep sleep.

The next day was more rushed. Without a thought, she threw on the magenta dress. The day moved quickly. Before long, it was seventh period. About half an hour into class, Karen fell off her chair and into a seizure. Mara felt more in control—less panicky. The class was more helpful, too—more mature about the incident. As Karen came to, Mara squeezed her hand tightly, marking a new bond between them. She wished, though, that there was something she could do to help. She was going to phone her doctor at lunch time—she thought she'd heard of a new medication to help epileptics. Karen thanked her and described her background, mentioning that her mother was a single parent and wait-ress. Mara wasn't quite sure what to say. "She has so many problems," Karen went on. "It's hard for her to always think about me—she really does do the best she can," added the girl, in defense of her mother. She went on about her twin and how hard it was. "They think I have epilepsy because I was born last and lost oxygen—they're really not sure," she added, looking down.

When the class left without further disruption, Mara knew she'd come along way as a teacher. Karen came up to her then.

"Mrs. Stein, it would be great if you could visit and meet Mom."

Mara promised she would, one day soon. She slouched at her desk afterwards, suddenly realizing she was wearing the magenta dress and that she had worn it the last time Karen had had a seizure. "What a crazy coincidence," she muttered.

The phone rang early Thursday morning, the first full day back for Paul at Vanderwall and Smith. Mara dropped the coffee mug and ran to answer it.

"Hi, Mrs. Stein. Dr. Boyd here. Why don't you stop by after work—I'd like to talk to you about something." In a flash, Mara felt jittery. "Is it serious?" she asked, watching small bumps form on her pale arms. Dr. Boyd got off the phone quickly.

Mara felt distressed all day, before speeding to the doctor's office, having asked one of the teachers to cover her last period. She couldn't wait any longer. The doctor was cool and confident, a short man with a cherubic face. He looked at Mara contemplatively and said, "Mrs. Stein, your last blood test was positive for extreme anemia. We checked again and we believe you have a mild type of leukemia. We think we can control it, but you . . .but you must terminate your pregnancy."

Mara couldn't move—couldn't say anything—for a time. "Is there any chance I could still have the baby?" she begged. She studied the roundness of her stomach, as if she were looking through it. She began to visualize the child, feature by feature. After realizing it was not a possibility, Mara asked if she could have the abortion ASAP. She did not want to feel more attached to the child. Dr. Boyd agreed. She wanted to call Paul, but she'd withheld too much and knew she couldn't tell him now. She couldn't understand why she'd undertaken her burdens alone.

She got to Bayville Hospital by six a.m. A Dr. Heller was going to do the procedure. She was worried about it because she'd never met him.

He mentioned it had been a girl. "Caitlin!" Mara shouted. "Oh, no, my little Caitlin!" She began to sob. She had only seen him draw a small plastic mask over her face. It had been over before she realized it was happening.

She dressed quickly, feeling a great deal of blood on the sanitary pad. It was seeping through. She sighed, drawing a long breath, grabbed some pads from the table and left against the doctor's orders. She drove around in circles, refusing to go home. She wound up at a mall. It was a few weeks before Christmas and the place was festive and crowded. When she started to feel weak, she remembered that Karen lived nearby and phoned to ask if she could stop over. Karen was thrilled.

The house was old and unkempt, the teal blue paint peeling. It reminded Mara of the homes she'd passed in the back woods of the south, on the way to Florida. Karen's mother—a tall woman, with broad shoulders and long, brown, straggly hair—opened the door. She was very clearly checking her out. "Glad you could visit." She smiled sincerely and thanked Mara for being kind to Karen, who ran out and hugged her. "We really appreciate your concern," Mrs. Solis added softly, as she fried Spam for dinner. Mara joined them. The simplicity and humbleness of

Karen's home soothed her, and she was glad she had visited.

"You look white," said Mrs. Solis.

Mara lay down on the sofa, until she regained her strength. Before she left, she went out to the car to get a box of old clothes she'd been saving for Karen. Karen opened the box and tossed the clothes over the couch. She picked up Mara's magenta dress and looked at her. "Gee, Mrs. Stein," she said, "I went *off* when you wore this dress."

"What was it about it?" Mara asked, curiously.

"I don't know. It was just something bloody, something … pinky."

Feeling weak, Mara repeated the words, "Something bloody, something pinky," and shuddered.

She pushed hard to get up and leave the warm home, forced herself out the door. As she made her way to the car, she pulled her jacket closed. She'd never had the patience to button her coats. The air was hazy, moist—unusual for the beginning of December. She noticed Karen at the smudged window. She was waving slowly, as if in a slow-motion film. Mara noticed the girl's dimples for the first time and wondered if Caitlin might have had dimples, too.

She found Paul sitting on the sofa, struggling to light his cigarette. His hands were unsteady and the matches kept going out. The odor of the dead butts in the ashtray was still strong. The sunshine had gradually thinned out and its faint glow was casting a shadow over the dull Formica counters in the kitchen.

When Paul finally lit his cigarette, he inhaled deeply. He seemed satisfied for the moment. She looked down at him. He seemed more depressed than ever, his hair sticking out in soft curls, his face unshaven. The circles above his prominent cheekbones were deep and dark.

Mara sat next to him and rested her head on his chest. She wished she could tell him everything—let it all out, but this was not the time. She knew he probably couldn't feel anything right now. She listened to his quick heartbeats that sounded like the rapid little beats of the baby's heart and touched her still-swollen stomach. For a brief moment, she even thought she felt the baby; that maybe the procedure had failed or had never taken place. She pressed hard over there for a time, but felt nothing. "Tell me, Paul, how do you feel?" she asked sympathetically.

He closed his eyes tight, without answering. The room was growing darker. The residual holiday lights broke through the dimness. She covered her face and saw only red and pink prisms. "Caitlin was doing so well," she muttered under her breath.

Paul sat, hardly moving, except to raise the volume on the TV and squint uncomfortably. He finally hit the mute button. The room fell silent, but for Mara's voice, inaudible to Paul. His eyes were blank. He could hear nothing. Mara was sure—quite sure—of this.

YOUR SHOW OF SHOWS

Three weeks after Dad's cousin Maxie gave my family a TV (we were the first family in Williamsburg, Brooklyn, to get one), the spare room, no longer a place for solace, had become a nightly hangout. That little wooden box with the five-inch screen changed everything that year. At school all I did or thought of was related to the new TV.

I would rush directly home at day's end to sit on the high-rise couch and catch Kate Smith singing "When the Moon Comes over the Mountain." In a few months I was starting to look like her, since the ritual included devouring an entire box of Mallowmars-the ones that had jelly between the marshmallow and chocolate. It was the only time I could be alone with the new TV.

The neighbors started hauling in about 7:30 p.m., just in time for dessert. My dad rushed around borrowing chairs while my mom slaved over the old oven, baking *rugalach* and cream cheese cookies. I was just thankful that my sister and I were able to catch Laurel and Hardy without the fuss, especially since our appreciation of their humor was about all we had in common.

I was soon playing with my friends less often, fearful of missing a favorite program. It was almost comforting not to care if my best friend, Rozzie, was playing dolls without me, or if I was just an extra on the punch ball team. Sitting safely on the high-rise was far better than losing at stoop.

Willie and Nettie came in time for Milton Berle. My father called Nettie "the Queen." My mother complained, "Does she think this is a Broadway show? She's so *fahrputzed!*"

"I love your outfit," I'd say.

I was in awe of her appearance, and wished I could look as stunning.

Her makeup was perfect. Her lips were bright red, as was her shiny nail polish. Her shoes always matched her dress, and the thing I loved the most were her false eyelashes and long black cigarette holder. Her immature ways appealed to me. I just wanted to be her friend. She never said my name. "Little girl," she ordered, "can you be a sweetie and get me some ginger ale with just a tad of ice?" or "Little girl, be a dear and ask your mother to get me a cushion?"

When Willie turned to her, she said, "Don't give me that look, Willie. You know how bad my hemorrhoids have been acting up." Willie had little facial hair. He was considerably shorter than Nettie. He would look up to her when he spoke and acted more like her butler than her husband. It was a strange relationship based on unwavering loyalty.

I didn't mind running around for her, because she was the closest thing to a star I knew. I didn't grasp my mom's dedication toward her. She tried to explain: "Delly, the poor thing never had children—that's why she's that way." There seemed to be a love-hate thing going on between the two. My mother was used to the martyr role as well. Sometimes, Willie got so livid that he would actually speak up to Nettie: "Don't be such a *nudnik*—what nerve." Nettie's face turned crimson, and she seemed to hold her breath for a time like a little kid.

Abe and Sadie usually arrived after Willie and Nettie. Abe, stiff-shouldered and somewhat arrogant, was the best-built guy in the neighborhood. My mom thought Nettie had a thing for him. He'd check himself out every time he passed the mirror in the hallway.

Short, stocky Sadie naturally despised Nettie and always sat away from her, on the opposite end of the spare room. Whenever Nettie started her little girl routine, Sadie glared at her and took off to the kitchen to dump her stuff on my mom. "She thinks she's so high-falutin', that hag. No wonder poor Melvin couldn't live with her."

Melvin had been Nettie's first husband. Rumor had it that she'd gotten an annulment because he came too fast and couldn't have normal sex. "What a terrible sickness," my mother would lament with a sad nod. I didn't get why she thought it was such an affliction, since she was always telling her friends that sex was no big deal—"Believe me, I could take it or leave it."

Sadie was my mother's dearest friend, so naturally there was a close bond. She'd hold my chin strongly to the point when it actually hurt. "What a *punim*," she'd say to Abe, who smiled faintly and answered with a grunt. I was amazed when he spoke to Nettie because of his hidden abilities to articulate.

There was usually a squabble about what to watch. They only agreed on the Milton Berle Show.

Jakie, my aunt Harriet's estranged husband, often showed up at some point. My father didn't like his limp, wet handshakes and lack of eye contact. But, even at my age, I couldn't blame the guy—he knew everyone hated his guts, but since he was so terribly lonely, he'd show up anyway. I figured that, since he looked like a Jewish Gordon MacCrae, it was hard for anyone to trust him—especially Harriet, who was so plain in comparison.

The thing Harriet had on him was the Williamsburg version of *Gaslight*. Harriet said he was writing weird notes and sticking them on the bell downstairs. In short, he had tried to drive her insane. "What did the notes say?" my mom asked. Harriet, though, adopted a strange look and never really provided anything specific. She had a tumor in her nose that was spreading to her brain, so there was always an underlying credibility issue about her stories. I guessed that was the only reason they let Jakie in the house. I was definitely on Harriet's side, and when Jakie got comfortable enough to focus on the TV, I'd stand in front of the screen and block it with my arms spread out. Poor Jakie stared at me patiently and never told my folks or yelled at me. But I thought he might be a child molester, too, so I moved away from the screen, sticking my tongue out and scrinching my eyes.

By the time my mother served dessert—saturated with perspiration and burns on her hand from the oven, since she didn't believe in potholders—there was usually something going on. Sometimes it was Harriet cursing out Jakie, but mostly it was a conflict between Nettie and Sadie.

The last TV night got physical. Nettie and Sadie, for some reason, wound up sitting next to each other on the high-rise. "Oh, no," my dad called out, his face and palms moist. "Nettie and Sadie are having *some fight*."

Mom entered the spare room with a ball of new dough in her hands, only to find Nettie and Sadie kicking at each other while sitting down.

Finally Willie spoke up, this time in defense of Nettie. "She a classless slob," he declared, referring to Sadie.

At this casting of the gauntlet, Abe dragged him to the bathroom and tried to heave him into the bathtub. They both fell heavily on the hard tile floor. Willie grabbed Abe by the collar and began to sock his head. Nettie cried out, "For God's sake! *Stop* them!" Sadie brushed by Nettie as she charged into the bathroom.

Willie, pulling himself up from the floor, was groping for words. He pushed his fingers through his hair and straightened his clothes. My father turned to Abe. "You bastard," he said, "how could you do this in my home?' Abe's face turned crimson. He picked up my mother's favorite Lenox vase and flung it at the TV screen as Trigger was neighing. He grabbed Sadie's arm, dashed toward the door, and looked back at my father in disgust, as though it was his fault.

Willie and Nettie followed in a more civil and dignified manner, and even offered to pay for another TV. Strangely enough, they seemed to be annoyed at my *parents*. I didn't get that then, and haven't since.

As war unites, this incident created a temporary union between Harriet and Jakie. Yes, they had acted like true allies in the battle, and they started to communicate. Jakie was unable to make direct eye contact with her, though. "What animals!" declared Harriet.

Jakie nodded affirmatively.

But after a short time, he started to feel uncomfortable about communicating with Harriet. "Rita probably needs some help," he suggested. "Why don't you go in there and help her?"

Harriet looked a little disappointed. I guess she still hoped that things might get better between them. Jakie left; it was the last time she, or anybody else, ever saw him. My father slumped on the high-rise, looking forlorn, and leaned against the crimson velvet throw pillow that Nettie always used. It still smelled of her tea rose perfume. "Rita, get in here!" he called out in a panic. "Everyone's *gone*—stop *baking*, already!"

My mom entered the room with flushed cheeks, wiped the moist residual dough on her apron, and proceeded to pick up the shattered particles of the screen, sighing and tsking the whole time.

I tried to sleep, tossed my head around on the pillow. My dad came in and sat on the foot of my bed. "Don't worry," he assured me, "Maxie will get us another TV.

"When?" I whimpered. "Howdy Doody is on tomorrow, and it's *Peanut Gallery* Day!"

He was silent for a while, encouraging me to call Rozzie. "You really should start playing with your friends again," he suggested with some emphasis in his voice.

I thought of what might happen after school the next day. No Kate Smith or Laurel and Hardy with my big sister—I knew I'd go back to being an extra in punch ball. I knew that Doris had become Rozzie's best friend by then. I wandered into the kitchen.

My mother turned toward me as she scraped the oven walls. "Tell me, Delly, what am I going to do with all the *rugalach*? I guess I'll have to freeze them." Her eyes were tired and watery. I knew she was going to miss all the company. She loved being a hostess, loved serving her friends—these were the things that made her happy. She bent down to line the cleaned linoleum with newspapers. "At least the kitchen will stay clean now," she concluded, and let out a long, deep breath of relief.

AMY'S PLIGHT

Amy had just turned fifty-three when she met Ralph. She knew it would probably be the last time she would find a man with whom to share her life. It was the first time that she had even considered dating again since her ghastly divorce from Howard.

Howard, a divorce attorney himself, had destroyed her during the divorce proceedings. He had known all the divorce court judges in the county. She hadn't had the money to retain one of the better lawyers. There was no chance to come out ahead. She lost everything: her home, her kids, and especially her self-respect.

Her pathetic state frightened both her eleven-year-old son and fifteen-year-old daughter. Their warmth and caring disappeared with the determination of the court case. Amy was a lost soul, devastated and depressed. She had no family to speak of.

There was no one to offer emotional support. She was homeless, jobless, childless, and lived out of her ten-year-old Ford Mustang. The court system had simply tossed her into the armpits of life. She didn't think she'd ever be able to function again.

Somehow, an inner strength kicked in at a time when it was sorely needed. Amy eventually edged her way back into society. She found a job, furnished a small apartment with hand-me-downs, and began the painful task of reestablishing relationships with her children.

She met Ralph at a singles function. He appeared pleasant. He was a CPA, from a similar background, and about the right age. He had good sense of humor and seemed quite caring.

They dated for several months. One time during that period, Amy and Ralph were at the market. She was about to purchase milk, juice, and cereal. Most of the men she dated had insisted on paying for such inconsequential items. She noticed Ralph standing firmly, however, arms folded across his chest, without a hint of approaching the cashier. He never offered to help her pay for the groceries. Of course, it crossed her mind that this might not be a good sign. But she had been through so much that she shrugged it off. She was not about to be picky at that point in her life. Ralph was caring in other ways, and good company.

She thought she was lucky to have met a guy who was educated, the same religion, about the same age—she couldn't have expected to do better.

She and Ralph agreed to live together. He bought a lovely co-op in an upscale area.

After many grueling court battles, Amy was finally awarded a restorative alimony. Ralph thought it would be appropriate to use the money to pay the maintenance on the co-op. Amy was so happy to have found someone she could love and trust, so thrilled to be living in a decent place again, she didn't hesitate to pay the maintenance, though Ralph refused to allow her any ownership of the co-op. Even without legal ownership, she happily used her alimony to renovate the apartment. Amy was sure it would all work out. She just wanted to live a good life, regardless of the shaky situation. After all, Ralph was a nice guy, albeit with some obvious problems. But who's perfect?

GOES AROUND

Gail seemed melancholy for days. Most of her colleagues thought she might be heading toward a deep depression. She had to push herself to do the usual things.

Although she loved teaching on a college level, especially after having worked in a high school for so many years, she procrastinated in getting to class each day and got ready in a state of bewilderment—though she Owed It to Her Students, she told herself.

She decided to take off on Mondays. It was something she had to do; she needed time alone. She'd have a late breakfast at a French bakery.

Gail enjoyed sitting on a window stool, watching everyone intently rushing by.

One Monday, she noticed a man on the sidewalk. He wore camouflage khakis and a faded blue shirt. He was sitting on a small chair, strumming Clapton songs on his guitar. His hair was braided and tied with a calico scarf around his forehead. His look emphasized strong cheekbones and white teeth. Everyone who passed by stopped to listen. They'd throw some change in a cup near the chair. Gail gazed at his face. She knew him—yes, she was sure of that—but she couldn't remember the circumstances of how they met.

She couldn't comprehend why he didn't pay attention to the money in his cup.

He paused just long enough to tune the strings. She knew he needed the money, but he seemed more concerned about adjusting the old wooden guitar. She finished her coffee and left the bakery. As he started to wrap up his belongings, she moved closer and put a dollar in the cup. Her glasses were low down on her nose; she peered at him over the black-wired frames. When he smiled at her, she felt assured that the mystery would end. But he smiled at everyone the same way. He finally counted the money in the cup and slapped his thigh in joy. He gathered up his blanket and chair, shifted the guitar onto his back and strolled off with a light, cheerful gait.

Gail quickly caught up to him. "Sir?" she called out. "Sir?" she said again, more emphatically. "Do you recognize me? I know we've met."

He smiled at her warmly without saying anything for a time, just shifted his weight to alleviate the heaviness of the chair and instrument. He looked at her as if he knew her thoughts.

She invited him to join her for lunch. He agreed. They went to an outdoor café down the street. He fidgeted, yet responded to her in a paternal way. He ordered a corn muffin and black coffee, gobbled up the muffin, and offered to pay for the food.

She insisted that she would, so he left a tip. They sat around for a while, making small talk, until an artist displayed his paintings on a fence near the restaurant.

When Gail turned toward him, the guitarist commented about the work of the artist, who painted women mostly—in dressing rooms, cabarets, parks, and boudoirs. "That young man has great potential," he said as he studied the paintings. He went on about the artist's style and technique. He spotted areas where mistakes had been covered up. Gail was impressed and pleased with his assessment.

He picked up some residual muffin crumbs with his right pinky. As he licked them off, Gail noticed that a section of his finger under the dark, crusted nail, that had been sliced off. This sparked her memory. It was coming back.

He noticed her inquisitive look and turned toward the door.

"I'm Gail," she said assuringly, and reached out to shake his hand. "And your name is. . . ?"

He smiled, "Matt, but my family likes to call me Matthew."

The name didn't sound familiar. All she could recall was addressing him as "sir."

He reached into his jean pocket and took out a small leather book. He fumbled through the parchment-like pages quickly, as if desperate to find a name. "Oh, yes, here it is," he whispered.

"Sir—I mean, Matthew—is there someone you have to meet now?"

"No, miss, not right now," he replied politely. He glanced at a man in the crowd, then squeezed Gail's hand tightly. Suddenly, he dashed out. "I'll be around, sweet Gail, I sure as heck will." He melded into the crowd.

Nursing her latte, she recalled a party in the Berkshires a few years back.

She'd recently been divorced then and felt it important to start socializing. Yet she had had negative feelings about going so far from home to her cousin's party. The cousin wasn't the kindest person she'd ever met, and she feared unnecessary remarks, but decided in the end to make the trip after talking to her closest friend, Louise. Louise was an attractive woman whose style Gail envied. She had silken, wavy chestnut hair, a tall thin frame, and piercing green eyes.

Jason, Gail's son, suggested that Louise had the Midas touch. She was a successful stockbroker and on her third marriage to a man named Michael, every woman's dream. He was smart, handsome, generous, and warm.

"Come on, honey," Louise told Gail. "It's gorgeous in the Berkshires. You really have to meet new people You can't hang out with your fuddy-duddy married friends forever."

Gail had phoned Samantha, her daughter, to let her know she'd be staying overnight.   Samantha had not been herself since the divorce. Gail didn't know if she should leave her alone. "I really don't want to go, Sam," she'd said. Samantha had assured her that she would stay at her friend Julie's house.

That was comforting, since they, Julie and Sam, had been friends since elementary school. Gail adored Julie's parents. The expression on Gail's face changed from its sullen pallor to a rosy-cheeked glow. "I love you, Mom," Samantha had said. "Have an amazing time!"

Gail had excitedly gathered her things together, placed dress after dress in front of her, scrutinized each one in the full-length mirror, her wrinkled forehead softening when she found the right one, and thrown cosmetics and toiletries into an overnight case. It had been years since she packed, and she felt that she was going on an exotic vacation.

She slipped into a royal blue sheath with gray pearls and matching earrings, took off her glued-on Ugg boots, and grabbed her favorite black suede shoes (the ones with high heels and open toes). After straightening up the house (just in case Sam's friends decided to party there), she glanced at the stairwell for no particular reason, checked herself out in the hallway mirror, and trotted to her chipped and rusted gray mini-wagon.

Gail was exhausted by the time she reached Lainey's place. She would have fallen asleep at the wheel if she hadn't been listening to a Kabbalah tape about the fate of the soul after death.

Her cousin was standing at the front door with her fleshy hands on her full hips. "Better late than never," she snapped.

Lainey had resented Gail for years—Gail, the star of the family, had married well, raised two beautiful children, and lived in a lovely home in an upscale suburb. Lainey had never married. She was a bank teller. The family consensus was that she "had no *mazel*."

"Gail, what the hell is this?" She was looking at Gail's open-toe shoes. "Where did you think you were going? This is Berkshires, and it's winter, hell*o-ooo-ooo*? And your car is blocking mine!"

Gail thought about going back home. "Lainey, give me a minute to settle in before you attack me, will you?"

Lainey shook her head and led her into the quaint cottage. It smelled musky.

The couch and upholstered chairs were heavily quilted. "Here she is, everyone. She made it, " Lainey sneered. She was wearing a short, clingy pleated skirt and a ruffled blouse. The blouse accented her round face and small, mean hazel eyes. As she walked, she kept pulling at the skirt. No wonder she never met anyone, Gail thought. She had no clue how to pull herself together.

Gail managed to keep her distance. After a few glasses of wine, she mingled with the other guests. She met a man who was personable. She hoped she wasn't intruding on Lainey's turf.

Lainey would sweep by every so often and intentionally squint at Gail, who after a while felt uncomfortable and moved on. Lainey kept on doing it.

After a couple of hours, Gail went into the empty kitchen and eyed the sloppy joes and desserts. She licked the whipped cream from the endless row of cakes. It was her idea of payback. She was thrilled to disturb the perfectly parabolic whipped peaks.

She had long realized the consequences of such encounters with Lainey—scenes created in public. They had visited the Guggenheim Museum the previous winter. Gail had chosen holiday greeting cards. "Which box do you like?" she had asked.

Lainey had taken the box she didn't approve of, thrown it into the air, and shouted, "Why the hell can't you make a friggin' decision on your own?"

I should have stuck with my gut reaction, Gail thought. There were always the beginnings of grief when they were together. She went to the bathroom and applied more lipstick and blush. She was fine, and that, she told herself, would trump her cousin's behavior. She despised the dated lace curtains and frilly knickknacks in every corner. That's so Lainey, she concluded—a tight-lipped, harried old maid.

Suddenly, there was a loud knock on the door. "What the hell are you doing in the bathroom? There's a line out here."

Gail opened the bathroom door and encountered Lainey's enraged, glossy eyes. She seemed to soften a bit when Gail edged out. "Look, my little cousin, you came all the way from Jersey. Why would you want to sit in the john? Get out there and meet my friends.

The crowd was on line at the buffet table. Gail chatted with those around her. Her spirit was soon coming back. She shone in her black velvet dress, her gray eyes filled with delight.

Gail's cell phone rang. She went into the hallway, since the reception was muffled. "Is this Mrs. Rosen?" asked a voice she didn't recognize.

"Yes, yes," she replied.

"Mrs. Rosen, I have some bad news."

She'd heard these words before. It was always the same—a strange, somber voice: "Bad news?"

"Your daughter is in the hospital."

Could this be an infuriating trick, she wondered, to obliterate her momentary pleasure? "Is she . . . is she . . . ?" She couldn't finish the sentence. "Oh, no, it can't be! Dear God!"

"Your daughter is alive, Mrs. Rosen," said the man in a more controlled manner. "But she's in intensive care."

"Oh, no! God, please don't!" she howled.

"It was a car accident," said the somber voice. She lied, thought Gail with a start. She said she was going to Julie's house. "She was on her way to the city," said the man, this time in a more indifferent way.

"Lainey!" shouted Gail. "Sam's been in a car accident! She's in the hospital!"

The gathering came to a screeching halt. She'd hoped someone would offer to drive her back. No one did. She flew out, high heels digging into the icy mud. "Why are you so irresponsible?" wailed Lainey after her. She turned to her concerned guests. "Things like this always happen to her," she snapped and looked out the living room window.

Later, in the kitchen, Lainey was shocked to see the dessert tray with the ruined whipped cream on all the lovely cakes.

Gail ran to the car. The car keys were digging into the palm of her hand. The lock was frozen, so she chipped at it with the keys. She looked back toward the living room window. "Where is everyone?" she muttered. She strained to see if anyone was in the living room. There was a steady white light, but the room was empty. It seemed as if everyone had crawled into a corner. "Where are they hiding?" She was dazed with anger. Perhaps they were in the kitchen in awe of the puddles of whipped cream over the cakes.

She feverishly pushed the keys into the car door lock. She pressed her lips together. She was wasting time, she thought. The fog hung over the mounds of snow.

She hunched over to get closer to the windshield. The thick moisture blurred her view. She passed unfamiliar houses and buildings. Finally, there were signs to the highway. This was comforting. Just the thought of getting closer to the hospital alleviated this nightmare somewhat.

The Palisade Interstate was flooded with state troopers who issued a lot of tickets.

Gail noticed a friend's old cigarette butt in the ashtray. She grabbed it and lit up. This was the first time she'd smoked in over ten years. The strong stench of the used butt created a strange energy. She sped onto the highway. She knew she'd be stopped. The car raced at eighty five miles per hour.

The red and yellow flashing lights were blinding. She ran her fingers through her hair as she broke into a cold sweat. "Holy God, this can't be," she wept, as if it was an unexpected event. Maybe I just need to talk to someone, even if it means getting a ticket.

The state trooper was tall and broad-shouldered. Gail could not look up when he tapped on the window. When she saw his handsome face, it was calming. How could anyone who looked like that be mean, she thought.

"Ma'am, license and registration, please." He spoke like a robot. He looked at her without expression.

"Officer, my daughter is in the hospital. She's in ICU— I don't have the time for you to write out a ticket!" she pleaded.

He studied her drained face. His flashlight turned toward the back of the car. The door of the police car was ajar, and he slid in.

She saw him speaking as he glared at a screen above the dashboard. He slowly opened his car door to walk back to Gail. He firmly placed the license and registration in her hand. "You have to take it easy from here on," he uttered softly, as if whispering. He straightened his heavy beige jacket. She read his name: *Paul Moran*. She'd had a classmate with that last name. He, too, was a good guy, she recalled.

"Well, good luck! Hope your daughter is okay," he said with concern.

Gail breathed in deeply and methodically placed the keys in the ignition. She looked in the rear view mirror. The officer had left. She knew the lucky break was a good sign. Maybe it symbolized a positive change. She drove on intently, knowing her daughter would be all right.

When she arrived at the hospital a nurse directed her to the ICU floor. As she entered the dismal room, a male nurse approached her. He appeared out of nowhere.

He was wearing loose green pants and a matching shirt, and was dark skinned. "Your daughter is no longer here," he said cheerfully. He sounded Jamaican. Gail followed him to her daughter's bedside. Gail breathlessly ran toward Sam.

"Mom, where were you? It took forever for you to get here! This is Matt." Sam turned toward him with a loving grin. "They couldn't get me up. He spoke to me and didn't stop. I didn't know what he was saying, but whatever he said woke me up. No one else could do it, no one," repeated Sam.

"Yes, there was a change in her luck," Gail muttered. Sam's words were clear as a bell. Matt held Sam's hand and squeezed it. She looked at him adoringly. Gail had never seen Sam appear so angelic. Matt's eyes were piercing yet soft and kind as he glanced toward her. He took a Bible from the nightstand and placed it in his back pocket. It was then that Gail noticed his damaged finger and crusted, curved fingernail.

"Sir, is there anything you need—anything I can do for you?" She was overwhelmed and didn't know what to say or do. She just knew Matt was not a run-of-the-mill nurse. He patted Gail on the shoulder, as they sat together watching Sam. She was resting peacefully.

Matt had stayed till early morning. He had placed his arm around Sam's shoulder, comforting her throughout the night. He was the only one there for her.

There was no one else.

"Sir," Gail uttered automatically, out of respect, "when will we see you again?"

He knew Gail and Sam needed someone, but it couldn't be him.

"I goes around," he replied with a West Indies accent. He studied Gail's lost gaze. "But, you and Sam will always be a part of me."

Gail went back to the French Café. She sat at the window in a reflective manner. Her eyes followed Matt as he walked through the crowd. He approached a frail man.

The man looked underfed and sickly. He patted the man on his shoulder and held out his hand, as he had done to Gail. Gail felt the strong healing vibes. He quickly turned back toward Gail and nodded. She could hear his words again and again, "I goes around."

Gail stretched her neck toward the window and smiled, hoping he would see her. She knew she was out of sight. Her spirit lifted, knowing she would likely see him sometime again, down the road.

KNOCKOUT

Marnie was an exquisite woman. She appeared to be in her early twenties, tall and slim, like the girl from Ipanema. Her lightly tanned and flawless complexion drew attention to her blue-green eyes. She was the starlight of the gym. This led to envy and unnecessary gossip.

I'd talk to her in the locker room from time to time. She was humble and warm. I thought this unusual for someone like her. Most good-looking women I'd known had been aloof and terribly self-centered. I thought she might let me in on some beauty secrets, some special diet or the name of a good dermatologist. I had just gone through a difficult time and needed to pull myself together. She seemed to be open and helpful, willing to be a friend.

"You know, a few extra pounds wouldn't hurt you," she said. It was clear that I had not been taking care of myself. It was most upsetting standing next to her in front of the mirror and seeing my dull complexion and unkempt look. It would be a good thing to hang out with her, I thought. We made an appointment for lunch the next day.

I sat in the corner booth of the Chinese restaurant near the gym. She got there twenty minutes later. She was wearing jeans and a short leather jacket.

All heads turned as she made her grand entrance. Her beige silk blouse draped softly over her narrow hips. "You look great," I said.

She eyed my pilled orange crew neck and sighed before she sat down, as if she were about to begin a lecture. "I know that you're having a hard time, don't give into it," she advised. "I've had my share of grief and, in the end, it was a blessing." I wondered what she'd been through. She appeared to be leading a charmed life.

She spoke about her life in Argentina. Her voice was deep and sultry. It didn't go with her look, really. "How lucky not to have lived your entire life in Bergen County," I said.

"I hated Argentina," she went on. "Too many has-been Nazis and over done women with gaudy jewelry." She tilted her head, "I feel free and alive here—and it's close to the city." She stared me down before she sipped her tea. "Why do you always have that needy look?" she asked assertively.

"Look, I'm just getting back to myself—I wish you hadn't said that about looking needy."

She smiled. "Come on, don't be so sensitive. If you were a total loss, I wouldn't have said anything. It's not that you appear pathetic, just helpless and trapped."

I tried to change the subject. She was exotic and different, and I knew she had a curious past. She felt my need for further conversation and company, so she invited me to her apartment. She lived in a lovely condo that was stark white except for a crimson accent wall. There were some fine paintings, mostly abstract, except for an Andy Warhol print of Marilyn Monroe. There were photographs of her family on the sill, and a crinkled unframed photo of her father. The resemblance was amazing. He was a handsome man with fine features, his facial structure was strong with high cheekbones. "Women usually look like their dads," I said. She quickly showed me a photo of her mother and younger brother. The former was petite and plain, with dark brown hair tied back in a long braid. Marnie's brother resembled her.

Marnie turned to me in support of my theory. "I guess you're right. Luis looks like my mom." When she picked up the photo of her mother and brother, I had noticed her unusually long fingers ad broad hands. She felt self-conscious when she saw me do so and said, "I know they look like I'm a fullback."

"Do you have a picture of yourself somewhere?" I asked in an overly inquisitive way.

She looked down, and for an instant her attention was diverted. "There I am," she said with a forced excitement. It was a photo of her at a dance recital. She was dead center and stunning.

I spotted Marnie in the noisy, brightly lit gym several weeks later. She was sluggish and hunched over. Usually, she would run as gracefully as a deer. When I walked in, she glanced at me with watery eyes. The usual police activity distracted me. More often than not, there was an argument regarding time spent on a machine. When the gym was crowded and the tension was strong, there was an increased odor of sweat.

I recalled several months back, when an overworked gym rat approached me. He'd demanded that I get off the elliptical. I had paused and looked at him intently but continued to work out. He'd backed down somewhat.

"Okay, lady, how much longer will you be?"

"I guess about fifteen minutes," I had replied meekly.

"You've been hoarding the machine, so get the hell off, and *now!*" He'd clenched his fists toward my face. I'd had no choice but to report the incident. When I approached the front desk, the manager had been on the phone with other complaints.

"Look," he had groaned, "these guys are not rocket scientists, the fees are a bargain, so just grin and bear it."

I had.

Marnie avoided these altercations like the plague. If someone even hinted at, or seemed annoyed regarding, her time on a machine, she'd quickly get off.

She eventually approached me. "What's going on?" I asked her. "You look like the weight of the world is on your back. "

She nodded and commented only on the lack of modesty in the women's locker room. "They really take their time about getting clothes on." Marnie always changed in the little space behind the curtain.

I dressed as fast as possible. We went to the local diner for lunch. It was dark, sleazy, and needed renovation. We shared a Caesar salad, which I nervously devoured. She tugged at her bra often. It seemed as if it was a foreign object, as if she wanted to rip it off.

From the look on her, I sensed I was going to hear a sad story. I was harboring my own grief, though, and didn't think I could handle hers.

Suddenly, her mood changed. She looked at me with smiling eyes.

I was wearing a replica of her short leather jacket and newly purchased designer jeans.

"Well, look at you!" she said proudly, pleased that I had taken her advice to get it together. She commented joyfully on my perfectly applied make-up. I had gone to Bloomie's and, with a purchase of twenty dollars, was entitled to a free makeover.

"You look hot," she went on. "It's time to get out there and meet someone."

"Do you have a boyfriend?" I asked reluctantly.

"Oh, yes, and he's a real find." It seemed as if she was uncomfortable talking about this subject, yet she continued to describe him. "He's very tall, very blond, with huge blue eyes, quite the Scandinavian. I must confess, I do prefer the Latin type. He's a good guy, though, and very creative. Jon works for Ralph Lauren, and he's an *unbelievable* designer of women's clothing."

She opened her sleek silver compact and studied her face as if it was the first time she had seen it. She pouted after applying fresh lipstick, forced a grin, and shut the compact. She seemed pleased, as if she were the artist who had created her reflection.

Marnie mentioned that her family was coming in for a short visit from Argentina. She seemed distraught about this. I, then, knew why she was feeling uptight and melancholy. She had mentioned that she'd kept her distance from them over the last few years. Her father was a diplomat and politician.

"He's overwhelmingly critical of every move I make," she whined. I couldn't imagine why he was unkind toward her. After all, she was charming, pretty and good-hearted. "I try not to think of them too often," she confessed, almost in a whisper. "My doctor agreed that they are bad for my health. I was hoping that you could spend some time with me when they're in."

"I'd love to," I said appreciatively.

"That's great! I think it'll keep things more even."

So I accompanied Marnie to the St. Regis. She immediately strutted toward them as though she was modeling on a runway. The hotel was *luxe* but not overdone. The doormen and concierge were helpful and attentive. Her family was sitting around a huge coffee table with a Waterford vase filled with lovely white orchids. Marnie approached Luis, her younger brother, and embraced him with extraordinary warmth.

"Meet Luis Nunez," she said, turning toward me awkwardly. She seemed to have forgotten that I was there.

"Wonderful meeting you," I said excitedly. He was short and somewhat plump. He wore oversized sunglasses. He would take them off periodically to wipe his eyes. I didn't understand why he was so emotional and tearful. He was elegantly dressed in a Georgio Armani suit and dark brown Ferragamo shoes.

Hilda Nunez, the mother, sat next to him. She wore a navy blue suit and black Lycra undergarments. She was far more sensual and alive than her photo. Her dark brown eyes pierced through me. She looked at me as though I were a puzzle of some sort. She shook my hand firmly. "What a cutie," she said in a soft manner. She patted me on my head, as if I were a puppy. "Great to meet you! I saw a photo of you, and I must say it didn't do you justice." She smiled warmly and turned toward Marnie. "My love, you have no idea how I've ached to see you again."

"Your daughter is so beautiful," I blurted and, for no apparent reason, glared at Mr. Nunez, who was at the opposite end of the sofa. He looked down as if he had noticed an untied lace on his shoe. His face was taut and drawn. He was quite handsome but appeared years older than in the crinkled photo Marnie had shown me.

We walked toward the bar near the restaurant. Mr. Nunez gave his name to the maitre d'. "Will it be a long wait?" he inquired. The restaurant was decorated in burgundy and grays: the walls, the tablecloths, napkins, even the plates.

While we were waiting, I glanced at Mr. Nunez's narrowed eyes. They were like sharp bullets about to go off. I was taken aback by his frustrated, malicious glance at Marnie.

"Mr. Nunez, your table is ready," exclaimed the maitre d' with a sigh of relief, feeling the tension and their need to be seated at once. Marnie and I noticed the busboys hurrying around an oversized booth in the corner. We took our seats. It was comfortable to be in the back of that room.

The waiter brought out a bottle of champagne in a silver bucket.

Mr. Nunez ordered Dover sole. The rest of us preferred the blackened sea bass. The waiters moved about conscientiously. When the food finally arrived, the headwaiter de-boned the bass as if he were performing a surgical procedure. It felt like we were in one of the finer restaurants in Paris.

Mrs. Nunez asked Marnie about life in New York City. I felt the need to change the subject and took it upon myself to describe her apartment. He seemed to listen attentively and sat overly erect and expressionless.

"It's really impressive," I bragged. "It's a loft—stark and ultra-contemporary. The art work is incredible. Marnie has a flair for decorating."

Luis began cleaning his glasses. It seemed as if he didn't want to hear about Marnie and her city life. Mrs. Nunez asked if I had a fiancé. I thought the question unnecessary, but I told her, "I did. We were high school sweethearts. He died in a car accident three years ago."

She moved closer to Luis, hoping he would think of something appropriate to say, since she was too devastated to speak. Marnie suggested we meet the next day.

We left before dessert. I moved toward the other end of the lobby, near the Steinway. Someone was playing a Gershwin piece. It was soothing to be there after the tense overtones with Marnie's family.

"So what did you think of them?" she asked in a challenging way.

I took it as a hint to be honest. "They were wonderful," I said and meant it.

"Allow me to clue you in about the Nunez men," she snapped. "They're small-minded and dumb! My dad is dreadful. Didn't you notice how mad at the world he appears?"

"Yeah, kind of," I admitted.

"We never connected. He's an egomaniac. If things don't go his way, forget it!"

I had felt the hostile undercurrents over dinner.

"I hated sports," she went on. "When I'd read GO or even Architectural Digest, he'd complain about how I should get out there and play ball."

I sat up, wide-eyed, hoping that nothing more catastrophic would follow.

"Remember when I told to you to get it together? It wasn't just about you, really—I'm the master of that category." She was determined to get to the point. "Can you imagine what it's like to have a brain that clashes with your body?"

I wasn't sure what she was trying to tell me. I leaned over the end table to smell the fresh flowers. She nervously went on, weaving her long fingers through that silky auburn hair, "You know, I wanted to be a model, but my dad wouldn't have it."

Had he wanted her to be a tomboy? I wondered. He certainly didn't appreciate her femininity. Was her beauty a threat to him? I asked, "Why didn't you do it on your own? I mean, the modeling?"

She sat speechless, then bent toward me as if she couldn't let anyone else in on what she had to say. "You remember the new Year's Eve party I told you about? A few of my gym friends were guests." She looked drained, and she blushed. "Well, I got smashed. We were talking about our teen years—where we went to high school, and that sort of thing. I poured out my guts, how it'd been the worst time of my life, how I'd tried to commit suicide. 'Why?' everyone asked in a concerned way. So told them: *'I was a boy!'* The room was still and silent. Everyone sat there in disbelief, except for one of the guys. 'I *knew* you were a daffodil,' he said. I staggered out in tears."

I, too, could not think of the right thing to say. Marnie tried to lighten things up. "Time to find another gym, don't you think? . . . My dad is sharp as a tack and very intuitive. He knew there was something deeper than the possibility of being just a gay guy. He would have been okay with that, I think. He's worldly. He's been everywhere and experienced everything. But his trans-gender problem put him over the edge."

I looked at her hands, her arms, her deep voice—it all fit. She couldn't stop speaking. She had to get it all out. "I despised my muscular limbs and deepening voice. I was taught that these thoughts were sick and sinful. My life was at ground zero, and I couldn't live with the labels at school: 'sissy,' 'queen.' I tried those Evangelical places to be 'cured.'

There were so many like me who became dangerously sicker after attending their Exodus classes.

I felt spasms in my abdomen an didn't want to know or hear any more.

Marnie's family spotted us. They sat down near the Steinway. I knew they could tell that Marnie had spilled the beans. They just talked about restaurants and shows. I shakily wrote the name of a restaurant that had the best Italian food in town. Mrs. Nunez held my hand and gazed at me knowingly.

When they left, Marnie told me how she had conned her dad out of five hundred thousand dollars to get the operation and hormones needed for the transition.

"In the end, it was all worth it," she affirmed. "I'm not trapped in a strange body, and I feel free. I have a loving partner—and you know what? He thinks I'm a knockout!"

LADY 911

"Get in here, Ann," Stu shouted. Ann stopped applying the deep wine lipstick. Stu was standing stark naked in the shower—except for the disturbing black soft cast. Water was all over the place. "The goddamn faucets fell off the *wall!* Call the friggin' landlord."

Ann wasn't quite ready to deal with Stu's hysteria. He'd shout even when water spilled from a glass. This, of course, was different. She muttered nervously to herself as she slowly made her way to the bedroom window sill. The magnifying mirror fell, and so did all of Ann's makeup. It all landed on the soft, cream-colored carpet.

Even though it was more important to deal with the bathroom nightmare, Ann couldn't stop rubbing the dark-pigmented bronzing powder into the carpet, hoping it would disappear.

It was the summer of 2006. Ann had been thrilled when Stu had agreed to rent a house in East Hampton. They looked at several within their budget. This was not an easy chore, considering the area.

They found an inexpensive, yet charming, cottage in the Springs section of town. It was a real deal, Stu had thought. The exterior of the cottage was a cobblestone brick entwined with dark green ivy. The backyard was unusually large for a small home, as was the triangular pool.

Ann had had a difficult winter. She'd had some medical problems that required surgery.

She thought this might have been the reason Stu went along with her desire to be in East Hampton. Ann had hoped that he had made the decision before the surgery. She wasn't the same Pollyannish Ann after the surgery and radiation treatments. Her friends had remarked about her weight loss and sallow complexion. This had upset Stu. "They're a bunch of sadists," he had said. "We have to get out of the city this summer."

Stu would drive out on the summer weekends. Ann had thought she'd be lonely with this arrangement. Strangely enough, she was calmer when he was away. That weekend proved it.

"Ann, what the hell are you doing? I'm drowning! I can't get out of the tub—my cast is falling off!"

"Okay, I'll be right in. I spilled my makeup all over the carpet. Greg is going to be livid!"

"Are you insane? The bathroom is flooded, and you're worried about a stain on that rotten egotistical landlord's carpet! Call the bastard! He ripped us off with this shithole."

It was a Sunday. Ann tried to call the real estate agent, Greg, and also the plumber. No one would pick up. The water was flooding the house at this point. Ann called 911.

"East Hampton Police. What is the emergency?" said an indifferent voice.

"I'm at 25 Lily Lane. Our house is flooding. The faucet detached from the tile in the bathroom."

"Are you renting?"

"Yes, we are," said Ann humbly. She'd heard that the police hated renters. She remembered going to a French restaurant the previous summer. She'd asked the waiter to heat up the soup. Somehow, he had known they weren't one of the East Hampton regulars. "This is what you get in August," he'd said as he reluctantly ambled toward the kitchen.

Ann knew it would be difficult to get help, since they were only renting.

"We're not plumbers, lady. Did you call someone like that?"

"I called everyone!" shouted Ann. "*Please* get someone over here. We're going to drown, and I have a pet rabbit that won't let me hold her."

The woman's voice softened. "Is someone hurt?"

If this was the only way to get help, Ann had no choice but to lie. "Yes, my husband broke his leg!" It wasn't a total lie, she reasoned. He was wearing a cast and he had clearly been injured.

Ann was relieved to see the red and blue lights in the driveway. She ran to the door before they had a chance to knock. The officers seemed surly and mean. "You realize it's Sunday," said the thinner cop.

"I know," whimpered Ann. "I tried everyone, and no one got back to us."

The same cop walked into the bathroom. He was prepared. He wore knee-high rubber boots. "You do have a problem! We know Greg. He's not going to be happy about this."

Ann pictured him with a Nazi armband. She thought he'd be a perfect extra for an SS trooper. The other cop was a bit more sympathetic. "Where's your husband?" he asked in a caring manner.

"He's sitting on the bed," she answered wearily.

The cop entered the bedroom and looked at Stu's cast. "I thought he just broke his leg. How did he get the cast so fast?"

Ann stammered, "That was the other—I mean, the old injury. I was talking about the new one. He fell in the bathtub and couldn't move his leg at all."

The cops looked at each other. "It's against the law to call 911 without cause," the sympathetic one said.

Stu turned toward Ann. "I didn't break it now," he whispered.

Ann was astounded. "Oh, God! How could you say that now! They could have *heard* you!"

"If you had turned the water off in the basement, this wouldn't have happened," said the Nazi look-alike.

Ann knew this was true: Stu couldn't put a nail in the wall. He had no clue where the water valve would be, forget about knowing how to turn it off.

The cops wrote some notes and left without saying a word.

Ann was infuriated. "Thanks a lot!" she called out the window. "It's a good thing you're not in the city. You'd be out of work!"

They chuckled, took off their hats, got into the car, and zoomed off.

"Ann, why did you start up with them?" Stu demanded. "You know the Hamptons and how everyone knows everyone. The cops even know Greg, and they caught you lying."

"I didn't lie! Shut up! Whose side are you on, anyway?"

Ann paused before the bathroom mirror. The usual glow she would get after being in the sun was no longer there. Her friends were right. Her complexion was yellowish. The room had a mildewed odor, and the tiles were moist and warped. She was trying to recall why she had so much wanted to rent a home in the Hamptons. After seeing the doctor at least a dozen times and answering unending questions, she'd thought that it would be a good way for Stu and her to get over the despair of her health problems. She knew he was less attracted to her now. They hadn't slept together since the surgery. He also had issues. He was unusually high-strung and had lost his appetite.

She opened her hand and swallowed one of the many pills she'd been taking since the surgery. She had begun to loathe the Hamptons: the stars, the star-struck and the pseudo-intellectual assholes from the city. The half-open screen door allowed the cool morning air to slide across the buckling wooden floor in the living room.

From the bedroom, she could hear Stu muttering under his breath. "That S.O.B., I can't wait to get him on the phone. This place is falling apart. It's a piece of crap." He came out of the bedroom fidgeting with his tie.

Stu's position at his prestigious law firm was becoming shaky. The senior partner's son had just graduated from Harvard Law, and Stu felt he was getting the cold shoulder and wouldn't be there much longer.

Stu massaged Ann's shoulder softly. "Are you going to be okay in this mess?"

She nodded.

He continued, "I'll be back Friday, and everything should be in decent shape by then."

"Bob said he'd stop by today," she said. "That'll be a blessing." Bob lived in their building in the city. He was her confidante. She confided in him, although she knew he couldn't totally be trusted. He was always there to lend an ear. Since he was gay, she knew there were no ulterior motives.

"Don't share your dirty laundry with him," Stu advised. She thought she *should* be a bit more cautious about sharing her problems with Bob.

A few hours later, she was sitting at the bay window overlooking the pool. She loved the forest-like setting and the garden in front of the window. The ambiance was soothing.

A black car pulled into the driveway. It didn't look like Bob's car, so she thought he'd probably rented a new one. She smiled and waved at the car. The windows were heavily tinted, so she couldn't see in. Then the doors opened. Ann couldn't believe her eyes.

There stood the two officers who had come to the house on Sunday.

Today was Thursday. "What could they want?" she mumbled nervously to herself. She stepped back in awe, stilled by the dread of what was to come. The SS-type officer briskly walked toward her with handcuffs.

"Mrs. Sandler," he said, "you're under arrest for calling 911 time and again without cause."

They handcuffed her and practically carried her to the black car.

"You've got to be kidding!" she protested in tears. "I...I did not call without reason. You guys are crazy! Let me out of this car immediately or this will be the biggest lawsuit that ever hit the Hamptons! I know you hate renters."

Total silence descended. The cops just looked straight ahead. Ann doubled over with spasms.

"You'd think with all the terrorists and thieves around, you would have better things to do," she said, weeping.

They drove off to the East Hampton Courthouse, opened the door of the car, and guided her in. She was placed in a holding cell. She pleaded to make a call. They allowed her to do so immediately.

"Stu, Stu!" She burst into tears. "The cops came back, and I've been arrested for calling 911! Please, get here fast and get me the hell out of here!"

He gasped, "Are you kidding? They're nuts out there! Don't worry. Cool it—I'm on the way!"

She suddenly thought about Bob. "How am I going to explain this to him? He's probably been standing at the door for hours. When he finds about what happened, it will be all over the building!" She doubled over again, phoned her daughter, and howled into the phone, "Stacey, I'm in jail!"

She hesitated before calling Bob. She felt guilty knowing that he probably had been waiting at the house for hours; he would be suspicious and judgmental. Not now, she thought. She would think of a good excuse, when she got back to the cottage.

An hour later, Stacey arrived. Ann was thrilled to see her. She rarely saw her in work attire. She looked like a stockbroker. Her dark navy suit and patent leather pumps gave her an authoritative air.

Stacey glared at her mother in the holding cell. She wanted to scream at the cops. She bit her lower lip. "Sir, would you kindly get my mother out of that pen," she demanded.

The officer told her to see the clerk and give her the bail money. Stacey marched to the clerk's desk.

"You look like your mom," said the clerk in a friendly way.

Stacey, taken aback, felt awkward. "This isn't a party."

She returned with the bail receipt. The officer opened the cell door. Ann's mouth was drooping. Her eyes appeared opaque. She walked toward Stacy like a zombie and seized onto her arm as if the girl were a pole.

They exchanged comforting words. Ann's anger lessened. She stood up straight, her, posture exaggerated, as if ready for war.

"I'm not going to be a renter after this is over!" she shouted. "You guys will hear from me in my Georgica beach house next summer—*if* I should happen to need a favor!"

The two officers near Stacey smiled. They were more than polite by then. Stacey shrugged and smirked at the cops. "We'll be in touch, *ciao*! . . . Where's Stuey?" she asked her mother. She wasn't particularly fond of her stepfather. "Daddy had more brains in his pinky than Stuey has in his whole pumped-up body."

Ann could not dispute this statement. Donny, Ann's deceased husband, had clearly been more intelligent and savvy. But he had also been a womanizer and intimidating. She was comfortable with Stu's less arrogant ways.

"You know the cops were right on the money. Why the hell didn't he think to shut off the water?" "That was a no-brainer," whined Stacey.

"Yeah, and he said I could get arrested for lying about his broken leg in front of the cops," Ann confessed.

"Mommy, don't you get it? He was doing a gasser."

"What do you mean?" asked Ann defensively.

"Come on, you know what I'm talking about. His usual *Gaslight* routine."

Ann was about to call Stu. She slammed her cell phone on the kitchen counter. "I've had enough. Shut up already."

Stacey's face twisted in shock. She ran her fingers through her hair.

Ann looked at her sympathetically. She would always play with her hair when she was stressed. "I'm sorry, baby," she whimpered.

Stacey was silent. She brushed the lint off her navy jacket, pulled at the rusty, warped sliding door and looked back at her mother. Ann's face was pressed against the mesh of the screen door. Stacey shuddered. It looked like Ann was in a jail cell. "Mom, remember to tell Stuey to get you a lawyer. I'm broke."

Ann shakily grabbed her cell phone. She called Stu. There was no answer. She left a voice message: "Where are you when I need you? Get back here!"

The glaring August sun hovered over the cottage. Ann stumbled into the kitchen. She turned toward the living room avoiding the brightness. She tore through the cabinets, seized the last of a Godiva chocolate bar, and devoured it. She poured some red wine into a glass and opened the utensil drawer. She noticed an unread copy of *Dan's Papers* (the popular Hampton News). She spotted an article that read:

> *911—Ann Sandler, 62, 25 Lily Lane, phoned 911 fourteen times, Sunday, August 2. She reported that the house at Lily Lane was flooding due to detached faucets in the bathroom. Ms. Sandler also reported that her husband, Stuart Sandler, had broken his leg due to this incident. She was cited for a misdemeanor for reporting an untruth. The hearing will be held Tuesday, August 11, at the East Hampton Municipal Courthouse.*

Ann burst into tears, pressing her face against the paper. She walked onto the sun deck to study the print as if she hadn't read it clearly at first. She grabbed her cell to call Stacey. "Stace, it's in *Dan's Papers*. Everyone at the gym is going to know my age!"

"Is that the main event? So what, Mom—who cares? You're getting crazy over nothing. My anti-Christ-like boss is hovering over me. Gotta go—just get a lawyer and get rid of this absurd mess. Call me later."

Ann tried to phone Stu again. "Shit, I hate that goddamn voicemail! *You have reached … at the tone…*how annoying!" Ann sat perched on the edge of the sofa. She grabbed the mirror on the end table. No one is going to believe that I'm sixty-two, she thought. She held onto a velvet throw pillow, frozen and expressionless.

Stu tugged at the screeching sliding door. "That friggin' traffic," he growled. "It took forever to get here, that one lane thing drives me nuts. What's goin' on?" he asked in an overly concerned manner.

Ann jumped up and dashed into the kitchen. Her heart thumped as she placed the article in front of him. She examined his face as he read the paper as if it were a legal document. She expected him to be livid and vindictive. Instead, he just chuckled. "This is hysterical. There's nothing going on here—I guess, they have to write about something!" he snickered. "God, Ann, why are you wearing my socks?"

"How could you be so *insensitive*? You wouldn't find it funny if it was about *you!* God forbid the stuffy lawyers at your firm should see this. You're not going to laugh when you hear the going rate of a legal retainer down here." She laid the estimate on the coffee table. Stu gazed down and read the numbers: *$2,500.00.*

"That's the Hamptons!" he complained. "You 'd better call one of your rich relatives."

"Really? Have I lived with *them* for twenty-three years?"

The light in the room faded. She looked out the door. The clouds blurred the sun. She turned toward him. "I thought it was going to be a nice day," she said mindlessly. There was just a hint of a nod from Stu. He dropped his cap on the end table, neatly folded his blue blazer, and draped it over the wing chair. He slouched into the sofa, his eyes half - closed. His mouth was open, as though he were about to say something but couldn't think of the words.

She nudged his arm. "Stu, get up—you can't pass out on me like that!"

He woke up with a start. He didn't look at her. He picked up the *Times* and read through the weather section. She sat next to him. She knew he'd had a lot on his plate, too.

"This place is a curse," she whimpered.

He spread his fingers and rotated his hands in circles over her back. "Don't worry, baby, we're going to get someone to help us tomorrow, okay?"

"Okay," she agreed.

Ann awoke at four a.m. Cranes at a construction site somewhere in the neighborhood were acting up earlier than usual. She didn't reach for the lamp on the night table. She sat with her chin resting on her hands and considered going back to sleep, but fumbled through the yellow pages for *Lawyers (General Litigation)*. Her cell phone cast enough light to read the names that she circled: *John Courtney, Esq.; Thomas Tierney, Esq.; Robert Flynn, Esq.* She knew that the judge, the cops, and the clerks at the courthouse were all Irish. They were connected in the Village of East Hampton. She was, clearly, on the right track.

The last name she circled was *Stan Levy, Esq.*, something she felt she had to do, maybe for good luck.

She thought of the other house they had thought of renting. What a waste. It had been larger, more contemporary, and in a better area. It had also been the same price. She still couldn't fathom Stu's words: "Daphne eats wires." Daphne was their pet rabbit. She didn't get why he had wanted to ruin the possibility of renting that lovely place. "Why does he constantly have to torture me?" she muttered.

Stu began to stir. She studied his face. He had never looked so drawn and exhausted. She knew that the firm was killing him. He was not a trial-lawyer-type, hardly a type-A personality, for that matter. He should have done forensic work. He was starting to lose his hair and gain weight. He didn't know how to dress, either. He looked out of sorts and sloppy most days. He seemed more frustrated than ever. He'd revealed this to her inadvertently, which was why he had admitted *the truth* about his broken leg to the cops and why he had made that stupid remark about the rabbit. He resented everything, really, especially her. She was beginning to believe Stacey's theory about him.

He yawned, stretched his limbs in an exaggerated way, roused himself from the bed, and limped toward the bathroom. She rose, too, then reclined on the floral wing chair in the corner of the bedroom and lit a cigarette. She rarely smoked in the morning. "Get out of the shower! I have to get ready, too," she called out.

He started to mumble angrily. He'd stay in the shower for almost an hour when he was stressed. She realized the water and warmth were comforting when he was in that state of mind.

When he finally finished, she showered quickly and quietly dressed. Everything in her closet was too beachy to wear to an office. Luckily, she did have her conservative beige sheath dress that fell below her knees. She tried it on. "Perfect," she declared as she stood before the full-length mirror. She brushed her soft brown hair and tied it in a severe bun. "Uggh!" she said to herself. "Do I not look like a D.A.R woman? How could someone like that think of lying to 911?"

They ate breakfast at the small table near the screen door. The pool looked inviting. The foliage was lovely. "Why couldn't I just enjoy this place?" she asked herself. "It wasn't all bad." She looked at Stu resentfully. He always found a way to rain on her parade.

He picked up the folded phone directory and read the names of the lawyers that she had circled. "Why these guys?" he asked.

"They're Irish," she said. "Anyone who's anything here is."

"You have some weird ideas," he said, giggling.

They drank coffee, studying the circled names, buttered the rye toast, and munched away in the sunny corner. She decided to phone John Courtney's office. The receptionist gave them a late morning appointment.

Stu slid out the door to get the car. It was the first model of the Sebring. The fifteen-year-old car was rusty and in dire need of repair. Stu didn't know what was going to happen at his job, so he was afraid to spend money. Ann crunched over to get in. They drove slowly past a row of Hampton properties. She would usually comment on the lovely array of homes; that morning, they gazed at them silently.

The receptionist at Mr. Courtney's office was sweet to a fault. "What is the problem?" she asked meekly. Ann said it was private and asked when she could see Mr. Courtney. The receptionist scampered into his office. Ann heard muffled voices.

The woman scampered back out and said, "You can go right in, Mrs. Sandler."

The attorney was tall and broad-shouldered. He looked like an ex-football coach. His gray hair was neatly parted and it appeared as if he had just shaved. His handshake was firm and reassuring. He invited them to sit. Ann and Stu chose to sit at the far side of the room. Looked into Ann's eyes, Courtney could tell she'd been through hell. "So what's going on?" he asked sympathetically.

"The faucets came off the bathroom wall," she said in a rush. "The house was flooding, and there was no one to contact. My husband had an injury and it was hard for him to do anything. He *did* have a cast! 911 said we could only get help only if it was a-a medical emergency— and it *was*, sir," she exclaimed. "*Dan's Papers* stated that I *lied*. They said I called fourteen times. These are all lies and exaggerations. They said it was a misdemeanor. They even revealed my age! If this isn't slander, I don't know what is!"

Courtney swiveled his chair around and looked out the window tugging at his chin, before turning back to her. "I'm not getting involved in a civil suit, Mrs. Sandler, but I will try to get this case on the calendar tomorrow, so I can get a quick dismissal."

Ann looked around the room. There were Citizen of East Hampton Village Awards, Little League and Soccer Appreciation plaques. There were photos of Mr. Courtney and the Mayor of East Hampton. She had chosen the right guy.

"That would be great!" she said appreciatively. "I'll call you later to firm it up," he said.

The following morning, Stu and Ann were waiting for Courtney. As soon as he arrived, the judge entered the courtroom from a door behind the bench.

Courtney approached thim before acknowledging Stu and Ann. When he was done, he turned back toward her. "It's a done deal," he said in a low voice. "We just have to go through the process." Ann felt drained and rubbed her eyes. She looked at the cops who had arrested her. They smiled at her almost in an apologetic way. She managed to smile back.

The calendar was arranged alphabetically. When they finally got to her name, the judge reviewed the brief and dismissed the case. He said, "Keep your nose clean from her on in, Mrs. Sandler."

Courtney leaned over and warned her not to speak, but she was flushed and angry. Her eyes filled with tears as she retorted, "I-I didn't do a *thing!* What are you referring to, Your Honor?"

The judge did not respond. She was about to say more when Courtney hotly whispered, "*Leave* it. He's an old devil—he's on his way out."

She remained silent and thanked the attorney. Stu held her hand as they left the courthouse. She couldn't wait to phone Stan Levy about a civil suit. He wasn't one of the connected guys and she knew he would do it. He probably even had an office in the city.

She walked to the beach. The midday dunes were silky white. She sat beside a reef and watched the gulls. They appeared willful and determined to take on another day. She noticed Stu's legs wobbling in the sand. He looked relieved, yet his eyes were twitching—his nervous state obvious. The gulls lifted her spirits. She decided she had to get back to the gym.

She got to the gym at the usual time. She knew she would see the same crowd and worried about their reaction. It was a place where words were few. She expected that the members she knew would keep their distance. She was sure they had read the article.

She cautiously approached the treadmills. Usually, they were all in use. Suddenly, a crowd in the corner called out in unison: "Welcome back, Lady 911!"

One of the men agreed that the cops in the Hamptons were S.O.B.'s. Someone else, who rented a house, said, "They're always pulling something on us. They hate renters."

But Ann knew why the whole thing had happened. It was Stu—he'd never back me up, she thought. Why did he have to say that his leg wasn't broken? She was aware she had to work on their relationship. Things were always getting screwed up with him around.

She went back to the cottage, took off her sneakers, and put her feet up on the sofa. Stu was working on a brief. She sat next to him and tried to touch his face. He turned away to focus on his work. She got up, went into the kitchen, dropped a huge scoop of ice cream on a plate, dug into it with a spoon, and started to lick the ice cream from it.

Stu said, "Ann, don't put the potato chips in the fridge. They taste weird when you do."

"Stuey, this thing didn't happen for no reason. I will never be 'One of Those That You Only Get in August,' like the waiter at that French restaurant said. I will always be *Lady 911!*"

www.ingramcontent.com/pod-product-compliance
Lightning Source LLC
Chambersburg PA
CBHW021843010726
47493CB00005B/1532